Fallen Empire

Volume II

Overrun

OVERRUN

J.F. Holmes

The rise of Private Mercenary Companies with the signing of the Treaty of Kepler Sigconis in 500 Post Conquest / 2642 AD filled a void left by the major combatants. The withdrawal of Terran Union, Charee, LaChan and New Empire ground forces from the Demilitarized Zone worlds enabled low intensity conflicts to flourish as old rivals settled scores.

The Old Empire had kept the peace while fostering the mixture of various species throughout the worlds. Xenophobia, racism, economic competition, military competition among the Great Power intelligence agencies, corporate rivalries and more all contributed to the conflicts. They were fueled by leftover military hardware, unemployed veterans and the confusion that went with the times.

Many of the major former Imperial worlds were already devastated by first the Grausian Civil War and then the Succession Wars or were themselves independent enough to have powerful military forces. There were, however, many minor planets with smaller populations that couldn't afford standing armies but still had it out for their erstwhile neighbors or former friends.

Excerpt from *"The Rich and the Dead: Private Military Corporations in the early 27th Century"* by Thomas Meagher © 2686 / 544 Cannon Publishing Ltd, Armagh, Eire, Terran Union

Prologue

Gliese 3293b, August 3rd, 503 PC
Firebase Cribben

He awoke to darkness and choking dust. No idea how long had passed but his left arm was pinned by a fallen beam, probably one of the roof supports and he couldn't see his watch. Second Lieutenant Lishar An-Selene, platoon leader, heavy weapons platoon, Bravo Company, Second Battalion, The Irish Brigade, Hibernia Arms LLC, lay quietly, listening before attempting to move. He heard nothing except wind whistling overhead and the drip of water. What he smelled was death and decay mixed with the moist odor of the jungle.

What caused the smell was the corpse lying across his legs. Thankfully the Grausian olfactory senses were less sensitive than humans, because the body pretty much ended at the chest cavity. He found this out by touch, sticking his hand in a pile of guts. A bit of flexing made the corpse roll off into the darkness but he was still trapped by debris.

Next was to assess his physical condition, first flexing each joint on his right arm. The upper then the lower elbow, the three segments giving him excellent strength and flexibility. Pinned, but they moved and nothing seemed broken. The timber lay on top of his wrist, the ancient timepiece Colonel Meagher had given him on graduation from OCS probably smashed and his hand felt numb. The rest of him ached, probably an after effect of the explosion that had collapsed the bunker. No concussion: the Grausians had a distributed central nervous system that made a catastrophic injury that much harder. Some small cuts and his right eye was swollen shut, maybe crusted closed with dried blood.

He tried to move his arm, drag it out from under the beam. No use, it was a heavy piece of timber that had held up the roof and hundreds of pounds of sandbags above it. Selene lay there, thinking about what to do next.

Chapter One

A week prior

Bai Alng, Capital of the Republic of Therer, Planet B, AKA "El Reino de Dios", Star System Gliese 3293

"And so we welcome this peace treaty between our two great nations, in the hope that we can build a new world in the wake of the Empire!" The tall Grausian leaned forward and scribbled his name or something on the archaic piece of paper, followed by his human counterpart, then they stood and shook hands over the table.

"Blah blah blah, shut your blathering mouth and get on with it," whispered Sergeant Major Huy, his red face remaining stone still. The Iryllian could get away with things like that, though he didn't say it very loudly. Most Sergeants Major knew when it was appropriate and when it was not and he stood at the far back of the formation.

"PRESENT .... ARMS!" called Colonel Meagher, echoing the command of the Theren national forces down the line. Second Battalion, minus Charlie Company out on the firebases, brought their SBR-86's vertical to their chest and then held them straight out. Across from them the mercenaries of 1st Reconnaissance Regiment, the 'Hispania de Tercios,' did the same under the flag of *Los Estados Unidos des Dios*. Both units were smaller than when they had arrived on the planet four months ago; the fighting had been brutal, though they had rarely faced each other across the lines. Merc units tended to try not to; you never knew when you might be working alongside someone who you had in your sniper scope a year ago. Still, there had been incidents, including an Irish Brigade patrol missing in action and a nighttime assault to recover POWs that left some dead on either side. The distance between them was a good thing; never knew when a troop might take revenge for a buddy and things were … delicate in the wake of the Terran Union brokered treaty.

The troops had to hold the rifles out in the sweltering tropical heat as ceremonial units from both armies formed up and marched on parade. The Therens were a majority of humans mixed with Grausians and the minor races of the fallen Empire, followed by a regiment of EUD troops, all human. It had been, like so many of the wars being fought in the DMZ, a bit of an open ended question as to what race would control the future of the planet.

"Just keep marchin, ya Dagos, we kicked your asses," someone in the row behind the heavy weapons platoon leader said a bit too loud. Second Lieutenant Selene made a mental note to find out who it was and deal with it later. A bit of pride was good, but too much and it could cause trouble and a Sergeant Major could speak where a new private could not. No need, as he heard the soldier's platoon sergeant growl, "Shut yer trap, Emerson." Nobody argued with Master Sergeant Nikova. No one. The rest of the parade passed in the stead thrum of marching boots as one company of the Tercios and Alpha Company of the Irish passed by, the mercenaries' own ceremonial contributions.

"READY … TO!" called Colonel Meagher. The Bravo company commander, Captain Tormund, echoed him and Selene dropped his salute. More waiting and then they were dismissed. The troopers headed off to spend their pay and the leadership to their endless meetings, this one covering their embarkation to Eire.

*****

"Bravo, you're last, so sorry. I want you to keep running patrols out of Firebase Cribben. The locals are taking over FB Hercules and FB Dennis," said Colonel Meagher. The CEO and commander of the Irish Brigade was a short, intense man who came across as larger than life. The ex-Imperial Legionnaire and former commander of the Terran Marine Corps 5th Regiment held his troops to a high standard but drove himself even harder. He pointed at the S-2 and Major Iona Keely stepped up, handing out paper copies of her intel estimate to the various members of the command group. The scar on her face was even paler with the tan her fair skin had eventually turned to under the harsh Gleise sunlight. Since being promoted out of her command of Bravo Company, First Battalion she had let her red hair grow out a bit to the point where curls were starting to show, but that was her sole concession to not being on the line anymore. Otherwise she looked like what she was; a former Marine officer and competent soldier.

"Our INTSUM," she stated, "shows the Dios regulars pulling back to treaty positions, with armor being laagered in Terran Union monitored cantonments. Their infantry hasn't moved yet, but remember, it's a staged drawdown. They won't start shifting forces until all foreign elements are off planet."

"You mean us expensive infidel mercs!" interrupted the S-4, Major Muhammad. The logistics officer smiled to show no ill feelings towards Keely, who was a Catholic.

"They mean you infidels and all the alien troops," she answered.

His smile grew broader and he said, "Good point!"

The attitude of the briefing was a lot more relaxed than usual, since the fighting was pretty much over. The Irish Brigade, or more properly the "armed" part of Hibernia Arms, LLC, based in New Dublin, Eire, had been contracted along with other mercenary units to provide troops and firepower to the Republic of Therer as they elected their first government after the fall of the Empire. Problem was, Los Estados Unidos des Dios, the United States of God and the current planetary government, had a problem with the breakaway province. Apparently religious tolerance was some kind of threat to order, as was having a large non-human minority. Unfortunately for them the Republic's economy had done better during the Succession Wars and they could hire a decent defense to supplement their militia. The Irish Brigade, along with a battalion of engineers from the Hooligans and a squadron of Black Snakes for close air support, had turned back every attempt by the Dios to force the issue. The fact that it had also almost bankrupted the newly independent country wasn't the mercs problem. As long as they got paid.

Besides, thought Keely with a smile as these things ran through her head, *it's merely a transfer of wealth from the government to the local bars and whorehouses.*

"Our threat assessment is minimal, based on intel provided by the Theren Intelligence Agency. Of course, we take that with a grain of salt," she finished.

"Which is why," said Meagher, "Bravo Company will be staying back. Two weeks and you'll be lifting via the merchant freighter *Scranton,* but until then, you're to remain here as a stabilizing force observing the TU peace agreement until the 3rd Marine Regiment gets boots on the ground."

Captain Tormund spoke up, "Sir, I'm sure it's all in the OPORD, but what does that mean? Presence patrols, raids, liaison with the civilian government? What's your intent?"

Major Ichna, the S-3, or Operations Officer, explained. "This is an add on to our contract and a pretty piss poor one at that. Two platoons only, heavy weapons and a second platoon for VERY light patrols. We'll fulfill the terms of the contract, to the letter, but nothing more. Basically enough to provide self-defense and a presence." The LaChan was an excellent tactician, but he had a bad habit of flicking his tongue out and testing the air as he spoke, making him hard to understand. "Let the TU figure it out, we don't want to lose any more trooperssssss this late in the game."

"Understood, not our fight anymore," said Tormund. The big Asgardian gave the LaChan a thumbs up and Major Ichna waved his tail in response.

The meeting broke up when Colonel Meagher stood and everyone else came to the position of attention. Mercenaries they were and fighting for pay, but every one of the staff was either former Imperial Legion, Terran Marine or some other planetary military and old habits die hard. He walked out with a motion to Major Keely to follow him and the room burst out into conversation, plans being made and satisfaction with a job well done. The Therens had maintained their independence and that was dear to their hearts of veterans of the Succession Wars.

*****

"You wanted to see me, Sir?" asked Keely, stepping into the office that the energetic Meagher sometimes used as a stopping place.

"Have a seat, Iona. This is personal," he said, pointing to a folding chair in the corner. When she sat down he said straight out, "I'm leaving you here as the OIC of the withdrawal, but I want Captain Tormund in command of the combat troops and the actual day to day. Sergeant Major Huy will handle logistics."

"I don't understand, Colonel. What am I supposed to do?" She looked genuinely puzzled.

"It's my opinion, backed up by your own threat assessment, that the Dios have gotten their fill of fighting. I was on the horn with General de Brigada Guillermo from the Tercios; they're about packed up and will be gone tomorrow, same as us." He saw a sour look come across her face and headed her off at the pass. "Listen, they're mercs like us and they fulfilled their contract. That's the nature of the business, you know that as well as I do. Next week we might be fighting alongside them. They're tough troops and good."

"It's … well, in the Marines we always knew the good guys from the bad guys, except the Lizards." The LaChan, the weakest of the former Imperial races as far as territory and military capability, had been notorious for switching sides several times during the war. "Even then, they were up front about it. Remember Signus 3? Just sat there."

"Of course I remember, I was your commander!" he said with a grin. "But that was then, this is now. I want you to RELAX! Take some time for yourself, get some sun, go snorkeling, learn how to surf." Therer was a coastal province, separated from the EUD by a mountain range, and it had beautiful beaches in a tropical climate.

"I'm not sure I know how to relax, Colonel, honestly," she answered simply. "It's been one fight after another, you know? Going on what, almost a decade now?"

"I do know, which is why I'm giving you time off. If you're worried about security, I'm leaving Corporal Thog with you. Someone in the Terran Union Intelligence Agency has gotten a bug up their ass and the Sons of Terra have been hunting Grausian 'mutants', so he needs to lie low on a non-TU world for now."

She actually laughed at that. "I'd love to see one of their bully squads up against him!" Corporal Thog was a failed Imperial genetic experiment, eight hundred pounds of bipedal Earth rhino crossed with a Cygnus puma, about as smart as a brick and absolute hell in combat. He was also completely loyal to Meagher and even more so to Keely, who had found him homeless on the streets after the war.

"Do me a favor. You have two weeks. Check in with Tormund daily, make nice with the Theren officials and military on a regular basis and be good to yourself. Maybe even get laid!" He had a wicked grin on his face when he said the last part.

"Colonel Meagher!" she spluttered, shocked. The residents of Eire were very old school Catholic and even ten years of military service hadn't driven it all out of Keely's soul.

"Don't make me order it. I want you to remember, though, that as the ranking officer, you're ultimately responsible for any decisions about unit actions. You're the official liaison between The Irish Brigade and the Therer government. If you see anything out of the ordinary, ANYTHING, you go screaming to the Therens, call in the Marines and hunker down. Now get out of my office!" he barked with a smile. In many ways he regarded Keely as a daughter he didn't have, though he wasn't quite old enough to be her father. She stood up, saluted, her face still beet red but with a smile, turned and walked out.

Chapter Two

"Is this seat taken?"

The redheaded woman looked up at the darkly handsome face of the man standing at her table. He made a slight bow and waited. She folded the old paperback book she was reading, marking the page, then pushed out the chair with a sandaled foot. "Captain Paco Mateo," she said in an almost accusatory tone. He wasn't sure if the chair had been moved as an offer or to block him from moving towards her.

"Major," he replied, nodding his head, ID'ing her rank despite the t-shirt and khaki pants she wore. The gun she carried wasn't at all unusual in this culture. "I see intelligence work suits you."

She laughed, her smile in direct contrast to the burn scars on her face. "I'd be wasting Colonel Meagher's and our client's money if I didn't know the head of the Tercios' Special Operations platoon." Under the table her right hand slipped down to the needler in a drop holster on her leg, flipping off the safety.

"That is true," he replied, smiling. "Major Iona Keely, late of the 5th Terran Marine Regiment, hired in 501 Post Conquest by Hibernia Arms LLC, initially commander of Bravo Company, awarded the Star of Valor by the Holcomb government for stopping a coup attempt. Now the Irish Brigade 2nd Battalion intelligence officer and commander of the stay behind party. And, if I may say so, a serious thorn in the side of our operations over the past few months. A few of my men are buried on this crappy little planet because of you."

When she spoke there was no trace of fear in a voice that was as cold as her skin was pale. "You've done your homework well, captain." Her arm tensed and she prepared to die with a smoking gun in her hand, but he was going with her. "You probably should have just used a sniper rifle on me."

He burst out laughing and held up his hand for a waiter. The Charee came over with two glasses of iced tea, the same thing she had already been drinking. "Thanks, monkey," he said in Spanish and the four armed xeno scowled. Keely dismissed the casual racism; it was all too common among veterans of the Succession Wars. "No, Major, I came …" said Mateo and he leaned towards her to whisper in a conspiratorial tone, *"… to invite you to a party."*

She also leaned forward and placed an elbow on the table, taking a sip of her own iced tea, ignoring the ones he had bought. *"Oh really?"* she whispered back.

"Of course!" he smiled, flashing perfect white teeth, "we call it a 'rumba'. Our contract is done, so it is time to spend our money and celebrate the end of this stupid little war, until we go on to the next one. Don't you Irish get roaring drunk after battles?"

"Before, during and after. It's kind of our way." She leaned back but kept the palm of her hand on the butt of her pistol. "But not mine. We board ship tomorrow, as you well know. In fact, I thought you all left last week." The Triceros had been based out of the capital of the EUD and the cease fire monitors had given them the all clear.

"Not me or my platoon," he said. "I'm going into business for myself! You are looking at the CEO of Acción Directa, Limited!" He smiled again, actually quite a nice smile, and stroked his mustache. "It is time for someone to pay me a

LOT of money for my genius! And my good looks will make an excellent recruiting poster." He did, she noticed, have some very sparkling brown eyes.

This time she did laugh and took her hand off her gun, flicking the safety back on. Maybe he was right, it was time to relax. Tomorrow was shipment back to Eire and then some other war and there wasn't any "no fun" clause in her contract. "I'd like to, but then I'd have to bring Corporal Thog and you don't want to see him drunk. Let me rephrase that, you don't want to see him pulling down a building on top of you for fun."

"OK, so no rumba. How about dinner, then? I know a restaurant with some great Lonestar Cluster grass fed longhorn steaks?" He made an open palm gesture with his hands. "And since neither of us got a bonus for winning the war, I insist that I pay."

Like any good catholic girl, Iona Keely had a devil on one shoulder and an angel on the other. This time she distinctly heard the devil say, "Do it!" and not a peep from the angel. "Oh, what the hell. THOG!" she yelled and there was a bellow from across the street. "Of course, you'll have to feed him too."

The smile faded from the man's face as the eight hundred pound genetic experiment that was her bodyguard lumbered over and stood above both of them, getting the usual stare from someone who hadn't seen the Grat up close. That more than anything convinced her that Mateo was on the up and up. If he was running an op, he would have known Thog was nearby. "Hungry!" the bodyguard grunted in Imperial.

"Good, because we're going to eat," said Keely, standing up.

"Cat?" asked Thog, with a hopeful tone. The massive mouth opened up in a feral grin, sharp pointed teeth contrasting with the horn on his nose.

"Not on the menu tonight. Raw steak suit you?" She winked at Mateo, who groaned. There went his pay for a week.

*****

It was dark in the hotel room, a warm breeze blowing through the open windows. Keely lay satisfied with her back to the man lying next to her. It had been … a very long time. She didn't dare fraternize with anyone in the Brigade and she was never 'home' long enough to form any real attachments on Eire. Plus, well, her countrymen tended to be a bit old school and conservative. This … this felt good. It was something she had needed and Mateo seemed the same way. Two soldiers who wanted to celebrate being alive, in the most basic human way. No virgin, but training and being a leader tended to shove personal things aside.

Dinner had been good, and she had politely fended off his very blatant attempts at recruiting her for his company. Once she had made it clear he had shifted into a very smooth attempt at seducing her. "After all," he had said, "if we can't do business, then maybe we can do pleasure?" accompanied by his infectious grin.

She felt him get up and head to the bathroom and thought about getting dressed herself. Her watch showed 00:47 local time, with Gliese using a twenty three hour clock. She was due at the firebase at 07:00 to assist with the turnover of equipment and facilities to the Theren army and then loadout at the spaceport at 17:00. *A few more minutes,* she told herself as Mateo ran the water in the sink. Her eyes had just started to close when she saw multiple flashes scattering light around the bedroom from the curtained window. That was artillery, not lighting, she knew it more intimately than the sight of her own family and it was confirmed a second later by the sound of the detonation shaking the building. Long range fires hitting command and control posts outside the city, she immediately thought. Her hand dove for the pistol that lay with her crumpled clothes and she started to yell for Thog, guarding the door outside. Before she could move more than a foot Mateo's fist slammed into her face, breaking her nose. Stars danced and she fell back, stunned, shaking her head as blood ran from down her face.

"I'm sorry," he said, pointing a handgun at her, "but it's part of our first contract. Had you joined me, well, things would be different." He listened to the artillery landing and continued, "Those idiots started early, or maybe I just spent too much time enjoying myself. In any case, I know you have your own orders to call in the Marines if anything goes badly, so ..." Keely felt a heavy punch to the chest at the same time as the soft POP of a suppressed pistol, a sharp pain that took her breath away, unable to move as a red haze settled over her vision, fading to black. Behind Mateo the door opened and two troopers came in, fully armed and wearing tactical gear. She heard him say something in Spanish and then they vanished. The last thing Major Iona Keely saw as she spilled off the bed into darkness was the massive figure of Corporal Thog lying in the hallway.

Chapter Three

Mateo closed the door and stepped around the prone body of Corporal Thog. The creature's eyes were open but saw nothing, courtesy of the hundred pounds of steak laced with animal tranquilizers that he had eaten. Moving him to a prison camp was going to be a bitch, but Colonel Meagher would pay a pretty penny to get his pet back. Or they could sell it to the Sons of Terra. Let them execute it on live vid.

"Ready up?" asked Sergeant Major Arroyo, covering one side of the hallway. Mateo paused, looked back at the woman's body sprawled on the floor and then nodded. To be fair, he did feel some guilt over what he had done to a woman he just had sex with, but it only lasted a moment. In combat, well that was all the time you really had to think about things anyway. Eliminating the highest ranking officer of the remaining mercenary unit on planet had been a necessity, as was what they were about to do in the city. Casualties and hearts be damned in both love and war and he had enjoyed his time with her, but she could have caused a lot of trouble. With her out of the way and the two Irish platoons isolated at their firebase, the Dios would have one less thing to worry about and no one to lodge an official complaint with the Terran Union. They could after the fact, but with no one in the capital to bring the 5th Marines down on them and stop the invasion they were less than useless.

"Let's go," he said and they pounded down the stairs.

Arroyo looked at his sideways as they descended. "Hell of a way to start our own company, Jefe! Shooting a fellow merc unarmed, a woman at that."

"It's business, sergeant major, only business," replied Mateo. "I'm tired of taking orders from people with less brains than a Grat. So now we do this for our own profit. I noticed," and they turned the final landing, "that you didn't turn down the high salary I offered you."

"I'm not stupid, boss," replied his top NCO, and they exited the stairwell through a rear door into an alley.

"Just think of the money, then. Acción Directa Limited is going to make us all very rich men, starting with this contract."

Outside were two vehicles, a ground effect van that sat very low to the ground with its fans turning slowly and a six wheel truck that contained the rest of his first squad. The other members of his platoon were out in the city hunting key officials of the Theren government but he had reserved the toughest job for himself and his best people.

No one said anything as they drove the five minutes to the Theren HQ, taking back streets to avoid frantically running civilians and random military vehicles. They knew their target and had spotters on the roofs overhead, tracking movement. The convoy carrying the Theren High Commander, a Grausian ex-legion Tribune now called General An-Uthre, had left her home two minutes after the artillery strikes started and was making its way towards the Government House command complex. There was no way an air or missile strike could make it this deep through the ADA purchased from the Terran Union, but where men had the will, technology often didn't matter.

"Are you sure this is going to work?" asked Arroyo of the Charee in the back seat. The four armed alien was fiddling with a set of controls, remote steering the van in front of them. Mateo' dislike of the species didn't extend to not using them where the situation warranted it. The subcontractor guaranteed that his tech would do the job and so far so good. Remote control of weaponry was one of the things that had been banned during the Empire but the past fifteen years of war had, like all wars, spurred exploration of old suppressed technologies and new innovations.

"I need to get within visual range," barked the Charee. "The radio is low powered to avoid detection, I can only control it line of sight. Move, human!"

"Arrogant shit, but we need him," said Mateo in Spanish. "Just do what he says, for now." The driver grunted and sped up to close the distance to the van, going against his instincts. That was how you get trapped and killed in an ambush or blown to hell by an IED. Which was, considering what the van was carrying, fairly ironic.

"Pull over here," ordered Mateo and the truck slowly rolled to a stop, the van slightly ahead of it.

"Kilo, thirty seconds," came over the team radio and everyone tensed. The Kilo OP was the last one on the avenue before the wheeled Armored Personnel Carrier carrying the general turned down the approach street. The air in the truck grew close with the smell of human sweat and Charee musk.

"Kilo, ten seconds."

"Execute," said Mateo calmly and the Charee flipped a switch. The van shot forward into the square, ground effect howling, aiming for the convoy that was just appearing on the video screen. There was an incredibly bright flash and a deafening CRACK as a shaped charge detonated five feet away from the APC. A sheet of copper lining the inside of the explosive turned into a pencil thin jet of plasma that burned its way through the ceramic armor and into the passenger compartment. The General was just off to one side of the penetrator and she lived for a moment longer than her Chief of Staff, who was cut in half. The jet then impacted on a fuel cell and fire shot out of all the gun ports. A second later the two thousand pounds of high explosive packed in the back of the van blew, shattering the lead escort armored car and flipping the rear one on its side. The main gates had just opened to let the vehicles in and the two guards on either side were cut down by shrapnel.

The compression wave shot into the alley where the Acción waited, chunks of rock falling and a swirl of dust surrounding the truck as a mushroom cloud rose over the square. The driver slammed on the gas and they shot forward, aiming for the gates and swerving around the blazing wrecks. Mateo leaned forward on the dash and when the driver slid to a stop, he opened the door and rolled out. The entire compound was mapped out in his mind and he lined up his SBR from memory, searched around and took a shot. The guard at the east tower fell before he could slew his crew-served weapon around to face the compound. Firing once more to make sure, Mateo turned around, leaned back in the door and put a three round burst into the Charee contractor's face. With a grin he turned and ran after his men as they disappeared into the depths of the Theren Defense Command HQ.

The guards on the inside were down with headshots and one of his men was watching their backtrail. The actual entrance to the command bunker was sealed tight already, dog legged around a corner with a machine gun firing down the corridor and rounds hammering at the far wall at even the hint of movement.

"Suicide to charge that, Jefe," said the sergeant major.

For a moment Arroyo stared at his boss. There was a bit of an insane light in his eye, but Mateo finally nodded, "Good thing that isn't the plan. Just keep them occupied. Their QRF should be here in probably," and he looked at his watch, "three minutes." As if to punctuate his words a siren started wailing.

"Sierra," came the call over the team freq from the OP watching the barracks. Good, two minutes. Time to go.

"Zulu," he ordered and nodded to the sergeant major. "On three. One, two … three!"

Both men had unhitched EMP grenades from their belts, new stuff straight from Mars Arms Unlimited. They whipped them down the hallway and ran. There was a crackle of electricity and the lights in the corridor went out. The doors to the bunker were now without power, effectively sealing it shut.

"Vominos!" yelled the sergeant major and the team headed out of the building. The rear guard was exchanging shots with several Theren soldiers who were using the wrecked gate as cover. He emptied his magazine as the squad passed, swapping out a fresh one as he fell into the rear of the line. Another trooper threw a smoke grenade and the courtyard filled with a gray cloud as they made their way around the corner of the building, leaving behind a gunfire simulator that popped and rattled. At the wall they unfolded an assault ladder under the tower with the dead guard and clambered over, dropping the street below. Another vehicle was waiting and they piled in, moving with the precise movements of soldiers who were confident in their success.

Thirty seconds after they were gone the Theren QRF crashed through the gate, three armored trucks filled with infantry and mounting crew served weapons, laser sights making red lines through the chaos. The first one charged into the smoke and the Imperial Legion K-36 demolition charge in the back of the attacker's truck, dialed in to 0.5 kilotons, detonated.

Chapter Four

Forward Operating Base Cribben

"CP, this is OP three, we have two vehicles approaching. Low speed, white flag, over."

Captain Lars Tormund acknowledged the incoming call and told them to hold their fire. He had spent the last hour watching artillery land on the nearest Theren army positions five miles down the road and a procession of armored vehicles moving down the highway past the Irish Forward Operating Base. In his night vision he counted almost a full brigade worth, led by the light vehicles of the 1st Reconnaissance Regiment. Vehicles that were supposed to be loaded onto the same freighter they were going to leave on later that day.

"Were," he said out loud, correcting himself. *"Were* going to leave, ain't happening now."

"What was that, sir?" asked the weapons platoon leader, First Lt. Lishar An - Selene. The Grausian had been taking spot reports from his heavy weapons team, ensuring that they were ready to shoot AND knew not to. There was a time to fight and a time to die and this was neither.

Tormund shook his head. "I don't think the *Scranton* is going to be giving us a ride anytime soon."

"Are you going to surrender? I really don't think this is in our contract," asked Selene.

The captain shook his head. "I can't without word from Major Keely. She's technically the ranking officer dirtside." The fact that she hadn't checked in made him wonder what was going on at the capital, a hundred kilometers away down the valley. Probably nothing good. They had pulled in the last of their patrols prior to moving out later that day with the Therens picking up the slack. Obviously not enough slack, though. "I'll give them credit, it takes a lot of balls to pull off a stunt like this with Terran Union Marines landing tomorrow," continued Tormund.

"Not really, Captain, I'm sure someone in the Marines was tipped off," said Selene. He was watching the vehicles stop and a man get out. Leaving Tormund and the XO to the big picture stuff he turned to one of the NCO's in the TOC. "Hit the floods, Sergeant Yar."

Three glaring flood lights lit off, throwing the base behind it in shadows and ruining any night vision devices an attacker might be wearing. The man standing at the car was revealed to be wearing the uniform of the EUD army, major's rank gleaming on his shoulders. He held up his arm to shield his eyes from the glare and waved the small white flag that he held in one hand.

"OK, let's go see what he wants," said Tormund. "Selene, you might want to stay here. You know how the Dios feel about Grausians."

"Well aware, sir," the xeno answered flatly, with as little emotion in his voice as possible, but Tormund knew that it irritated him beyond words. Then again, being part of a race that had basically ruled the known galaxy for almost a thousand years and sometimes pretty brutally, well, people didn't forget.

Tormund set out on the short walk to where the road breached the perimeter. The fifty or so Irish troopers were manning defensive fighting holes and bunkers, fingers nervously tapping on buttstocks for the younger troops, the veterans kicking back in their fighting holes. They were all alert though, since nobody wanted to die in a war that they weren't getting paid for, one that was now none of their business. Even so, most sat up straighter as their commander walked by. No one wanted to let him down because the big Asgardian, a former Terran Marine NCO, took good care of them. He was bold where he needed to be and cautious when it called for it, not spending lives for his own glory.

Tormund stepped out into the light and saluted the EUD officer, a courtesy since, as far as he knew, there were no active hostilities between them. "Captain Lars Tormund, Bravo Company Commander, Second Battalion, Hibernia Arms Incorporated."

"Yes, of course," replied the man, returning the salute, "I am Major Inigo Juarez, aide to Mariscal Compton, the 54th Independent Brigade Commander. I am here to discuss status of your forces." The man was a bit … stuffed, was the only way that Tormund could describe him. Stuffed into a uniform a little too small. Or maybe swelled up with importance. Many of the staff officers in the EUD Army were civilians who had bought their commissions and, like the majority of the DMZ worlds, had sat out the Succession Wars. The last three months of conflict between the EUD and the breakaway Theren province hadn't been long enough or brutal enough to get rid of this type. Whatever, the contract was done and the most important thing was to extract safely. And get paid, of course.

"Well, sir," replied Tormund, "I am not at liberty to make any decisions about the surrender of my men since my senior officer is not present. I am sure you are aware of the status of forces of private military contractors as per the treaty two weeks ago. Though things do seem to have changed," said Tormund, with a bit of irony in his voice.

The major seemed surprised at Tormund's words. "Surrender? Nonsense! All we ask is that you and your men remain stationary while this operation is carried out. Our legal officer assures me that there is no obligation in your contract to conduct offensive operations in support of Theren forces. This is a completely different matter than the -" and the man's words were cut short as his head exploded showering the car with blood and brains.

*****

Two hundred meters behind Tormund, on top of a bunker close to the Operations Center, Private Jeanne Trudeau looked at her SBR with amazement. She had been watching the exchange between the EUD officer and Captain Tormund half out of interest and half out of boredom. The young Alpha Prime native had arrived as a replacement three weeks prior, had yet to see any combat and she was still dealing with being the "New Guy" in her squad. All she knew so far of deployment was filling sandbags and walking patrols through a steaming jungle, nowhere close to the beaches the recruiter had told her about. She had shifted the red dot of her scope over to the EUD officer, playing with sighting on him and imagining what it would be like to pull the trigger, when the stock had suddenly slammed back into her shoulder with an accompanying WHAP from the suppressor.

"WHAT THE FUCK DID YOU JUST DO!" yelled her team leader from the next hole over and the other person in her fighting position, Corporal Mahkah, just said, "Holy Shit!" in Lakota.

*****

Tormund stared at the major's body as it sprawled over the low slung hood. Then his eyes rose to meet those of the driver, who had exited the vehicle as they talked. He saw his shock and surprise mirrored on the other mans' face, but there was something else. Fear. The driver scrabbled at the pistol in a cross draw holster on his chest but fumbled it and dropped the gun on the ground, Tormund clawing at his own submachine machine gun that had been slung at his back. Up top in the vehicle's small open turret a woman struggled to get her light machine gun around to fire on Tormund. Another CRACK from the hilltop and she was slammed backwards to fall bonelessly through the opening and disappear, dead hands squeezing the trigger and sending a stream of tracers up into the sky.

"DON'T DO IT!" yelled Tormund, the former Terran Marine reacting lighting quick, the gun in his hands and sight lined up on the terrified man who had grabbed the pistol. The EUD soldier seemed to pause and then lifted it, hands shaking and Tormund put three rounds into his chest as the plasma pistol sparked. The Irishman fell to one knee, grabbing his shoulder and yelled a curse.

Behind him there was a WHOOSH CRACK as an Imperial plasma blower from one of the bunkers erupted and slammed into the escorting vehicle behind, turning it into a ball of flame before the occupants could react.

*****

In the CP there was a stunned silence as the echo of the gunshots died out. Then the landlines and radios erupted with a confusing babble of voices stepping over each other on the nets. The company XO, Lieutenant Ferguson, picked up a hand mike and bellowed, "CLEAR THE NET! CHECK FIRE CHECK FIRE CHECK FIRE!" then turned to Selene and said, "Get the boss, NOW!"

The Grausian turned and ran out of the TOC. The Quick Reaction Force was already hauling ass down the road and he put on a burst of speed to catch up to them. As he caught up he put a long arm on Staff Sergeant Morales shoulder and yelled in his ear, "Secure the captain, get him back to the TOC, then have your guys reinforce the gate."

"We're gonna be in a world of shit, ain't we, LT?" asked Morales, but both already knew the answer to that question.

Chapter Five

"One round into the shoulder, you're going to be in a lot of pain, but no arteries or broken bones. It's gonna hurt like a sonofabitch but one of those fancy little plasma pistols aren't going to do jack shit because they burn through instead of punching like a bullet. Matter of fact I wrote a paper last ..." Doc Knowles trailed off as he finally saw the look on Captain Tormund's' face. "Anyway, you're good to go if you don't get a nasty infection from this shithole and those burns are going to have to be treated or you're going to need some serious nano therapy when we get back home."

"Good enough, thanks Doc. I'm going to need you on the perimeter, a world of shit is going to come down on us." Then Tormund turned to his XO. "Where ..." and he looked paler as a wave of pain washed through him, "is Selene? And Lt. Collins?"

"I've got Selene moving the heavy weapons around, concentrating them towards the road. When they hit us, it's not going to be anything fancy; they're too busy dealing with the Therens. Collins is putting together a forward OP across the road so we have eyes on what's coming." Ferguson was making notes on paper, redrawing the defense. "Back side, too."

"Good," grunted Tormund as the medic tightened a bandage. "I want you to start drawing up an exfil plan into the jungle and keep trying to reach the EUD leadership. What's our coms like?"

"Sir," interjected Sergeant Yar, "I think I got a message out to the relay beacon, but can't be sure. I'd say fifty fifty, but there's really hard jamming on all freqs. That includes all the Theren nets. We can't talk to anyone."

"OK, I want you to find the biggest white sheet or whatever and run it up the flagpole. It MIGHT stop them, but I don't know. Any input?"

"What do you want me to do with that kid that fired the shot?" asked Sergeant Major Huy. The Illyrian NCO had been sitting quietly, thinking and taking everything in. His red face was darker than normal and the scales on his skin were hardened bumps. He expected a fight, or at least his body did, tail swishing from side to side.

Tormund turned to him and said, "You're leaving, now, sergeant major. Get to the Illyrian trading delegation in Bai Alng and get off planet. Get back to the boss and tell him our situation. At the least he'll be able to claim our bodies."

"Yessir," said Huy simply, picked up an already full ruck and disappeared out through the canvas flap that covered the bunker entrance.

"Think he'll make it?" asked Ferguson, who had transferred from Alpha Company in First Battalion only two months ago and didn't really know the xeno that well.

"If anyone can. I bet he has civilian clothes in that pack, some nasty surprises and a ton of gold along with a platinum Illyrian credit card. Remind me to get him to tell you his story about breaking out of a Grausian POW camp." Tormund actually smiled at that before wincing in pain.

******

It was quiet. The Dios bombardment of the Theren positions had stopped and the artillery was probably shifting positions to follow the attacking brigade. The armored column had trickled off to be replaced with trucks carrying infantry and supplies.

"You know, max range on a blower is two thousand meters. If we hit one of those fuel trucks..." said Sergeant MacDougal, almost in idle speculation. She and LT Selene were sitting in the heavy weapons platoon command post at the front of the base, a sturdily constructed bunker that also contained one of their two plasma blowers and a heavy machine gun. The air inside was humid, stinking of sweat and jungle and MacDougal was using a piece of rubber to clean the contacts on a hand set. She was the platoon commo sergeant and took her job very seriously, making sure the hardwired field phones were up and running between the CP and the forward positions.

Selene finished his thought for her. "It would snarl up traffic, disrupt supply of the forward columns and maybe give the Therens time to organize a defense. And draw even more attention to us."

"Heads up, OP reports company coming," came the voice Lt. Collins, the other platoon leader over the field phone.

As if in answer to their conversation four APC's appeared and diverted towards the fields between the firebase and the road, followed by half a dozen trucks. Infantry began to dismount and Selene could see through his night vision that they were a bit disorganized, leadership actually kicking and shoving some of them to get into an assault position. He picked up the hand mic and called in the spot report. "CP, looks like we've got about a company's worth of light infantry with four Rhinos to back them up. I'm thinking they aren't their front line troops."

"I'll be there in a minute," said Tormund, *"make sure everyone holds their fire."*

"Roger, weapons tight." A feeling of calm was coming over the Grausian, something that he had experienced before. Being a male his gender had been bred for war but not for leadership. That was reserved for the females and he was still learning his way from the humans. Fighting, though … well, this was going to be a fight. He could feel it in his bones and instead of fear a thrill shot through him. MacDougal wished him luck and then headed out to the next bunker.

Sitting in front of Selene looking through firing ports that pointed off at oblique angles were the two heavy weapons teams. He poked Corporal Greene on the shoulder to get his attention. "Remember, you shoot that OUTSIDE the bunker. Got it?"

"I know what I'm doing... sir," answered the human, with a bit of a dirty look. Most in the Brigade respected Selene for his actions on Holcomb and the raid on the space station last year, but there were some who held onto a bit of their prejudices. Selene just looked at him until the human turned away. The unblinking Grausian stare could be very unnerving.

"Greene, no seas gilipollas," said Staff Sergeant Morales, who had just slipped into the bunker. "The LT is just looking out for you. Matter of fact, beat feet outside and get ready." He turned to Selene and said, "Just checking the range card on the Mark 13," referring to the machine gun. The sabot round fired a thirteen millimeter shot that sent a tungsten penetrator downrange at fifteen hundred meters per second. It could blow off a track on a tank or damage a side skirt pretty damn badly and go end to end through the Rhino APC's if it found a weak spot in the armor. The blowers, on the other hand, pretty much could nail anything up to a light spaceship. Problem with them is that it left a bright line back to the firing position that quickly brought return fire. It was a trade off, really and two blower teams could work in tandem, shooting and moving. Selene designed a brutal training regime with Staff Sergeant Morales pushing the crews hard.

When Greene had left the bunker Morales' tone changed and became much more that of a friend than a subordinate. "What I don't understand, Thal Selene," he said, using the Grausian's formal title, "is why you're even here anyway. I mean, you own a frigging PLANET now and you're richer than shit." He was referring to Selene's inheritance, against female dominated Grausian tradition, of his family estate. The fact that the estate was the entire planetary system of Holcomb IV and rich in rare earth minerals, well, that was land ownership in the Empire.

Selene gave out a dry rasp, a Grausian laugh. "Tell me, what would you do with an entire planet's worth of wealth?"

"Well, screw myself silly, first, or course," smirked Morales. He winked at MacDougal, who shot him the finger. Their encounter the night before in the latrine had been great, relatively. Today was all business.

Selene shook his head, almost mournfully. "Not an option for me. Imagine the politics. Plus, well, male Grausians are kind of at the mercy of females when it comes to mating," he grimaced. The females choose their mates, not the other way around and often it wasn't exactly a 'choice'.

"Hmm. Good point. Honestly, past that, I dunno." It was true, Morales really couldn't think of anything. He was a soldier; many days he woke up surprised he was still alive. A year from now was an impossible thought.

"You would be right here, staring down an enemy, spitting in the eye of death, feeling alive," said his commander and his friend. "Maybe it's different for humans, but for a Grausian, it's a thrill. Or it was, before the Empire got soft."

"Nah, humans are the same way. I mean, it gets old after a while and I think we were getting slack too before the Empire kicked the crap out of us. Heads up!" finished Morales as Captain Tormund slid into the bunker. He was followed by a female human wearing privates' rank who looked pale and scared. In her hand was clutched a white t-shirt, probably civilian gear taken from someone's duffle.

"Selene, I want you to take this idiot, go out there with a flag of truce and explain what happened. If it goes sideways, just get to cover, we'll come get you." It was a command and not one to be argued with.

"Yes sir. Terms?"

Tormund thought for a moment then said, "Armistice with small arms and transport off planet."

"They aren't going to accept that," said Selene. He spoke it with a finality tinged with some fatalism.

His commander nodded, but then said, "That's the difference between you Imperials and us humans. We never give up hope. Ever. Another lesson for you. Now get to it and don't get yourself killed."

"What about her?" asked Selene, nodding to the ashen faced Private Trudeau. "We could hang her as a show of good faith," he ventured.

Again the momentary consideration as the captain weighed the good of the many against the good of the few. "I suppose she'll get hung eventually after a court martial back on Eire, but I can't make that call. Of course, if she redeems herself in the next few minutes that will go in her favor."

Chapter Six

"Well, here goes nothing," said Selene, standing outside the bunker, SBR slung across his back and Private Trudeau standing next to him, holding a stick with the white t-shirt tied to it. He started walking towards the entrance to the base, taking note of the two plasma guns set up on either side. The positions were sandbagged well enough and nervous tension showed on the faces of the mercenaries stationed there. He wondered how many would cut and run. Some, maybe. It was hard to spend money that you died for, but the veterans wouldn't leave their friends.

Well, as Colonel Meagher would have told him, that was leadership. Getting people to do things that, on the face of it, were insane. Lishar An-Selene squared his shoulders and walked calmly forward.

*****

For Private Jeanne Trudeau, it was like walking to a firing squad. Her mind was close to the breaking point with disbelief and anguish. Nineteen years old, just missing the final draft for the Succession Wars and she had gone and freaking enlisted in a merc company instead of college. It had all seemed like a game, making friends, training against electronic targets, her past few weeks walking patrols after she had arrived on planet. Now she was going to die on some godforsaken world, dozens of light years from home. Tears streamed down her face as she walked next to Lt. Selene and she sobbed gently. Hell, she was still a goddamned virgin.

"It's beautiful, isn't it?" asked the alien, his cat's eyes looking toward the sky.

Momentarily driven out of her stupor by the words, she stopped and said, "What?"

"The sunrise. On Holcomb we don't have a lot of water and dust usually keeps the sun obscured until it's well above the horizon. This world, well, the sunrise is beautiful." He had stopped also and since the firebase was set up on a hill, they could see the blueish white hot star rising, bringing with it this world's equivalent of birds to full waking. The jungle literally exploded with sound at the touch of the sun.

"If it's one thing I've learned in the past two years, each day might be your last. Appreciate it and hope that the Empresses of us all notices your attention." He said it almost in a chant, as if a prayer. In response she crossed herself, glanced around at the sky, muttered something and started forward again. Selene walked on beside her, ears tilted, listening to the shouts of the Dios infantry getting in position.

"OK, far enough," he said. "Start waving that flag like your life depends on it and be ready to run your ass off."

There was a blinding flash of light that dazzled Selene's eyes and he heard a chopped off scream from the woman next to him. Diving to the right after the flash he could hear the whip crack of supersonic rounds passing by him, then the ground smashed into his face. The Irish Brigade machine guns opened up, a heavy tattoo that he felt through the ground.

"SHIT SHIT SHIT!" screamed Private Trudeau at the top of her lungs .

"Where are you hit?" yelled Selene. He was blinded by the dazzler and it wouldn't pass for a few minutes. It was a Terran weapon, designed to affect Grausian neurons, but it worked on humans too, just much less effectively. He guessed the Dios militia were throwing every surplus piece of weaponry they had into the fight.

"I … I'm not!" said Trudeau and she broke out in peals of hysterical laughter.

"CAN YOU SEE?" he asked urgently. Overhead the firefight had turned into a massive exchange of shots. No one was going to come out and get them any time soon but they were safe enough if they stayed where they were. She was only a few feet from him and a dip in the road gave them slight cover.

There was no answer for a long moment and then she said, "I think so, sir, yes, I can! I'm going to get help!" with a note of hysteria in her young voice.

"NO! STAY RIGHT WHERE … damn," finished Selene. He had heard the dull THWAP that a large bullet makes going through flesh, then the sound like someone dropping a heavy duffel bag. That was followed by a splatter of hot coppery smelling liquid and something wet and squishy that landed on his neck. He brushed off the still warm piece of meat and lay there, waiting for the fire to die down, A rumbling through the dirt of what could only be a tracked vehicle and the faint shouts of the infantry screaming as they charged forward. Time to get out of there. He started to low crawl back down the road towards the entrance, a million kilometers and twenty meters away in hopefully the right direction.

*****

Blinking back the dazzle from his eyes, Staff Sergeant Morales saw movement in front of the gate, a stirring in the shadows where sunlight hadn't touched yet. The former Terran Marine corporal knew what a dazzler did to Grausians; he had used them to good effect himself in the wars. If the LT just waited, he would be OK. Then all hell broke loose, incoming rounds hammering at the emplacements, a heavy plasma gun and two machine guns. He glanced over at Captain Tormund but the commander had disappeared out of the back entrance, heading for the main CP. OK, then, up to him.

"TAKE OUT THE CREW SERVED!!!" he yelled over the racket, slipping out of the back of the dugout to get a better view. Just then an incoming rocket impacted one of the far bunkers on the left side of the perimeter, silencing it and raising a mushroom cloud of dirt and dust. He heard a whistle blow, three short blasts and knew that the captain was sending the QRF platoon to deal with another attack, probably a diversion. Not his problem.

With a teeth grinding hmmm CRACK one of the blowers sent a jet of plasma straight through the lead APC, blocking the road. Corporal Greene might have been an obnoxious ass, but he handled the heavy tube like a sniper. The vehicle caved in on itself, ceramic and aluminum armor turning to superheated vapor and washing over the infantry squad behind it. Half a dozen figures spread out like little torches, wandering dizzily and then falling to the ground. Greene's laughter as he and his loader shifted to a new position almost made Morales' stomach turn, but he had a job to do. His next stop was one of the machine gun crews, directing their fire at the infantry, stopping their charge cold with bursts of suppressing fire that uncaringly, mechanically walked its way across the field.

*****

The blindness slowly disappeared from Selene's eyes, nerves finally coping with the overload. He stopped and stared at the road for a second, color perception gone but plenty of shades of gray. And black, too, pools of it. Off to one side sat the head of Private Trudeau, one eye blown out and the other staring at him accusingly, her mouth open in surprise. Selene looked away, plenty of time for nightmares and guilt later.

The gunfire dribbled off and then stopped except for rounds cooking off in the destroyed vehicles. He was about to start up and run towards the entrance when boots thudded on the ground and rough hands grabbed his harness, dragging him across the road and back to their position, rolling him over and dumping him into a dugout.

"ARE YOU HIT?" Bravo's medic, Corporal Akari, yelled in his ear, running hands up and down the Grausian's skin, sometimes going the wrong way and irritating the fine feathers on his forearms. Selene took a deep breath, letting the medic do his job. He had seen troops in the heat of battle get life threatening wounds and not notice until it was too late. When a bright light was flashed in his irritated eyes, though, he batted it away.

"Get me some sunglasses!" he ordered, sitting up. "I'm OK, but my eyes are screwed up."

Akari slapped his knee, nodded and took off running in the direction of another cry of "Medic!"

"You OK, boss?" said a voice. "Want to take a little nap or something?" grinned Morales, white teeth flashing on his tanned face.

"Jose, give me a report-" he started to say when the interceptor laser started whining, the beams glittering through the dust from the assault. At the same moment the incoming siren wailed, a deep BWAH BWAH that indicated heavy ordnance. Selene had made it halfway up out of the hole when Morales, who had been standing on the edge, gave him a tremendous shove with his boot that sent his LT tumbling into the bunker. Then the world disappeared in unimaginable loudness.

Chapter Seven

Firebase Cribben
Thirty six hours after the attack.

He tried to move his arm, drag it out from under the beam. No use, it was a heavy piece of timber that had held up the roof and hundreds of pounds of sandbags above it. Selene lay there, thinking about what to do next. Obviously get out, but he had a raging thirst. He felt around with his free hand and encountered the body he had shoved off. First he felt a face, human and sticky. Then he grasped what he was looking for, the end of a drinking tube. "Thank you, Empress!" he croaked and tried to pull it closer. It stretched a little but stopped more than a foot from his mouth. He silently cursed and let it fall, then grabbed frantically at the body, pulling it towards him with one arm, his greater Grausian strength helping him overcome his condition. Finally the tip of the tube was close enough that he could contort himself enough to reach it.

Selene took a long pull and then choked, spitting it out. The liquid was warm orange juice mixed with vodka, the taste of the alcohol bitter in his alien mouth. By the gods, he would have had that trooper whipped and this was HIS platoon! His exhaustion was replaced with fury at the dead soldier and with a burst of energy he pulled as hard as he could at his trapped arm. With a snapping sound the watch band broke and much of his skin tore but his wrist slowly dragged free with a cry of anguish. The pain was incredible and his breath came in labored rasps.

"Hey!" came a muffled voice from up above and then some words in Spanish, at the same time as some twittering from the darkness to his left. There were sounds of someone digging, two people talking back and forth, one a woman or a teen, the other an older man. Both humans. Holding his bleeding wrist to his chest, not caring about the dirt that must have been getting into the wound, he felt for his pistol that had been strapped to his leg. Gone, somewhere in the darkness.

"Help me!" The words startled Selene, computer generated ragged sounds coming from the debris on his left, underlaid by more twittering. There was an excited conversation above and dim light began to appear. With a crash a section of corrugated steel was shoved aside and brilliant blue white light sunlight flooded into the ruin, revealing an open space that had been the left side of the bunker. It shone directly onto the face of Private Orahst, a birdlike alien, one of the communication specialists who was a runner from HQ. "Thank you, please, help me get out of -" and then two puffs of dust on its dirty uniform as a burst of shots popped from above. Orahst groaned, shivered and laid still.

Selene reached over to his left side and placed his hand on the hilt of the ancient Imperial poniard on his belt. The vibro-knife's battery was long dead but the mono-molecular edge could still cut through steel. Then he lay very, very still, both eyes closed, listening to the work going on around him, debris being shifted. He didn't hear any Tricero or Dios ranks used, though he was familiar with them from the fighting over the past three months. He distinctly heard personal names. Looters, maybe, come to scavenge the battlefield.

That didn't make them any less dangerous, as Orahst had found out.

Shadows danced and he slowly opened his eyes. Unlike humans Grausians didn't have eyelashes, rather an inner membrane that they could open or close at will. To someone not looking very hard his eye remained closed, a thin film over the slitted iris and he saw two dark figures, backlit by the sunlight, climb down into the remains of the bunker, shoving aside pieces of debris to get at the corpses. One exclaimed with delight, pulling out a dirty SBR that lay jumbled in with a shattered commo unit. The other started going through the pockets of the dead soldier that lay next to Selene, expressing disgust at the smell that was coming from the spilled guts. The looter had a battered suppressed submachine gun slung across the front of his body and a large sack over his shoulder for holding scavenged items. He hummed to himself as he went through pockets, probably to keep his mouth shut against the smell. Then he shoved the body aside and reached for Selene, leaning over to move his arm.

With his wounded left hand the Grausian grabbed the man by the shoulder, double joints wrapping themselves around and pulling him close. His other drew the knife in one motion and slashed across, just under the gun, the blade cutting through cloth, skin and bone, from stomach up through lungs and into his heart. The man made a surprised WHOOF! and blood erupted out of his mouth, over the side of Selene's turned head. Another quick cut of the sling of the gun as the woman asked, "Arturo?". It was a locally manufactured 10mm issued to the Dios militia, one Selene had familiarized himself with. He shoved the dying man off him and looked at the woman, pulling the gun out and staring at her. To the looter he must have looked like an apparition from the grave, an alien covered in dirt, grime and blood. He checked the bolt, making sure there was a round in the chamber, flicked the selector to single shot and put two in her chest as she started to put her hands to her mouth to scream. She collapsed to her knees and fell forward into the hole, landing atop Orahst' body then rolling over.

The woman had a look of surprise on her face, which was by human standards not very pretty. Old and worn, which was good. Definitely looters, not part of any Dios force scavenging the base. He cautiously crawled over and pulled a canteen off her belt, sipping the water like it was more precious than gold. All the while he kept the gun trained on the hole, waiting for some response. Grenades, probably, in which case he was screwed. Nothing happened for almost a minute, time he used to drain the canteen. There was little he could do for Private Orahst, who had no heart anymore. Instead he recovered his own pistol, wiping futility at the blood and viscera covering it, until finally he just jammed it in his leg holster. The entire time he kept the SMG pointed at the hole in the roof. All this while crammed into a space not much bigger than his own body, with the dead all around him.

"Empress watch over me," he muttered quietly and shifted around to move to the new entrance. Slowly, ever so slowly he lifted his head just enough to see the immediate surroundings of the back of the bunker.

More dead bodies, many in Dios black with their distinctive crimson crosses and a few in Irish camo. They had swollen up in the summer heat and were starting to strain the uniform cloth. Looking closely, he identified one soldier of his platoon, Corporal Greene, locked forever in death with a

Dios soldier, knife in his guts and hands wrapped around his enemies' neck. Another was an infantry sergeant from third platoon, sword in his hand and five dead enemy in front of him. Selene could almost hear Master Sergeant Boru saying, "Well, here's a song to be sung in the hall on a cold winter's night." He nodded his head in respect to the two who had gone down fighting.

There was no movement anywhere on the base, though vehicles traveled on the main road a kilometer away. Every bunker that hadn't been hit by indirect fire had been wrecked by a demo charge and there were heavy artillery craters all over. A small, battered four wheeled powered cart sat at what had been the entrance, probably the looter's vehicle. From a broken commo antenna at the CP hung a tattered shred of green and gold cloth, maybe a quarter of the Irish Brigade standard with a burned edge and several holes from bullets and plasma. "Survival is the priority," said Selene to himself, mind still reeling from everything that had happened. It was the first time he had been involved in an actual defeat and he felt guilt as he looked at Greene's dead body. That was his troop, no matter how much he had disliked him and the Grausian had failed him. It tasted even more bitter than the vodka in the soldiers' water bladder and he couldn't spit it out.

"Well, survival second, more important things first," he said aloud to the dead man and made his way over to the battered flag. Someone had tied it to the whip antenna after the flagpole had been shattered and it was splattered with blood. With great care Selene cut it down and folded it, putting into the leg pocket of his dirt smeared uniform. Then he looked at the dozen bodies in a makeshift aide station where the Command Post had been. All had been wounded and bandaged to some degree, except for the single hole in each ones' forehead. Someone had shot them as they lay there and Doc Acari's brown eyes were open, getting pecked at by a bird.

"Now survival, escape and revenge." It was almost a prayer. "I'll be back for you, I swear," he said to the dead and slowly, with incredible weariness, he made his way out towards the jungle.

Chapter Eight

Bai Alng, Capital of the Therer Republic

Huy Yurtay, AKA Sergeant Major Huy, 2nd Battalion, The Irish Brigade, waited patiently in the shadows of a city at war. He had to give the Therens credit; they were putting up a pretty good fight for having gotten the crap initially kicked out of them. There was a running gun battle two blocks over between the truck drivers of a transportation unit and a platoon of Dios regulars with screaming civilians caught in between. Maybe now might not be a good time to insert himself into it, since he pretty much looked like the human idea of a demon, right down to a barbed tail, horns, red skin and sharp teeth. Panicked people would start shooting ANYTHING, much less a nightmare. That and bullets don't care who they killed once they left the barrel.

So he stuck to shadows and relied on his knife instead of his gun. His destination was the Illyrian trading mission by the spaceport. Huy was an oddity, one of his race who actually got involved in fighting. Ex-Imperial Legionnaire, Former Terran Marine, current mercenary, he had turned his back on the profit his people had made on wars of the last two decades and risen steadily through the ranks. That didn't mean he had completely walked away from his kin; after all, information was the ultimate currency and he traded on it often.

The hard part was going to be *getting* into the compound. It was guarded by its own contingent of LaChan mercenaries, six limbed lizard types who were the weakest political unit but some of the fiercest warriors in the Old Empire. Huy would have to take a chance to expose his identity to them and hope his species would gain him entry. He watched them from the darkness, catching occasional glimpses of figures moving behind bright floodlights. The next minute would either see him shot or safe, but it was better than dodging Dios patrols all the way back to the capital. That had been a nightmare, sneaking onto a militia truck full of ammunition and then jumping out ten kilometers from the capitol as it passed over a bridge. Then fighting his way through a refugee column of people of all species fleeing the city. Now he was exhausted and hopefully thinking straight, but maybe not.

Behind the spotlights there was a brief flare of a cigarette lighter and he caught a glimpse of a red face. The Illyrian wore the expensive robes of a senior trader and Huy immediately stepped forward, raising his hands to his mouth and shouting in his own language, "COUSIN!" It was an honorific, not necessarily true but good enough. Then he took a deep breath, counted to ten and stepped out into the spotlight, tense but calm at the same time. The next few seconds he'd either be dead or safe.

A spotlight shifted, pinned him against the brick wall, but it wasn't followed by gunfire. Instead a heavily armored trio of LaChan, one of their family triad fireteams, rushed out, moving incredibly fast in their loping four legged run. He placed his hands in the air and two of them knocked him down, cuffed him behind his back and heaved him up. The third stood, slaved power gun dancing around in time with the LaChan's bobbing, scanning head. Then they were up and moving towards the courtyard. With a thud they threw him to the pavement at the foot of the expensively dressed

Illyrian, whose only action was to draw deeply on the cigar clenched in his teeth and blow cigar smoke at the captive.

"Cousin, I claim sanctuary," said Huy. He didn't choke, merely luxuriated in the smoke. It was Terran, from an island called 'Cuba' and like most of his species, he was mad for it.

The Trade Guild official looked at him for a long moment then finally said, "Good evening, Sergeant Major Huy. I have been expecting you to come running back here like a hartr with your tail between your legs." The word was an insult, referencing a particularly dirty animal on the Illyrian home world. "What information do you have that would buy you sanctuary? Obviously you bring no goods to trade."

Thinking furiously because he was on dangerous ground, Huy answered, in the ritual way, "Information of the future is better than information of the now."

Another puff of smoke. "And what is this information of the future?"

"The mercenary leadership is possibly looking to form a collective within the next year or so to manage contracts and conflicts." He waited, letting the official take it in. The guilds probably had rumor of this already, but confirmation from a highly placed source was worth an immense price.

"And what do you require?" was the next question.

That was easy. "Transport off planet to inform Hibernia Arms, LLC, the status of the two platoons left here."

A grim smile emerged from his fellow Illyrians' face. "What platoons? Your firebase was destroyed early yesterday morning. So far as we know, there weren't any survivors." There was even a note of sympathy in the voice, even though Huy was considered an anomaly for actually becoming a combatant. He snapped his fingers and a LaChan came over, uncuffing Huy.

Burying his feelings, the immediate grief that struck him, the mercenary asked, "Did you know about this?" waving his arm in the general direction of the city. A red glow had started over by the warehouse district as something big started to burn and tracers still arched across the sky.

"About what?" It was obvious that his 'cousin' had known all about the offensive, but apparently the Trade Mission had decided that that information wasn't worth any price the Therens could pay. Or the Dios paid more for silence. "We have negotiated for your information and unless you have something else of such value, you have no need to know anything more from us in return."

Huy knew that the guild member wouldn't yield. He had plenty of information to sell, but nothing that wouldn't betray Colonel Meagher's' trust. "When can I get off the planet then?"

"We are waiting for payment on something … ah here it is now." A heavy duty truck pulled up to the gate and Dios soldiers jumped out, fanning out to form a perimeter. The LaChan stayed at their posts but ignored the humans as if they weren't there. A whistle blew and from the darkness came an answering call, then a column of figures emerged from the darkness of the same area Huy had been hiding in minutes earlier. With a start he realized that they were Grausians, tall figures with chains around their necks.

"Slaves? The Guild now trades in SLAVES?" Huy was furious as he rounded on the Guildsman, ready to rend flesh with his sharpened teeth.

"Hardly," said an accented voice and a newcomer appeared from the darkness behind the flood lights. It was another Grausian, but this one wore the high collared black uniform of a New Empire officer and sported the ranks of a

Legate, or full Colonel. "More like liberators." A half dozen Imperial Legionaries came forward as the slaves entered the compound, maybe fifty or so and they began unlocking the chains. The Dios soldiers ignored the Imperials, climbing back into the trucks and leaving.

Pulling Huy aside the Illyrian guildsman said in a low voice, "You'll be on the freighter *Printey K-Alta* in a few days and I have arranged for you to be dropped off at one of the DMZ worlds with a gate before they transit into New Empire space. Where you go from there is your business, but until then you may stay here. You have seen what you have seen and there is value, as always, in information." He stared meaningfully at the Imperial officer. "Along with you will be a representative of the former Theren government."

"New Empire messing around in the DMZ. There are many who would like to know that," mused Huy. "Why are you passing this on to me? What value does it bring you?"

"You are of the Yurtay clan, are you now?" said the tradesman.

Huy nodded. "This you know, but I have also been away for decades."

"You will pass a message then, to your elders. Certain younger members have seen fit to engage in piracy instead of commerce." It was said with a bitter element of disgust. "Your elders probably already know, but the message to them is this. 'Handle it or be cast out'."

"Piracy? Are you serious?" spluttered Huy. There were a few, like him, that joined the military out of a sense of adventure and sometimes at the direction of their Clan Elders, to gather information. Piracy, though, to become mere thieves, was abhorrent to the Illyrians as a race, seeing as how it upset the normal flow of trade.

"Yes. Apparently, it is a business deal with some Terran corporations. Insurance scams, theft, outright destruction. You will tell them, end it or be cast out. Hryty would be the preferred way. Perhaps you can attend to it yourself. After all, you are killer." With that the older Illyrian turned his back on Huy and walked away.

Chapter Nine

The militia had picked up Selene's trail the day before when he had stumbled into a prosperous but quiet farmstead. There were shirts hanging on a line and he waited until nightfall before snatching one, replacing his uniform blouse. The fatigue pants he could do nothing about, but now he had at least a chance of blending into the civilian population. He had expected some kind of guard animal but the house was quiet and as he pulled the shirt on the wind shifted bringing the coppery smell of fresh blood. Squinting hard he closed his inner eye membrane, changing the black and gray colors of the night into shades of yellow and red. A very few Grausians had a primitive form of infrared vision registered by the membrane, a legacy of some genetic tampering centuries ago. It wasn't something he thought often about; he had been scheduled for surgery to remove it as a child when the war broke out. More than ninety percent of the Grausians who were born with it eventually went blind from it before they turned forty; it was more a blessing than a curse, but he was grateful for it now.

There were three bodies, still slightly above the ambient air temperature. All of his own species, one smaller, a child, with splashes of blood showing dark against a wall. Anger blazed up inside of him and he made to step forward when a spotlight flicked on, blinding him.

"¡COSIGUELE!" yelled a voice and shots rang out. They impacted the dirt and he heard laughter and a truck engine revving. Selene ran as fast as he could towards the house and around one side, then down a garden path towards the jungle. More shots ripped past on either side, not coming close, herding him towards the tree line. Cutting left he dove behind a tree, pulled out his pistol and fired half a dozen times at the spotlight. He heard a yell and then a machine gun opened up, ripping high over his head and showering his position with twigs and leaves. Keeping the tree between him and his pursuers Selene ran as fast as he could in a straight line into the underbrush.

All through the night they had dogged his steps and he had no time to rest, heading deeper and deeper into the jungle. Their shouts were accompanied by laughter; this was a game to them and they gave him no rest. He kept moving, listening for the barking of dogs, stopping only to drink some water from the occasional stream, still going even after they faded away. Just after dawn he came close to a field planted with some root vegetables, across from another farmhouse, large, even more like a manor than a farm. Several Grausians were at the front, one in rich clothing, probably the estate owner and her field hands. There were a few humans also, maybe eight people total. Although this was a world that had been at the edge of the Empire the social divisions had carried over. Females ruled and males worked, but these males were all armed. Her retainers expecting trouble, but they carried swords and simple hunting weapons.

For a moment he thought to call out and get their attention but then he heard the fans of air-cushioned vehicles coming up the oil covered dirt road. Selene crouched down by a tree and watched as three battered trucks, one wheeled, pulled up in front of the house flying the cross and hammer of the Dios militia.

The female Grausian walked forward and started yelling at the militia men. One of them, dressed in a black uniform with an armband, dismounted and started arguing with her. Both rose in volume until the militiaman raised his arm and then dropped it. The medium machine gun mounted on top of the truck opened fire, mowing down the farmhands like a scythe through standing grain. They fell, some knocked backwards and others just collapsing, none managing to fire a shot. The farmer screamed and launched herself at the man. a head taller than him and stronger, but he hit her with a shock baton, a brilliant blue flash of electricity and a snap that Selene heard across the field.

That was when a bullet caught Selene in the smallest finger of his left hand as he watched, leaning up against a giant tree. He held his hand in front of his face, looking at the stump in amazement. The second suppressed shot TWACKED into the tree and he heard laughter echoing from far up the slope. Shoving the wounded hand into the opening of the simple peasants' shirt he wore the Grausian dove forward into the underbrush.

"RUN, IMPY DOG!" yelled a voice from behind him in Common, not Spanish. "WHEN YOU GOT TO HELL, TELL THEM JUAN DOMINGO SENT YOU THERE!" There was another burst of laughter and unaimed gunfire ripped overhead. Selene took a moment to look towards the farm house; the patrol had picked up the noble and was shoving her into the back of the truck. The shot had come from a hill back further in the jungle. So, two separate groups. He was tired of running and they had circled almost all the way back to the devastated fire base. The snipers had been herding him and that other patrol was probably there to be the anvil they would hammer him into. Time to show them what being an Imperial Legionary had once meant. They expected him to run, based on the last twenty four hours. Instead, he would fight.

Ahead was a gully, carved through the jungle by the frequent downpours. Water ran through it but this was the tail end of the wet season, not very deep. He ran to the far edge, making his prints obvious, then with a tremendous leap managed to clear the brush on the other side. Another jump and he rolled onto a thicket of brambles and thorns, biting back curses and holding absolutely still. With luck, they would think he had run up or downstream in an attempt to confuse the trail and would turn sideways.

He didn't have to wait long; the first thing that appeared was a hunting panther on a leash, cautiously stepping forward. It was an Earth animal, genmodified centuries ago to provide Grausian nobles with hunting beasts and Selene felt an icy chill run down his spine. This was an older one with burn scars on its face and an '82' painted on its side, the number of kills it had. A veteran, not likely to make a mistake. It followed his path right to the water's edge then looked both up and downstream. Selene held his pistol in steady grip; he loved animals and was reluctant to kill this one, but it was far more dangerous than the men who followed behind. He watched it sniff the ground, then it raised its head and looked directly towards where the Grausian lay and coughed once, a challenge.

"Cazar!" yelled the handler, hidden behind the trees with a long leash. He let it slip and the panther bounded forward, across the riverbank and directly at where Selene was hiding … and stopped. Both eyed each other; Selene deciding whether to shoot and the panther looking at the tangle of barbs and long thorns that had already drawn blood from his target. They held that pose for a long moment, each knowing that the other was likely to get a kill. Up close the panther was battered, face scarred, ears torn, ribs showing and fur matted from poor treatment. He had been abused and misused often since his days as a favored servant on some Imperial estate.

Then Selene said softly, "Go, my brother. No need to die today. I know you. Go be free," and rolled to expose his throat to the beast. He said all this in the old Imperial Hunting language, taught to him by his grandmother back in better days on Holcomb. The panther hesitated, not knowing what to do, confused by memories two decades and many wars away. The exposed throat was an act of submission, acknowledging the superior hunter and did not necessitate a kill.

"Dammit! I SAID HUNT!" yelled the handler and Selene winced as a spasm of pain shot through the beast, probably an electric shock delivered by the collar around its neck. He crawled forward on his back, keeping his throat exposed, thorns ripping his clothing to shreds and drawing more blood, ignoring the obvious hate in the animals' eyes as it glared back towards where the handler was. Then he lay in front of it, waiting for the quick rip through its artery, continuing to talk in the hunting language, soothing words. The panther turned back to him, lowering on all fours and tensing to strike, misery on its face. Here in front of it was one of the old masters, who had rewarded it with feasts of raw meat, not pain. Sensing the hesitation and before the handler could deliver another shock, he pulled out his blade and gently inserted it under the leather of the collar, a simple cut and it fell free.

The animal started, startled and Selene dropped the knife, exposing his neck again. The bond of trust. He reached out and held his fingers up for the animal to smell. Several sniffs and then it leaned forward, placing its jaws around his throat, feeling his racing heart. Then it backed away. Selene reached cautiously in his pocket and pulled out a candy bar, the last bit of food he had and held it out. The panther ate it greedily, wrapper and all, then started licking his face.

Selene started scratching behind the big cat's ears then leaned over and said, "Hunt."

Chapter Ten

"What should I do with you?" said Captain Paco Mateo. He held a needle point dagger in one hand and was using it to carve his initials in the table in front of him. "My offer to come work for my company still stands, you know."

The woman across the table was pale and dirty, chained to the chair. The mercenary officer was under no illusion about her being a mere female, even after a week's captivity. Not starved, not tortured, but the Grausian nerve agent he had hit her with had some serious side effects. Her skin was pale except for the burn scar on her cheek and her red hair was matted to her head. No, she was dangerous.

"You take your offer and ..." and she let out a long string of Gaelic expletives, though her face remained emotionless and she sat completely still in the chair.

"Come now, Iona, I was merely fulfilling my contract, same as you would have done. You could have caused a lot of trouble to my operation and probably lost your life, as well. My men were right outside the door, So you owe me that and ... I think you had a very good time with me in bed, too!"

He smiled, tapped out a cigarette from the pack and held it out but her face remained expressionless. "Póg mo thóin, you bastard," she responded flatly.

Mateo shrugged and lit it, drawing in a deep drag and letting it out slowly. Then he sat there regarding her for a long moment, as if assessing her for something. Finally he reached down to his hip and pulled out a data tablet, sliding it over the desk to her. It wasn't the newest TU model, some knockoff from the DMZ, but she could see what was written on the screen well enough. It was a personal ansible message from Captain Paco Mateo, CEO of Acción Directa, Limited, expressing regret for the misunderstanding that had led to the death of so many Irish Brigade soldiers. At the top of the list was Keely, Iona, Major, followed by Tormund, Lars, Captain. Every soldier from Bravo company was listed there, except for Sergeant Major Huy and Lieutenant Selene. Remains of which they wouldn't be able to produce.

"Only the ones we can provide bodies for, because your commander will want them shipped back to Eire. Of course, you can change that. We can explain away the live ones as miscommunication between our unit and the Dios. We rescued our valiant mercenary brothers form almost certain death, etcetera and so on."

"How many do you actually have?" she said in a whisper. "How many are alive?"

"Oh, maybe two dozen. Tormund saw the futility of any resistance and put up a white flag right away, but it took the locals quite a while to acknowledge it. He took it down and they fought until they ran out of ammunition. Killed more than a hundred and wounded twice that many. It was glorious, if you still believe in that sort of thing." The smirk on his face showed that he obviously did not.

"And what do you want from me?" she asked, staring at the names. Which ones were dead? Which were alive?

He took a sheaf of papers from a small briefcase and laid them on the table. "Well, as I said before, I'd like you to work for us. My new company, that is. We're all in it for the money, after all. Standard contract, with a bonus for special services rendered. A copy will be sent to your Colonel Meagher along with a letter of resignation. Dated prior to the attack, of course, to make it legal." On the next page was tacked a full color glossy printout of … her in bed with Mateo, stark naked and quite obviously enjoying herself.

"You're out of your goddamn mind!" she spat out at him, finally showing some emotion. Inside of her, though, there was despair. He had her and he knew it. What was her reputation compared to the lives of the soldiers she commanded?

He laughed and said simply, "Yes. But come on now, Iona, what have you got to lose, other than your life? Which is worth nothing and you know it. Either Meagher suspects that you had something to do with this or he'll be sure of it soon enough. In any case, you can never go home again. So why not take a decent paying job and save the lives of people who are going to spit on your memory no matter what?"

"You bastard!" she screamed at him and lunged forward, trying to pull her arms from the shackles.

"And you have no choice, being who you are. There are added benefits, also." He reached over and took back the contract, flipping to the pictures of the two of them in bed together. "You can't deny that we really do have some good chemistry in bed."

She calmly said, "Go to hell," and leaned back in her chair, face impassive again.

"Very well then," and he spoke into a mic clipped to his uniform. The door opened and two men came in, not the Spanish mercenaries but Dios locals. "Proceed," said Mateo, getting up. "I really don't want to do this. I could go with bringing one of your troops in here and shooting them in front of you, but … sometimes a little preparation goes a long way and saves lives."

Keely steeled herself for what was going to come next, but they merely unlocked her chains from the chair and lifted her up by the elbows. Seeing the look on her face Mateo smiled. "Just some time to think, bonita. Money, a career and the lives of your surviving soldiers." He turned and walked out without a backward glance.

The two guards said nothing, just gripped her arms tightly. She thought for a moment about trying to take them out, but even if she managed to disable both of them she was still in ankle and wrist cuffs. When she had first came too from the neurotoxin she had been dressed in a dirty prison coverall. It still clung to her, covered in sweat and dirt and she hadn't been allowed to bathe at all. Whatever; she had seen worse in the Marines, but she was still hobbled. They reached the cell that she had been held in, a regular barred room with a small window. The building had once been a barracks for the Grausian Legion that had kept order during the heyday of the Empire and of course there had been a stockade. She started to relax in preparation for the chains being taken off and being shoved in the cell but the guards didn't loosen their iron grip. Instead they carried her onward and down several sets of stairs, passing exits to basements. Finally they stopped at a room marked "ARMORY" in Imperial script and Spanish, the door to the darkness hanging slightly ajar. It was musty and empty, just a bare concrete floor. Without a word they threw her into and slammed the heavy steel door shut. She scrambled around, feeling out the cell and came across several cases of what she assumed was water and a box of military rations.

Once she had explored the limits of her cell Major Iona Keely sat alone in the pitch black and prayed to the Virgin Mary for the first few hours. After that she paced, planned her escape and slowly worked to keep from going mad.

Chapter Eleven

The cargo transfer from the lifter to the freighter was automated but there were still space suited figures out there among the stars. Sergeant Major Huy watched them through a porthole, thinking of the combat in the war, armored, suited Terran MIST troopers blowing holes in carrier hulls, venting them into space, jumping into shattered corridors to exchange fire with Grausian sailors.

He shuddered and picked up his duffle, heading towards the lock that connected the lifter to the main living quarters of the freighter. Huy was making his way through zero G to the cheap steerage cabins when one of the crewmen stopped him. "Hey demon," she said in heavily accented Common, using the Charee nickname for Illyrians but meaning nothing by it, "message from coms."

Huy thanked her and took the paper, slipping it into his pocket. He waited until he had slid into the small, dirty cabin to unfold it and read. It was simple, in common, but told him everything. "Cousin, a message to your father, some of his sons wish him well but were unable to make his birthday. His daughter has gotten a new job and will be doing work in her field." He crumpled it and put it in the recycler. Well, that changed everything. Major Keely and some of the troops were alive, though he didn't for a second think that she had actually joined another mercenary unit. His Illyrian 'cousin' had sent him the message to gain a debt from Meagher, but few in his species understood the human mind, even less so a female. She was his friend and former company commander when he was a First Sergeant, and nothing except the words from her mouth would let Huy believe Keely had betrayed Meagher's trust.

*****

Two weeks passed in transit, slow crawling across the Gliese 3293 system to the jump limit. No Gate here in orbit around the planet, a backwater system in a cloud of stars in the Orion Arm of the galaxy, just the jump on the edge of the limit. Then another long slow crawl down into a more important system on the edge of New Empire territory and hiring a fast packet after sending an ansible message to Colonel Meagher on Eire. Gate to Gate to Gate and then the yellow sun of Eire's home system, the planet hanging like a green and blue jewel beneath the massive ring. During that whole time he never saw the representative of the Theren government that was also on their way to Eire but traveling first class. It was only when they were disembarking that a note arranging a meeting was slipped to him by another crew member.

Huy was met groundside by Command Sergeant Major McRory and Colonel Meagher himself. The commander of the Irish Brigade was a short man, barely five foot six, and standing next to the giant McRory he looked even more diminutive. Huy often wondered how such a small human could contain the amount of energy and brilliance the colonel exhibited, but also accepted it. It was why, among other things, he worked for the man. McRory, who was a tall, muscular human who almost matched a Grausian in strength, grasped his hand in a powerful grip and grunted, "Welcome home, Huy," a strong show of emption for him. They climbed into a ground car and sped to the Brigade HQ, a low lying building on the outskirts of Dublin, making small talk about things that had been happening to the other units of the Brigade.

It was only when the three had sat down in a secured room, accompanied by Major Ichna and the XO, LTC O'Brien, that Huy spoke about what had happened. "I did get out to the firebase before I shipped, Colonel. As I had been told, there was a hell of a fight. The Dios don't really take care of their dead, but none of our people were to be found. I wondered at that, but I just supposed the Dios had gathered the bodies to be shipped back to Eire. I did find two civilian bodies at a bunker, locals looking for loot. I also found this," and he pulled a battered and broken ancient watch from his pocket, laying it on the table.

"That was Selene's watch," said McRory, handing it to his boss.

"I know, I gave it to him. Did you see anything else?" asked the Irish CO.

Huy nodded. "Some Grausian blood at the bunker where the two dead looters were as well as some expended cartridges, local make, inside the ruins of the bunker."

Meagher let out a breath that he didn't realize he had been holding. The Grausian had become, along with Iona Keely, something of a protegee to him. He had also been turning out to be a hell of an officer and the loss of both had aged him. "So one of the Grausian troops made it out." There were three, including Selene, on Bravo company's roster and he put the hope that it was Selene away. All his troops needed to be valued the same, or so he told himself. "Well, they're going to have to make their own way home best that they can until we have some info on their whereabouts. Sergeant Major McRory, make arrangements for the return of our troops' bodies. I'll make a formal protest to the Dios government, but there's not much we can do."

Huy hadn't said anything about the message, wanting to keep it from becoming known until he could deliver it directly to Meagher. "I also got a message from someone at the Illyrian embassy. Some of our troops are alive and probably imprisoned."

The atmosphere in the room immediately changed and Major Ichna took out a pad and started taking notes. Huy then dropped the second bomb. "They also said that Major Keely has gone over to the other side." That stopped everything and all eyes went over to Meagher.

"Opinion, Sergeant Major Huy?" said the Colonel.

"She was seen having dinner with one of the Tercios' the evening before the attack, Captain Paco Mateo, and left with him," answered Huy.

"And Corporal Thog?'

"Not seen since and I heard nothing on the street about a Grat anywhere," said Huy. He had spent the few days before transit gathering as much intelligence as he could find but the situation in the capitol had been a mess. Roving gangs of humans looking for aliens to beat had kept him from generally circulating and talking to people. "In my opinion she's probably dead or captive. There's no way she would turn on us."

"So Iona and other troopers are prisoners," said Meagher flatly. "Well, let's see what this Theren has to say." He pressed an intercom button and said "Megan, send in Mr. Baker." It was a pseudonym, but Meagher had met him before when they had first negotiated their contract.

"I'll get down to business right away, colonel," said the man, a mid level bureaucrat in the Theren State Department and a Reserve military officer before the attack. "As your sergeant major told you, we were caught by surprise. I'd like to hire the Brigade to liberate our province. I have access through the Illyrians of all our off world funds and, though it may bankrupt us, it has to be done."

"The price will be gold, Mister Baker, deliverable today," said Meagher flatly. "One Terran Eagle."

Baker sat for a moment, stunned. Then he grinned and dug through the change in his pocket. A Terran Eagle was a gold coin worth about a hundred credits and Meagher knew well that the Illyrians would have given the man some as traveling money. The coin glinted in the sunlight coming through the office window and Meagher took it, putting it in his pocket. "Mister Baker, they pulled a fast one on us and I was made to look like a fool. That and they have some of my soldiers prisoner and I'll go through hell or high water to get them."

When the man was gone Meagher hit the intercom again, asking his niece to transfer him over to plans and operations. When the duty sergeant answered he ordered, "Cancel all leave, get First Battalion out of the field and initiate Plan Orange." He hung up and turned back to his staff. "Sergeant Major Huy, meet me in my office in fifteen. You'll be working with Chief Wallace and Master Sergeant Aronda. Don't even bother to unpack your bags."

Chapter Twelve

Three weeks post - overrun.

There is something about humans, thought Lishar An-Selene, *that can forgive just about anything for the price of security.* These idle thoughts wandered through his mind as he worked with two other Grausians to clean rubble from the street.

"Keep your head down, boy and you might survive this," barked an old Grausian woman. Her fingers were callused and her face weathered, probably a farmer who had her property seized and who had been driven to the city by hunger. She and the other surviving Grausians had quickly become the bottom layer of society, doing menial work in exchange for small wages that barely kept them from starving.

"I am no flatu, honored mother," he shot back at her, using the Imperial word for idiot. They had been exchanging small talk as they worked, each being careful not to give any hint of their true identities. One a mercenary on the run and the other a formerly wealthy landowner, both subject to execution if found out. After all, they worked within sight of several corpses of their species, hanging from gibbets with white crosses painted on their rotting bodies.

"Speak Common, or I'll have to punish you," grumbled their human boss. He was a fat man who sat in a chair as they worked, swatting at bugs and sweating. There was no malice in his voice; merely exasperation. Selene suspected that

Senor Bastian's station in life hadn't improved much with the regime change.

Ignoring him, the female Grausian babbled loudly, "Wait until the Empire sends the Twelfth Fleet here to punish these human scum! Burn them down to the ground!" Yets Ji-Sheun was a middle aged female who had served in the Old Empire as a sailor on a heavy cruiser and Selene suspected that she had sniffed a little too much vacuum. She was forever babbling about the Fleet and what they were going to do to the rebel humans. After a day of trying to explain the last twenty years to Sheun, Selene had realized that the older female was living in a far different reality and had just let her be. "They're here, though," she continued, "Saw one the other day, wearing the gold and black. Legate. Probably a Legion commander."

Selene let that one pass too. He had also seen a delegation of New Empire military, here to evacuate the nobility and those with money. Then Sheun leaned over and whispered in a far different, stronger voice, "And Jicas, too, ... *Lieutenant Thal Lishar An - Selene*." The young Grausian froze for a split second then kept working. The name he had been using was Ordu Ji-Aklos, the Ji being a moniker for the peasant class. Someone might have remembered him from before, during the war; the Irish Brigade had been in the news a lot. This, though ... a chill went down his spine. The Jicas had been, in the Old Empire and still in the New, the field agents of the Legion's intelligence service. Their deeds were legendary, as were the rumors of their ruthlessness.

"I was at Sirius Major when we smacked the usurper's ships out of the sky like so many fireflies. What do you know about that, Senor Bastian?" Sheun said it loudly in Common but the human just gave her the finger and went back to swatting flies.

The Grausian Special Forces operator leaned over again and continued in Imperial, "Your unit wasn't wiped out. There are seventeen humans, no other species. They are on the upper floor of the old Legion Barracks. Your Major Keely was involved with Captain Mateo of the Tercios and hasn't been seen since the night of the attack. She is probably dead, traitors never get the reward they expect. It is possible that she is also being held separately, maybe as a bargaining chip, as the humans say,"

"Why are you telling me this?" he asked and kept moving rubble as they talked, slipping his hand off his knife. Instead of answering, the female just turned her back and started babbling again in Common at their overseer.

After a while she continued in Imperial, "The Empress gives orders and we follow, Jicas give favors and expect them to be returned. Your Colonel Meagher would understand and you, Thal, are still one of her Imperial Majesty's loyal subjects, no?" Sheun, who was probably the team leader, hadn't paused in what she was doing, sweeping up broken glass with a broom.

"I need passage off planet for all of us, weapons, plans for the jail and your full strength on an assault." He said it flatly, falling into the tone of nobility speaking to commoners.

"Aye, your grandmother said you were a throwback," said the Jicas commander. "Watch your male tongue, boy, noble or not, before I geld you. We've given you information, that's favor enough and a favor you owe to the Empress now, Thal." There was steel in her voice and he knew that he was dealing with a veteran soldier.

"I mean no offense, honored mother. It was merely concern for those that I lead. It was the Legion way, after all," and he quoted, "*I shall not abandon those I lead without suffering death myself.*"

She smiled at that and again there was steel in it. The other one, who called herself Uthar had ignored the whole thing once the conversation moved away from her, but Selene noticed that she stayed within striking distance. "We cannot … compromise our mission here. Perhaps a distraction," and Sheun paused as if to scratch an itch.

Grausians have a wider field of vision than humans, much more birdlike than classical predator and Selene caught a bit of movement on the edge of that wide field, from where a human thought he might be unwatched. The overseer had his head down and seemed to be whispering into his collar. If their vision was a bit wider, their hearing was worse and he had no idea what was being said. Even so it was something that set off his danger sense. He glanced at the older woman and she was still scratching her neck, but her attention was focused off to left, not in the general direction of the overseer but close enough for a Grausian to see. Her other hand, the one with the broom in it, had moved closer to her side. Beyond her Uthar maneuvered slowly to a position to cover her back.

When the violence came it was abrupt, like most violence is. It's hard for any creature that is the product of a civilized environment to turn that switch, to jump from the reality of peace to the reality of violence. Soldiers do it better, faster, criminals maybe faster yet with less discipline. Highly trained Special forces and veterans of sustained combat perhaps the fastest of all, but surprise usually wins.

With a whipping motion the broom in the hand of Sheun, powered by long, double jointed limbs, struck the overseer in the throat, crushing his windpipe. A second blow crashed into his temple as he dropped the pistol that had appeared in his hand, then the third one smashed the small radio that fell out of his pocket. "RUN, BOY!" said Uthar, who had a wicked looking machine pistol out, covering the far end of the street. She fired at the half dozen Dios militia that appeared from around the corner of the next block as her commander darted down an alley.

******

Selene fled, not looking back, and didn't stop until he reached the deserted warehouse he had been squatting in. He had been on the run for two weeks, at first hiding in the jungle and then making his way back to Bai Alng. The patrols hunting refugees had stopped after three of the militia had disappeared into the wet darkness. Lifting the piece of sheet metal that covered the entrance, he slipped into the darkness and called out to the cat lurking somewhere around. He knew that she had already smelled him, otherwise he would be a shredded mess on the ground right now. The panther came out of the darkness, jumping from the top of a wrecked milling machine. Instantly she stopped, perfectly still and he could feel a low growl rumbling from her. Without a wasted movement Ghost, for so he had named her, disappeared back into the shadows.

Outside there was a shift in the afternoon sunlight and the mutter of voices. "He's in here, has to be," said a male Grausian voice in Imperial. The shadows passed the sheet metal and he tracked their voices with his pistol, mind racing furiously. The Jicas were all female and none of the Dios had any use for Grausians, other than as cheap expendable labor.

"Here's the door," said another voice, younger. The shadows turned into silhouettes in the doorway and Selene raised his gun. Then he lowered it as one of them leaned up against the glass and wiped at it. They were unarmed that he could see and young. No more than teenagers. Stepping back into the darkness he held up his hand and made the silent signal for his hunting animal to stay, waiting and watching as the two rattled the locked door. Finally one picked up a piece of bar metal and used it to pry the door open. *Strong but stupid,* he thought to himself, *bread to it like all Grausian males.* He corrected himself, thinking back only two years to when he had first joined the Irish Brigade. *Untrained.*

They stepped inside, blinking in the darkness and one called out, in Imperial, "We know you're in here and we want to talk, Thal!"

The use of his title was interesting. Keeping the gun up but slowly stepping sideways, he answered, "Put your hands in the air unless you both want to get shot. Good. Now lie down. Cross your feet and put your hands on the back of your head." He finally stood behind them and asked, "Now who the hell are you and what do you want?"

"You're ... that mercenary. One of the ones fighting those Dios bastards!" The kid had a note of excitement in his voice and his crest was flushed red. The other one lay there mute and Selene could literally smell the fear coming off them.

"No, I'm not. I'm just a farmer like you, hiding out." He said it calmly, but his mind was racing. How many others might have recognized him?

The talker turned his head slightly and said, "We saw you, our mother brought fresh produce to the base. You were standing right there, right in the middle of all those humans! A male, with weapons!" The kids' accent was purely local hick farm worker.

Selene sighed and said, "Get up. Go take a seat over there. Ghost, come!" he ordered. Both the Grausian's eyes went wide as the cat slunk out of the shadows and their crests stood straight up in fear. He secured the gun in a side pocket and stood in front of them. "So, as I asked, who are you and what do you want?"

It was obvious the younger one was the talker and smarter. "Honored Thal, I am Hurin and this is my brother Huor."

"That's a joke, right? Those are seriously your names?" asked Selene.

"Yes, Honored Thal. We were named by the Lady of our House, after two great warriors far in our past." Hurin said it with evident pride.

"Of what house?" asked Selene patiently. He didn't have the heart to tell them that they had been named after fictional warriors in an ancient Terran fantasy book, one the he had read at the suggestion of then Captain Keely. He had to remember that these farm hands had even less education than some of the mercenaries he had commanded. If they were able to read he would be lucky.

"Uh, we were, we were of An-Try but the estate is no more." The genuine sorrow in the kids' voice, more than anything, convinced Selene of their sincerity and that they were who they said they were.

"And what do you want to do? Why did you track me?" he asked, genuinely interested.

The older one finally spoke, a deep rumbling. "We want to fight. For the Empire." And they both stood up and rendered a fair imitation of the now dead Old Empire Legion salute, left arm out, right palm on second elbow.

Lieutenant Lishar An -Selene, Thal of the planet Holcomb IV and the ruler of Holcomb system, one of the richest in the DMZ, stood in the dust of a deserted warehouse, a penniless refugee from war, and burst out laughing.

Chapter Thirteen

"Do either of you have any experience with weapons?" Selene asked. In the Old Empire, males of the lower classes had been forbidden anything more complicated than a bow, but perhaps things had changed. This was also a different world, with more aliens than Grausians and maybe different customs.

"I know how to work an SBR, honored Thal," said Hurin. "Our lady, after the time of troubles, made all of us learn."

"Please call me Lishar, both of you. If we are in town and you keep calling me by a noble title, the Dios will hang us all from the nearest light pole. Do you understand?" he asked.

Hurin picked it up immediately but his brother had a bit more trouble with it, rolling the name around in his mind. Selene could see the thoughts going through his face and he realized that Huor might be a few rounds short of a full magazine. He looked, however, like a tank. Many centuries ago, when the Legion line troopers had been almost exclusively male in a female dominated society, genetic experiments had sometimes resulted in things like Selene's extra vision membrane or, in Huor's case, masses of packed muscle. There was always a price, though and the Convention had forbidden any further experiments on Grausians themselves. The recessive gene the young farm boy had inherited to gain such mass would cause him to die of heart failure before he was thirty, if not treated.

"Here," he said, digging out the locally made sub-machine gun he had recovered from its hiding place in the jungle and handing it to Hurin. He saw with approval that the young Grausian checked to make sure it was unloaded.

To his brother Selene handed his knife. It was more like a short sword than a combat blade, a smaller version of the vibro-sword so prized by the Legion. Centuries old, the tiny fusion battery was long dead, but the mono-molecular edge could still slice through any armor worn by soldiers in this day. Huor took it with a gleam in his eye and a nod to Selene. As far as the farmer was concerned, the slightly older Grausian from off planet had just become his liege, to fight for and to die for. "Don't lose it; the blade was a gift and I'll want it back."

"Yes Thal!" was the reply from both of them, which he automatically corrected. Then he told them to start cleaning the warehouse.

"Now, to plan a jail break and steal a starship," he muttered out loud.

*****

Two days later Selene felt like beating his head against the ground. "No, again, we are doing this by stealth. It does no good to get INTO the prison if we can't get out. Therefore, you two are going to be our distraction and then will cover our escape route."

"But we want to fight like Legionnaires," answered Hurin. "This is a human way, cowardly. The Legionnaire dies with their face towards the enemy and a sword in their hand!"

In contrast his brother sat and stared at the drawing in the dirt. It was an outline of the streets around the jail and the route leading to the spaceport. "What if ..." he began slowly, "what if, Thal, I mean Lishar, we attack the jail and lead the enemy away? It is like when we face a pack of thriables, going after the herd. Sometimes ..." and Selene could see the wheels slowly grinding in his head. "Sometimes we would take blood from the killing and lay a trail to draw the pack away to a place where we could slaughter many in the canyon."

Hurin spit on the ground. "We are not farmers anymore, brother, we are of the Legion! Are you a coward?"

In the blink of an eye they were both rolling on the ground, wrestling and punching at each other. Selene watched them; Huor was stronger but Hurin was fast and apparently knew better than to let himself get bound up by his brother. It was actually amusing to Selene as he had never had any siblings and had been so sure of gendering female before puberty. He let them beat each other until both sat, exhausted and superficially bloody. Then he drew his pistol and aimed it at them. "In the Legion, I could have you shot for violating standing orders for fighting in front of a Pretorian. In The Irish Brigade, I could have you whipped for striking another trooper in front of an officer." For a moment he actually thought about it. They were potentially very useful and also potentially a liability.

"Get up," he finally said, putting the gun away. "Let's get all that bullshit about the legion out of your heads. Do you know why, ultimately, we lost to the humans? Because they are weaker than we are, don't have a distributed cognitive system -"

"A what?" interrupted Hurin. Smart, but definitely not educated.

"Never mind. Huor, can you break a human's neck?" he continued.

The bigger Grausian grunted and made a twisting motion. "Yes. I'd like to!"

"Good. I know a human who stands three tine," and he held up his hand about five and half feet off the ground, not even close to Huor's shoulders, "by the name of Master Sergeant Boru. He could choke you out using ancient human fighting techniques before you even laid a hand on him. They win because they fight using every trick and asset they can. And that's what we're going to do. Do you understand me?"

"Yes, Thal … I mean Lashar," said Hurin. "We will do as you say, even though I don't understand. You are our commander and it is the Legion way." It was said in an almost reverential way and both of them rendered the hand down to the side legionary salute.

"Goddamned action holos," said Selene under his breath. "So let's go over the plan again," he said louder.

Chapter Fourteen

"This planet sucks. Too damn hot," said one of the Acción Directa troopers. "Why do we have to be here again? I got promised a hot job, not some bullshit police stuff against militia jerk offs, who are supposed to be on our side anyway." He slapped at a bug that had descended on him in the darkness.

"Why don't you ask El Capitan. Until then, focus on your job, Cabo Padilla." The sargento's word were said casually, a bit mockingly and they shut his subordinate up.

"Because this is our contract," interjected a voice from behind the squad. Padilla turned to see Captain Mateo standing behind them. "And we'll do it until ordered otherwise."

He turned and walked away, back to the idling truck. Sergeant Major Arroyo sat half in and out of the driver's seat, the motor slowly turning over as he checked over his rifle. As his boss came up he gave him a nod; they were ready to go. "The Grausians have taken the bait, they're rolling out of the Trade Mission right now."

"Time to teach those New Empire putas a lesson. And those idiot Dios militia, already selling out their own government for silver Realls." Mateo pulled himself into the passenger seat and they sat, waiting.

After a while Arroyo asked, "What about the Irish girl? She break yet? How's your plan working out?"

It took a long moment before Mateo answered; she was a sore pint between the two, and Arroyo thought it was half the reason their platoon was stuck here. His Jefe knew he thought that but neither had brought it up. "No," was the answer after a long pause, "but the plan stays. I will give her another week."

"And the rest of the prisoners?" pressed Arroyo.

"Unfortunately they've about outlived their usefulness. I'll use them as a lever one more time with her, and if nothing, then dispose of them." He glanced over at his old friend, who gazed steadily ahead. "It bothers you?"

"Of course it does, and it should you too. That could be us there, and if it hadn't been for that accidental shooting, they'd be off planet now." His voice was cold in the heat. "And we still haven't gotten paid yet for the job we did do. The guys are grumbling, asking why we're doing anything for the Dios if they haven't coughed up any money."

Mateo was saved from replying by the radio crackling. He picked up the hand mike, acknowledged the call and they rolled out.

*****

In the square was a standoff. Twenty of the Acción troopers stood, weapons at the low ready, accompanying two very uncomfortable local police officers.

Across from them, lit by the headlights of the mercenaries' vehicles, stood several humans in front of a huddled group of chained Grausians. Behind them were a dozen fully armed and armored New Empire Imperial Legionnaires.

The policeman stepped forward, holding a pistol in his hand. He said, shakily in Spanish, "Corporal Carlos Badia, you are under arrest for stealing the property of the government of the United States of God."

"You can go fuck yourself, they were going to get hung anyway tomorrow, cop," replied the leader in Common, a bearded man wearing a dirty Dios militia uniform.

"Be that as it may," said the cop, "you are a thief. Give me the chain and it will go easier on you."

There was a quiet moment as Badia considered his options. He looked at the heavily armed mercenaries, then at the Legion troops, finally throwing the end of the chain down on the ground with a disgusted sound. The police officer stepped forward with his partner and placed handcuffs on the three men. Bending down he reached for the end of the chain when a commanding voice rang out.

"STOP!" came the voice of the Legion commander and she strode forward. "You will let them go, now."

Mateo cursed under his breath. Fucking Impies. Striding forward, he passed the policemen quickly retreating back behind the Acción lines with their prisoners, leaving the captives still huddled on the pavement.

"Primus, you have no business here," he stated flatly, looking up into the vertical slitted eyes. He kept one hand on his pistol and thought o himself how much easier this was than dealing with contracts and not getting paid. A little action was all he needed.

The alien gaze stared at him unblinking and he returned it. Finally the Imperial said, "I would say that YOU have no business here, mercenary. This is not your world, and these are still citizens of the Empire, Old or New, and I am the Empress's representative on this planet. Stand aside."

"I think not. Move along or my troops will open fire."

Another long stare and then the Legion officer looked around, first at the captive and then at the Acción troops, calculating the odds. Perhaps it was the always-there

Imperial arrogance, the feeling of racial superiority. Maybe it was that she had never faced humans in battle before and underestimated them. Maybe she was raised on too many stories of Grausian knights on fields of honor. Maybe she was just as bored as he was.

"The old way. Single combat."

The Human looked at the Grausian for a moment, said, "Ah, what the hell. Do we shoot each other from ten paces?"

"Oh no, Terran. It is the Old Way, swords. You can borrow one from one of my Legionnaires," and the Primus smiled at him. With her powerful arms and longer reach, she was sure that it would be an easy kill. Turning her back on him she started to walk away, pulling out the long spatha and swinging it from side to side. The vibroblade started emitting that teeth gritting hmmm, almost in anticipation.

"Fuck that!" exclaimed Mateo, drawing his pistol and firing three quick shots into the back of her head. Then he dove to the ground and started firing at the Legionnaires. Laughing at the joy of battle.

There was a roar of gunshots, plasma cracks and screams. Mateo shot down two when he felt powerful arms grab onto his legs and start dragging him. He rolled to see the bloody face of the Primus and tried to bring his pistol to bear. His hand was clubbed aside and she straddled him, grabbing his head in both hands, slamming the back of his skull on the concrete. Stars erupted in his vision and he lay there, stunned. Once more his head was taken in two enormous fists and slammed into the paving stones. Just before his world went black he felt a tremendous weight fall on him.

******

"Jefe, are you OK?" There was a face looming over him, shining a light in his eyes. The light hurt and suddenly the figure split into two, then came back together.

"Unghh … agua …" he managed to grunt, and felt the blessed coolness of a bottle tilted to his mouth. He spit it out and tried to sit up but the world spun and he lay back down. After a moment he grasped the sergeant majors arm and pulled himself up, resting on him.

"Next time, boss, shoot for the neck. You forget they have a distributed nervous system. Gotta smash their airway or hit that big bundle of nerves right above the shoulder blades." His subordinate was trying to make light of what had just happened but he couldn't keep the concern out of his voice.

Mateo looked around at the square. The captives were all down, caught in the middle of the fighting, and his own men were collecting the Legion weapons and cutting throats of the wounded. "What's our damage?" he rasped, then drained the bottle of water.

"Two wounded, lightly. The Grausians held their fire trying to get to protect their captives. We got lucky."

The captain didn't answer that, instead he stumbled over, reached down and picked up the sword lying on the ground. The vibrating hum had stopped and he saw that a bullet had smashed the handle. With a curse he threw it down and started kicking the body of the dead primus.

After a moment he stopped and staggered again, the ground spinning. Arroyo helped him over to a vehicle and he sat down, letting the medic look him over and bandage his head. "Sir, you need to get to the hospital. I'm pretty sure you've got a concussion, and maybe a skull fracture," diagnosed the specialist.

"Fuck this world, fuck those Dios shits, fuck the Therens, I'm not going to some indig hospital. Sergeant Major, find the XO and tell him to start packing, we're leaving. Then take me to the jail. Some loose details to clean up." He dry swallowed the pain killers that the medic handed him and then closed his eyes.

Chapter Fifteen

Darkness lay over the city of Bai Alng, though it was never complete, the third moon hanging brightly in the sky created a soft twilight until the few hours before dawn. In Empire days Bai Lang had been a tourist destination, the twilight and warm ocean breezes lending it an era of romance. Now the twilight was punctuated by fires burning in the distance, refugee settlements of non humans which were more like concentration camps. High overhead the dimmer random stars that were Terran Union ships with the 5th Marine Regiment moved in a manmade constellation, parked in a holding orbit while things sorted themselves out on the ground.

Selene sat on the roof of a building five blocks over from the old barracks building. One thing that gave him hope was the fact that it wasn't purpose built as a jail. Next to him sat Sheun, the Pico commander, who he now knew as Centurion An-Karees, still dressed in the rags of a refugee. "You're a fool, Thal," the special forces soldier muttered. She was scanning the face of the jail with a thermal optic, whispering targets. Beside her lay Senior Sergeant Uthar behind the stock of a long barreled rail gun.

"But a rich fool," Selene countered, "and my guarantee of access to the training center on Holcomb for observation of certain units will be a feather in your cap," he answered, "so thank you for the equipment. I won't need it, but thank you. "

She snorted. "I doubt you would have been able to get in there without it. But yes, this will look good to the Primus."

"What would help more is if you would provide the distraction that I need." He made another count of the guards that he could see, two on the roof and four by the front door. There were two other buildings close by.

"Those two kruntu will get themselves killed nicely, no worries. Their names will be enrolled in the annals of the Golden Legion as members of the honored dead." The sarcasm rolled off her tongue but she never took her eyes off the target.

He started to retort but then remembered a favorite saying of Master Sergeant Boru, 'Nothing you can ever do will unmake an areshole.' Instead, he merely said "OK, as the humans say, I'm moving."

The Imperial answered, "Koiat!" which meant happy hunting in Old Imperial and continued to call out targets.

Selene went down a rickety fire escape, whistled once and scratched the ears of the panther as she slunk out of the darkness. Behind the big cat came Hurin and Huor, carrying a war surplus blower in a canvas bag with one reload. He went over the plan once more with them.

"One shot, then you move. Pick a light skinned vehicle, maybe a troop truck. Their crosses make great targets, right?"

"Uh," said Hurin in a hesitating voice, "Th, I mean, Lishar, we … We are Christians. To target a cross, I don't think that would be proper. The good Father Monaghan has been instructing us in the ways of the Lord Jesus for a few years now."

A growl of frustration came out of Selene's snout and his lips drew back in disgust. "NOW you tell me you can't kill Dios?"

"Oh no, Thal! Most assuredly!" answered Hurin. The young Grausian was extremely nervous, his head moving from side to side, a Grausian tell that they felt in danger. "It is just, well, the cross is the symbol -"

"I know what the cross is, idiot!" snapped Selene. "Do you think your God would want it profaned by placing it on a military vehicle that is killing innocents? No. You fire and burn that blasphemy right off the face of the planet, do you understand?"

"Yes, Thal!" they both said in unison.

"Then no more arguments. Go do as I told you, make sure you lead them AWAY from the jail and then get to the Illyrian Embassy." He had no faith that they would accomplish any of that but only the initial distraction was what was needed. If they made it, so much the better. They both gave the fist down Imperial salute and he returned it, palm out, left hand to the side.

*****

The waiting was the hardest part as he and the cat hid in the shadows of a darkened alley a block away. He sat, back against the wall, covered by a ragged cloak, one of many hundreds of Grausians and other aliens thrown out of work. The panther slid even further into the darkness on the other side of the street, invisible. Far off in the distance he heard a brief firefight, but that was towards the commercial side of the city, kilometers away.

As he sat there, waiting for the distraction, three human youths came stumbling into the alley. It was a Saturday and partying was in full swing for the victors. One of them lifted his fancy toga and started to piss on the wall when another noted Selene sitting there. She laughed and walked over, pulled back a sandaled foot and kicked at him, hard. Her foot connected to the submachine gun under the cloak and she yelped in pain.

"Hey, Tabru, come over here and beat this Impy's ass! He hurt me!" she wailed as she held her wounded foot.

Both of the human boys turned to him, one drawing a knife that flashed dully in the moonlight. The knife wielder was maybe seventeen, though Selene had always had a hard time judging a human's age. The kid stepped forward, holding it out in front of him and said "Hey, shithead, nobody hurts my sister!"

"I am sorry, my lord," said Selene, putting as much cringe in his voice as he could. This was the last thing he needed now; the deception was going to go off any second. "Your mate kicked me, as is her right, I am sorry she was injured."

"What did you just call her ?" asked the other youth. "That's MY girl, Impy shit stain!" He pulled a sap off his belt, the heavy weight hanging there in his hand and made to swing it at Selene's leg, aiming to smash his lower, more fragile knee; this one had experience hurting Grausians. Before it connected the mercenary lifted the SMG and fired through the cloak, a long suppressed burst that whipped through both the human males as they stood next to each other, showering blood and viscera on the brick behind them.

The girl raised her hands to her mouth in shock and started to scream, a high pitched shriek that stopped almost before it started. A hypervelocity needle fired by Sergeant Uthar hit the side of her cheek and blew through her nose. She fell to her knees, one eye hanging out, blood pouring from the ruins of her face and she started choking, inhaling wetly. Selene stood and fired once into the red tinged blond cropped hair, hating himself for it. Then there was a reflected flash and a whip crack that was followed instantly by an explosion.

All thoughts of the dead humans gone, he moved to the corner to watch for the reaction force to leave. They were sloppy, as he expected, taking almost two minutes to mount their trucks and race towards the attack, men hanging off the sides. In that time there was another explosion and Selene wished his proto-legionnaires well. He saw the first one, then the next sentry on the roof drop and set off down the street, whistling a command to the big cat. It ran ahead of him, dappled fur making it a ghost in the streetlight. He decided there that it was what he would name the panther.

There were two sentries at the front door and a parked van off to one side. One sentry had left his post and was trying to see down the street towards where the explosions had come from. His partner was lighting a smoke, the glow of the match briefly outlining her face. She looked up just in time to see the panther spring from the darkness at the unknowing guard on the street and started to shout a warning, dropping the lit cigarette. Selene stopped, took a knee and fired, trading time for accuracy, then was up and running again. He passed the bloody mess that was the first guard and Ghost fell in behind him.

Jumping over the woman, who was sitting on the ground trying to hold her stomach in, he slapped a breaching charge that the Jicas had given him on the center of the doors and crouched down off to one side of the steps. It went off with a muffled THUD and Selene was charging up the steps, kicking in the broken doors and moving into the building. Ghost followed, ignoring the dying human. Not his kill.

Chapter Sixteen

For a prisoner there are many ways to keep track of time. Iona Keely had been through Terran Marine Corps SPEaR school on Naya Ghar learning the basics of Survival, Prisoner, Escape and Resistance, but that was five years ago. Being a heavy weapons platoon leader when the war ended and working contracts for the Brigade she had little time to keep up on it. She didn't know how many days she had missed and she was sure her captors had varied her food and sleep times causing the first few days, or weeks, to be a blur and she had no idea how long had actually passed. Eventually Mateo had grown tired of hurting her and they left her alone, though he occasionally showed up at random times to beat her. She welcomed them in a way; a bruise healing was a decent way to keep track of time. Keely almost enjoyed the look on Mateo's face as he hit her. Although she might gasp in pain or scream as a fingernail was ripped off, she never let her eyes close and stared him straight in the eye. "I'm going to kill you, you know," she shouted after him each time he closed the door and each time he grew more uncomfortable and the beatings slowly spaced out.

When the door shut she instantly went back to working on her escape plan. Laboriously, because her damaged fingers were swollen, she rubbed at the hem of her dirty nylon prison suit leg until it frayed. Then ever so slowly worked a thread from the break. Keely didn't want the short ones that circled around her leg but the long up and down threads. Another rip and she had both ends exposed. Careful, slowly, so very slowly she teased out one thread then another, each a foot long. When a jailor showed up to feed her she attacked the food wolfishly, grabbing the plate from them and shoving whatever slop they had into her mouth. She acted, even felt, like a crazy person, driven mad by her torment. As soon as the door was shut and they retreated, though, she went back to unraveling. When one thread broke she wept bitterly for an hour, but then tried again.

Finally she had a dozen, more than a foot long in the old measurement still used on Eire. Tying two together and biting down hard on one end she stretched them out and started twisting them, winding them into a tight weave. One length per day until she had six much stronger threads. Then she repeated, down to three. Finally those three together formed a slim but strong string. A lop tied in either end reduced the length to less than nine inches, but that was enough. It would have to be.

Iona Keely hid her primitive garrot and knelt to pray to the Virgin Mary. Not for forgiveness or intercession with God, but for strength and victory in battle. Her religion wasn't fatalistic, whatever happened, happened. Rather God sent her opportunities and it was on her free will to take advantage of those chances.

One of those chances appeared tonight as the door opened to let in Mateo.

*****

Sergeant Major Arroyo sat in the basement room that led to the prison cells, playing cards with three of his soldiers. It was early morning, several hours after the firefight in the square and darkness still lay on the land, as dark as it ever got. The lights in the basement turned their dirty, blood spattered uniforms garish.

"I can make … four, maybe five," said the man next to him on his left . Arroyo looked at his own cards, some high suites and four spades. The man on his right grimaced and put his cards down.

"Where did you learn to play Spades, Corporal Deleon? From your mother?" said the sergeant major. "You are going to break your partner's spirit with your crappy bidding. Then he will be useless to me as a soldier."

"You know who is useless as soldiers? Those Dios fuckheads. I swear, if I have to spend another week here I'm going to go crazy. Thank God we're getting out of here, money or not." Sergeant Hanson, one of the few non-Hispanic members of the Acción, particularly hated the lackluster manner the local militia operated. "I mean, three weeks, their regular forces have up and left, we haven't been able to teach them to shoot straight and they spend all day running around terrorizing the shit out the people of this city then all night getting drunk. And after that bullshit firefight tonight and not getting paid yet …I mean, we could have all gotten smoked. That was some cowboy bullshit."

Sergeant Major Arroyo exchanged a look with his partner while they placed their bids. It was something they had been discussing the night before, without their captain. "Instruction of local forces is a classical special operations mission, sargento," said the fourth man, Lt. Molina. "We will execute our duties and fulfill the contract, but that's for the capitain to figure out. I can make three and a possible, sergeant major."

"We bid eight," said the NCO. "Besides, Sergeant Hanson, you are always free to quit your contract and leave."

"I might, if certain people don't pull their head out of their ass," grumbled Hanson. "The boss is losing it, but shit I don't blame him. Stuck here doing bullshit after pulling off a spectacular op like that, no pay. That would drive me crazy."

Molina put down a King of Hearts and said, "Captain Mateo has seen a lot of combat, many years. I trust him and that's why I signed on with his new company."

"Man's got to be a little loco to do what we do, but I think he may have slipped a few gears, LT," put in Corporal Deleon. "I'm serious, I think he's got something going on. Maybe his head is really messed up. He took a pounding tonight and he didn't look so good."

"Maybe," said the sergeant major, who had been worried about his old friend for a while, "and I'll try to get him to go to a hospital when he's done with the Irish woman."

They paused as they heard and felt a Thud from overhead, but to them it sounded like a heavy door closing. "Hanson, go check that out," ordered the Lt.

With a grumble the man put his cards down and got up from the chair, heading for the stairwell.

*****

"Ah," Mateo said, "I knew you would break. Three weeks," and he reached for a cigar, bending forward to light it. The special operations soldier straddled a chair, leaning on the back, monologuing at her. Keely had almost come to hate his constant prattling more than the silence of her lonely cell and her skin crawled with the thought that she had had sex with him. Right now he looked a complete mess, blood and guts all over the front of his uniform and a field dressing on his head.

"Your colonel, you know, is taking an incredibly long time to get back to us regarding the disposal of your comrade's bodies. It's making it a bit inconvenient to keep them alive as an incentive for you to work for us." He blew some smoke on the pathetic figure that huddled on the floor in front of him. "To be honest, I'm not even sure you're worth it."

"I've had a vision," she rasped, sobbing as she said it. "Mother Mary came to me and told me to sacrifice myself to save ...to save ...." She said it quietly, forcing him to lean forward on the chair, tipping it forward. She held her face on the cold concrete, watching his boots and the chair legs. Although he may have seemed off balance and vulnerable, the soles of the tan boots were tipped forward. Mateo was waiting for her to try something, not trusting her helplessness. After a few moments he put the chair back down as she continued to sob.

"It's a shame, honestly," he muttered, "but I've seen even stronger people than you break. She heard the chair scrape as he got up and the whisper of a knife leaving its sheath. "Still maybe I can get some enjoyment out of you."

"But … you said I could work for you!" she gasped out. In return he laughed and grabbed her greasy red hair, pulling her head up. A sawing motion and the long knife bit through her curls and he dropped her head down on the floor again. His laughter was getting a bit maniacal, louder and he drove a boot into her side. She felt it hit her stomach and she immediately vomited on the floor.

"Fucking bitch!" he screamed at her, laughing. Then he stumbled as he tried to kick her again.

She realized that he was actually over the edge and that she was in incredible danger. *Mother Mary, help me now!* she prayed to herself as another kick smashed into her stomach. Then there was a thump that both heard and felt. Mateo stopped, listening. Like any combat veteran he recognized the thud of high explosives. As soon as he did she swung her other leg out with a vicious kick, sweeping his ankle and dropping him to the floor. The knife clattered away as he started to roll into her and she whipped the makeshift garrote around his neck. Mateo tried to get his fingers under it then locked his hands on her wrists, pulling them forward. She dug her knee into his back and screamed, using his own weight against him as the rope cut into his neck. Over the past three weeks she had been doing a thousand pushups a day and the muscles stood out like cords on her arms, whereas the other mercenary was suffering from a massive concussion.

He rolled over on top of her and started bucking, trying to smash her head against the floor, scrabbling his legs. Then he let go of her wrists and grabbed the knife that they had moved close to. Keely felt a piercing pain in her side but held on, twisting the garrote and forcing it deeper even as it gouged into her thumbs. The nylon rope cut through his skin and blood started to flow out of his neck and across her face. Another stab at her side, feebler and his boots gave one more kick at the ground, body heaving.

She held on for another minute as his body pressed down on her, tightening the rope slowly until it disappeared deep into his neck. Then she let go, shoved him aside and lay there on the floor in a pool of blood.

Chapter Seventeen

"Banshee Six, shots close to target, location unknown, developing, stand by," and the incoming transmission cut off.

Colonel Meagher sat and waited. He wanted to be on the scene, directing the recon on the prison but he knew a good commander gave the plan and trusted his subordinates. The six man team consisted of Chief Warrant Rob Wallace, Sergeant Major Tim McRory, Master Sergeant Kirn Aronda and three troopers from the HQ Reconnaissance Section. They were due south of the building with eyes on in two man teams.

Their recon position was little more than three kilometers from the spaceport where the cargo carrier *S.S. Utica's* three container drop carriers slowly cooled after a long reentry. Slung underneath each were two enormous boxes, each fully a hundred meters long by fifty wide. Inside the containers the massed might of the Irish Brigade held itself in ready, three hundred troopers of heavy infantry strapped tight in Hellrider APC's. In the third hauler's containers were four Marauder tanks from the Drakes and overhead a squadron of the Black Snakes' suborbital Shrike close support craft had been attached to the *Utica's* hull, pilots disengaging from ship support and hours before and slowly drifting into strike position. On a Terran Union or Charee system, even a LaChan, radars and other sensors would have quickly discovered the squadron, but here in the DMZ the surplus out of date space to ground attack craft baffled the rudimentary traffic control systems. That and a bribe to make sure the Treaty patrol ships, a Charee light cruiser and a TU frigate, happened to be far out system doing exercises with the 5th Marine transports.

Sergeant Major Huy had arrived at the Illyrian Embassy two days before and quickly established, through lavish expenditure of Brigade funds, that Meagher's people were indeed being held in the old barracks. The following day the recon team had dropped down from the *Utica,* posing as settlers coming to 'live on a human and Christian world'. Now they were watching the route to the prison and the building itself.

"That was a blower," said Aronda unnecessarily, his genetically enhanced hearing making up for his lack of eyes. Every one of the Irish on the recon team were experienced combat veterans and knew the sight and sound of the war surplus weapon intimately.

"All units, hold position," came McRory's voice. No one answered and he didn't expect any. Wallace may have been a warrant officer but McRory was in charge of this operation.

"QRF rolling," said Aronda and his partner, Chief Wallace, passed the info up the chain. From Huy's information they knew that there was an incipient insurgency and there had often been attacks on Dios patrols by ex-Theren soldiers, but a blower …

"Slow reaction time," commented Aronda again, listening to the troop carrying trucks roll out in response to the attack. "More than two minutes."

"Whatever, I'm glad for the distraction. Less crap for Task Force Shillelagh to deal with. Hang on … Mhac Na Gall!" cursed Wallace, "someone just dropped the roof sentries!" He keyed his com and said with a bit of pressure in his voice, "Confirm, upper sentries are down."

"Confirmed," came back McRory's voice. *"Look like someone else is running an op. Sit tight."*

"Someone is moving, I hear claws on concrete. Sounds like a hunting animal," said his partner. "Boots, too, one set, moving fast."

"Hang on, that's an Impy hunting cat and … yep, that's a Grausian, both front sentries down!" He snapped a button on the long-lensed spotting scope he was using, catching the attacker's face as he squatted to one side. He instantly piped it to the Operations TOC for ID, if they could.

"That's Selene, from Bravo company in Second Battalion," said Master Sergeant Aronda. "I know his steps from when we were on Holcomb two years ago. We need to move and support him."

Chief Wallace never argued with his partner, the man's hearing and sonar was incredible, even if his missing eyes disturbed most. "Banshee, this is Sùilean, someone has initiated an assault on the Target Blue. Count one plus probable long range local assistance and one support asset. Assaulter identified as Objective Royal, over."

"ALL UNITS, EXECUTE," was the only reply.

******

"Snakes, we have a go order. Mission package alpha two niner seven. Get shot down and we'll try to come for you, no guarantees, lead out." This corporate work sure as hell wasn't like being in the war, with dedicated SAR assets ready to grab a downed pilot before the Charee roasted them on a spit. The flight leader almost said it over the radio, but what was the point? Sure as hell paid better.

In the sky above the main continent the Shrikes of the Black Snakes went nose down, using powerful directional anti-gravity to open a vacuum in front of each ship, a small sliver of negative pressure that prevented them from turning into cinders as they encountered atmosphere. It also allowed them to dive on a target with incredible speed. Getting back up into space again, well that was a different matter. Strap into a cargo lifter and sip margaritas. As they bled off speed and emerged from the heat each fired off two kinetic penetrators. They weren't in Theren airspace, they were high over the main military bases of Los Estados Unidos des Dios and each munition aimed for either a communications nexus or a command and control facility. The crafts were suddenly nimble in their hands as the missiles left their racks and each pilot turned and burned westward with the mission commander was the last to fire.

Instead of heading towards a military base the final two weapons, anti-matter munitions designed to allow space fighters to attack capital ships, leapt outward on a long ballistic arc and then down straight down into the side of a mountain. The titanium penetrator heads allowed them to bury themselves into solid rock for several dozen meters where the warheads detonated. Most of the side of that mountain slid into the pass connecting Therer to the rest of EUD territory.

The commander smiled to himself; shooting a mountainside with weapons banned under convention was one little legal gray area legality that would never have made it through JAG. Maybe there WAS some benefit to this mercenary crap after all.

******

In his command track Colonel Meagher hid his emotions behind a face of stone. Command in combat allowed for no distractions, however personal. Major Ichna, his S-3, however, felt no such compulsion.

"Yesssss," the LaChan hissed with pleasure. "That crazy Impy son of a bitch is alive!" As xenos in the mostly human mercenary company, he and Selene had developed a bond over several drinking sessions and were good friends, as much as their rank would allow.

Meagher let himself have the briefest of smiles but reserved any real emotion for when and if, Iona Keely was rescued. Instead he talked about the concept of the operations. "Major, in our old calendar year of 1992 Common Era, a light infantry task force was tasked with securing some high value targets inside a large sprawling city. Mogadishu, on the eastern shore of the continent of Africa. It was one of the bloodiest days for the old United States military in a time of peace."

"I've ssstudied it," said the LaChan, wondering where this was going. "It is very similar to the plan you have crafted,"

"In many regards. Ingress into a possibly hostile city, egress under fire. Some differences, in that we do face militia but the local population will be, at worst, indifferent. May actively help, even, but they know to steer clear of our guys. One of the things that come up in a discussion of the battle was this problem. A helicopter crashed -"

"Helicopter?"

"A rotary wing VTOL," said Meagher. "Well, it went down and a squad was sent to the crash site. Instead of securing the wounded and moving out the squad was ordered to attempt to extract the bodies of some dead crewmen. As a result, a dozen more soldiers were killed and the operation delayed, resulting in a political embarrassment to the United States government."

"It seems wasteful to sacrifice the living for the dead," said the LaChan. "Though we have similar concepts of honor, but the dead should lie where they fall, with their slain enemies around them."

"Well, that is the problem. A commander must weigh the risk of casualties against the objective. How much is a man's life worth? What are the costs versus the gain?" Meagher almost seemed to be talking to himself rather than to his subordinate. "However, it's never just a cost analysis. There's always emotion involved."

******

Ramps slammed down and the tightly packed APC's spilled out, forming four columns that thundered across the tarmac. Heavy caliber automatic guns raked the small squadron of VTOL attack aircraft that the Dios had left parked in a row. The semi armor piercing rounds were designed to penetrate the armor and create a storm of shrapnel inside the craft, avoiding rupture of the fusion containment modules. Modern military craft were, on the inside, filled with plastics and other hydrocarbons as well as munitions and the jagged metal was white hot. All six went up in flames along with service vehicles and facilities. The west end of the airfield quickly became a raging inferno, consuming military and civilian craft alike. A lone fire truck started to move out of a hangar then stopped, its crew spilling out and running for their lives.

Each of the columns was led by a tank from the Drakes. The one designated *Smaug* split off and its accompanying dozen APCs headed south, thundering towards the prison complex. The other three columns headed onto a broad avenue that went straight towards the Theren government complex, tanks hammering the few Dios armored vehicles that were occupying the city. At each major intersection an APC peeled off and dropped a squad of Irish infantry. They dug in, taking up good clear fields of fire and waited for the Dios response. It wasn't long in coming.

Chapter Eighteen

"So let me understand the plan," said Private Connors. "We're waiting here for some indig militia religious fanatics to shoot our asses while the rest of the company does a jailbreak for some of our guys who may or may not be dead. And behind those indigs are the rest of the EUD military who are going to come in here and kick our asses even if we do manage to bust out our troops, who may or might not be dead anyway. While the other columns attack the occupation government HQ. For money."

Master Sergeant Nikova absentmindedly smacked him on the helmet as she listened to the command channel. "Watch your goddamned sector, shit for brains Irish bog cutter. We're doing this because if it was your stupid Mick ass in that prison, the Old Man would come for you too."

"Aye Sarge, I didn't know you cared," said Connors.

"I don't and there isn't enough money in the DMZ for ME to come get you. So don't get captured." She moved off to the other side of the street to check on 2nd squad at the next intersection.

"I think she's sweet on you, Jimmy boy," said his squad leader. "Maybe you should ask her out when we get back to Eire."

"Hey Sarge, I got movement down the - INCOMING!" yelled another trooper across the street. The darkness was lit by the spark of a rocket that ripped past the intersection, missed the APC and continued on down the side street to detonate on the back end of a parked aircar. The response from the Irish was a single shot that echoed among the brick canyons and the rocket firer tumbled backward to lie in the darkness. Quiet fell again on that street, but to the west a massive firefight erupted as the other columns attacked the Dios military headquarters.

"Well, this is boring," said Connors a minute later.

*****

Keely stood up, no longer a prisoner. She took a deep breath, ignoring the smell of blood and shit from the corpse, ignoring the pain in her hands where the garrote had cut into them. If blood and shit was the smell of freedom, so be it. "Iona Keely, daughter of Eire and your fuckin DEATH!" she finished with a scream and kicked as hard as she could with her bare foot at Mateo's face. Her toes impacted and pain shot through her foot, making her hold it and hop around, feeling like an idiot and cursing.

First things first. She pulled off the boots and slipped her feet in, reminded that she may have to *actually* kick someone or run over rough ground. To her amazement they were slightly too small. "Matched your dick!" she muttered and grabbed at his keys. That and the knife; his holster was empty. Even in his madness he hadn't been that stupid.

The key fit in the door, she had seen him open it many times. With a *snick* she turned the lock and, fast as she could, pulled it open. The sentry outside barely had time to react before the needle point knife was buried in his stomach, just below his body armor. Keely swept the shocked mans' legs out from under him, wrapping an arm around his torso and hugging him to her as they both fell. She drove the knife over and over into his side then once more into the base of his throat. It was a thin stiletto and it snapped with the last thrust, but the guard was choking his life out.

She looked around, running on pure adrenalin, heart hammering. *Calm down, calm down, calm down. Fear is the mindkiller.* Slowly she caught her breath and searched the still twitching guard. Pistol, shock baton, ammo, a water pack, thank Mother Mary. She sucked greedily on it but was careful not to drink all of it. Next she washed her face off, clearing her eyes, getting the blood off her hands and wiping them on the guards' sleeve. She thought for a moment about exchanging clothes when her eye caught sight of a small window in the door at the end of the hallway.

Careful to show as little of her face as possible, moving very slowly, she looked through the lower corner of the window and swore softly to herself. There was a full squad of Triceros, including Mateo's sergeant major and several others she had studied the files on. Probably waiting for their boss, sitting at a table playing cards. Two she might take with surprise. Maybe three. Not five. Might be even more that she couldn't see through the window; their standard squad was eight and it was a big room.

Desperately she searched through the guards' equipment, looking for a grenade or gas incapacitant. Nothing. Standing up to go search Mateo when her eye fell on a heavily reinforced door marked "EXPLOSIVES" in Common and "EXPLOSIVOS" in Spanish. The door was slightly askew, the frame twisted, the mortar cracked and a heavy bolt lock had been welded across the front. She slid it back with a strong pull and managed to lever the door open.

The room was empty except for a massive bulk huddled in one corner. It was still as death, Corporal Thog's skin cold and gray. Keely dared not hope as she pushed her hand through the stiff folds of armor like hide around his neck and felt for a pulse. It was a long time coming, almost a minute, but she felt the artery move under her hand. "Oh Jesus, thank you and Mother Mary for your intercession." The Grat was in hibernation, a feature his Grausian designers had built into the massive genetic experiment for long spaceflights. What she needed now was food and lots of it. Fast.

Keely ran back out into the hallway, glanced at the guards' body and estimated her chance of moving it. The man had been very bulky, more than a hundred kilos she estimated and wearing heavy armor. Fuck it, she swore, continued into her cell and with a heave, managed to get her hands under Mateo's shoulders. She dragged the lighter body across the hallway and into the Arms Room.

Dipping her hand in the mess that had been the Special Forces officers' neck, she covered her fingers in his slowly cooling blood, then jammed them up Corporal Thog's nostrils.

"Wake up, Thog," she whispered. "Cú Chulainn is calling ye to go to war," she continued, using the words from his favorite war story, "and all Ulster needs defendin!"

His nostrils twitched and then his giant mouth opened in a yawn and she shoved Mateo's body towards the razor sharp teeth. Eyes still closed, Thog reached out one paw, pulled the head into his mouth and bit down with a cracking sound.

"Serves you right, you bastard," said Keely from a safe distance.

*****

Selene stalked quietly down the stairwell towards the basement, gun out and the panther slowly proceeding ahead of him. Each step was a measured movement through the semi darkness, listening more than seeing. Lamplight shone from under a doorway and he heard voices. They were speaking Spanish instead of Common, but Selene had studied it enough during the deployment that he got the general point.

"I'm telling you, sergeant major. The captain has gone over the edge. He is not right in his head. You know this!" The last point was made emphatically, with a slapping of a hand on a table.

"Go do what I told you, Hanson," replied another voice, older, probably the sergeant major. "He was supposed to be promoted and here we are stuck on this shit stain world. Training a Dios special operations company." The man sounded miserable.

A third man chimed in. "The only thing those asswipes did good was rounding up all those Imps and shooting them in the head. Especially the kids."

Outside the door Thal Lishar An-Selene, ruler of an entire planetary system, officer in the Irish Brigade, heir to a noble Imperial bloodline, calmly checked to make sure he had a round in the chamber of his submachine gun and put his hand on the doorknob.

Chapter Nineteen

Keely checked through the window one more time before she entered, hoping to memorize the initial positions before she burst in. Behind her Thog's hot breath fell on her neck, almost a comfort. She was tempted to let him go first, but he was her troop and she was his leader.

She risked a quick glance just as the far door opened to reveal a hooded figure with a SMG in his hands. There was a frozen moment as she recognized the bulky, muscular figure of a Grausian and instantly knew that something bad was about to go down. She watched as the figure stopped in realization that there were a LOT of bad guys. He fired at the closest one and grabbed at the door to pull it shut. In the instant before it closed she saw the Grausians' face and she recognized Lt. Selene then multiple guns were fired at him.

Rolling away from the window, putting her back to the door and grasping the doorknob, she nodded at the Grat. "Oh boy, Thog this is gonna be fun," she muttered out loud, holding the pistol straight up in front of her face. She was scared shitless but a deep calm had settled on her. In response the Grat merely flared his nostrils and peeled back his bloody lips to reveal his razor sharp teeth. Then he very gently reached out two massive hands and lifted her off to one side. She nodded and made the sign of the cross over him. Thog grasped the doorknob in one hand and pulled the door straight off the hinges.

*****

Selene staggered back with a grunt as a round hit the door jam and ricocheted into his shoulder. The door slammed shut and then banged back open and he was knocked to one side as Ghost hit him, a fusillade of rounds striking the back wall where he had just stood. Then the big cat was through the door and into the room, slashing and clawing. Unfortunately these weren't some shaky Dios militia but highly trained, veteran Special Operations soldiers who reacted instantly. A hail of gunfire plowed into the beast even as he tore out the throat of one soldier and eviscerated another. The cat's blood ran red into a pool with his prey but he continued to charge through the room like a buzz saw.

The Acción scrambled for cover, upending tables and moving to the sides of the room, firing measured shots into the stairwell when there was a crashing sound behind them and the door to the cell corridor simply disappeared. An enormous bulk was silhouetted against the doorway, a nightmare of teeth and blood that moved forward and then … stuck.

Selene heard the roar and recognized it instantly. Ignoring the wound in his shoulder he threw the door open and dove forward onto the floor, firing at several figures behind a table. As a wall of sound, gunshots, screams, roars, crashes all washed over him he crawled off to one side, firing at the feet of the men hiding behind tables.

*****

Keely was right behind Thog, cursing the too small boots, gun held out in a two handed room clearing stance. She moved as soon as the door was out of the way and crashed into his back, bouncing off and falling to the floor, pistol skittering out of her hands. A crashing wave of gunfire impacted the wall and she heard Thog roar and bellow in pain, but his shoulders remained firmly wedged in the doorway. With a curse that would have brought a beating from her Catholic nun teachers she crawled over, got her shoulder under his ass and heaved. A crunching sound, a roar and they both tumbled forward into the room.

When Dante Alighieri wrote *Inferno* he placed in the Seventh Circle those who had lived by violence. There those who dwelt in the first round of the seventh circle, the murderers, war-makers, plunderers and tyrants are immersed in Phlegethon, a river of boiling blood and fire. When Thog went through the door it seemed to Keely that she had stumbled into that very circle. He grabbed the nearest human, tore his head off and started swinging the body like a club. The corpse sprayed blood around the walls as it crashed into other bodies, bowling them over. When he knocked someone down the mutant jumped forward and landed on his victim, crushing them to a pulp, sending blood flying.

Then she saw the Grausian come through the door and land flat, fire and move to one side. She pivoted to cover the other. The sergeant major had a plasma gun lined up on Thog and Keely fired once into his face from twenty feet away. The rifle jerked to one side and went off, a dazzling brilliance that hammered across the room and set the table ablaze, a searing hot flame that caught the aluminum frame on fire. A man stood up from behind it, trying to beat out the flames on his uniform and the Grausian shot him, a quick double tap. It was a mercy, really.

"THOG, STAND DOWN! ACHYTAH!" barked Selene in Imperial, "ACHYTAH!" He screamed it again as Thog started stomping on the bodies.

With a thunderous roar the Grat turned on the Grausian, then stopped. "THAL!" he barked and took one knee, bloody steam rising off him.

Keely ran forward to meet her fellow Irish and was struck in the back by a hammer blow that threw her forward onto her face. For a moment she thought that she had caught fire because a searing pain shot through her, like a bolt of electricity. Behind her she heard shots and Thog roaring but all she could see was the floor. She tried to move her arms to push herself up floor but they didn't respond.

Chapter Twenty

"We got shots from the basement," said Master Sergeant Aronda. Down the street the armored column was advancing, now taking fire from various sides, dropping off squads to secure major intersections. They were still several blocks away as the recon team ran through the gaping front doors of the prison.

"I can hear it," said Chief Wallace.

"You two, take it," said Sergeant Major McRory. "The rest of us, up until we locate prisoners. Make SURE a floor is cleared before you move to the next one, we don't want any surprises."

Aronda and Wallace were through the doors to the stairs before he finished speaking, the four troopers from HQ heading up as they went down. "Holy shit, that's Thog!" exclaimed Wallace, there was no need for his partner's fine-tuned hearing. Then a reflected flash and the crack of a plasma gun. Both stopped and advanced cautiously rather than charging in but picked up their pace when smoke started to drift up the stairwell.

The scene that greeted them was chaos. Selene knelt next to Keely, who still had her face pressed to the floor. On the back of her prison jumpsuit there was a smear of blood spreading out from under the improvised bandage the Grausian was holding. As they entered Thog, covered in blood and gore, gently went to pick her up.

"No, Thog,' said Selene. He seemed not at all surprised to see his fellow mercenaries, as if he had almost been expecting them. "Chief, she's been hit in the back and can't move. We need a backboard and enough muscle to get her up the stairs without jostling her."

"Aye, Sir," said Wallace. "Banshee, we've found Fire, Royal and Mutant. Need full MEDEVAC, Fire is wounded and immobile." The radio cackled a response and then he knelt down, placing his face on the floor to look into Major Keely's eyes. "The shit some people do to get out of work," he said.

"Kiss my ass, Chief," she muttered, but there was a slight smile on her face. On the other side of her Aronda held à med monitor to her neck and there was a slight hiss as nanos were injected into her skin. "Tell the Old Man ... that I'm ... never taking a ... vacation .... again..." The world swam around her and then Major Iona Keely drifted off to a warm green country.

Epilogue

On a rooftop overlooking the front of the prison Centurion An-Karees watched the liberated prisoners being hustled out of the broken front doors. She and Sergeant Uthar lay hidden, the officer watching through a spotting scope while her NCO made steady adjustments to her rifle optics. The crosshairs danced on the head of Thal Lishar An-Selene as he stood outside the hatch of an APC, helping maneuver a stretcher containing a severely wounded Captain Lars Tormund.

"Permission to shoot?" There was no itch in her trigger finger, the rifle held rock steady up against her shoulder. The Grausian double joints and powerful muscles made for an excellent firing platform, but only with an order.

Karees waited a moment, thinking of politics and personalities. She had already given the standdown order to her reinforced squad, scattering them across the city to infiltrate back to the Illyrian trade mission. The original plan, to allow Selene to rescue what prisoners he could and then help him get off planet had, of course, been a farce. Yes, they would have gotten him off planet but then he was bound for an interrogation and reprograming. The Irish they would have disposed of or used as a goodwill gesture to Colonel Meagher.

"Denied," she said abruptly.

Sergeant Uthar said nothing, just started breaking down the rifle and stowing it in a sack, to blend in with their disguise as poor peasants. As she did the occasional hiss of suppressed laughter escaped her.

"So you disagree with my decision, Sergeant?" asked Karees. The veteran knew her boss well enough not to answer, but the broad Grausian equivalent of a smile creased her face. "Speak, Uthar. That's an order."

Taking a moment to compose herself, she finally said, "You've taken a bit of a shine to the boy, Centurion. But that is not the old way. Either take him as your mate or kill him if you are interested, that's how it was."

"It's a new way, Uthar, and yes, I do like him, but not as a mate. He cares about our people as a race and is loyal to his friends, of the People or not. The old ways are going and he can be a powerful ally if used properly. Maybe that is the new way."

Most Wanted

J.F. Holmes

Chapter One

Terran Union Bureau of Investigation
Section Six, War Criminal Apprehension

"Got a hot one!" Carla Pochinishy might have been a potato, overflowing the sides of her chair, but she was good at her job and that forgave a lot of things. The former Navy intel officer might have let herself go after she got medically discharged, but her mind was still a steel trap and had contacts *everywhere.* She hung up the phone and wrote down a few more notes.

Yeah, she *hung up the phone.* I know, the Terran Union Bureau of Investigation is supposed to be high tech and leading edge, first to get all the new whizbang things now that we're shifting from wartime to peacetime economy. Rediscovering all the technology of the ancients, like cell phones and computer networks, casting aside the Grausian limits on technology. Maybe other divisions, but the War Criminal Apprehension Unit, AKA Division Six, wasn't sexy and had no high placed friends.

Most people in the Union wanted to put the war behind them and I sometimes didn't blame them. When I started to have some doubts though, I just closed my eyes and watched a city disappear under an orbital strike. My planet, Naya Ghar, suffering under the plasma glow of a Charee orbital bombardment. It has been a beautiful place, a world more than six hundred years old founded by Americans of Indian descent in the Great Diaspora. Cool ocean breezes, warm tropical nights. It was paradise, but it had also housed a military hospital and the Terran Marine Corps School of Amphibious Warfare. Bitterness welled up in me and I wanted to get my hands around that furry monkeys' neck, Legatus Nisuim Cha Krat. Someday you little shit ...

"Hey boss, yo, did you hear me?" interrupted Pochinishy. She was waving

I sighed, all thoughts of revenge squished out by the job. "Yes, Carla. I heard you. Better be good."

"No shit!" I heard a voice from the break room between grunts from sit ups. "Not some bug hunt!"

"Does Major Johannes Hurtenger ring any bells?" she asked with glee. Well, she did have a nice smile.

Kira's voice came from the break room again. "The Butcher of Sông Thiên Đức? How did you dig that asshole up?"

"A tip from the S-2 of a merc unit called the Fixers, search and rescue guys. His name came up in a rumor about a planned op here in the Capitol. He disappeared right after the Treaty, probably had plastic surgery, so I started running local DNA crime scene samples and official whiffers in the inbound transit areas through the Impy widget. Took me three days, but no shit, I got a hit from KIX inbound. He passed through three days ago." There was a flush of excitement from the hunt on her face and she almost looked pretty.

"Three days is a long time, but he probably didn't figure on a DNA hit." It was a closely guarded secret that we had an Imperial genetic biocomputer in our unit, able to sample and decode over a thousand DNA samples in about five minutes. We dumped whatever we could recover from a suspect area and about one time out of ten thousand it spit out a name and a time since the person had been through. By Shiva, I hated talking to that thing and let Carla do it. It was pretty much her pet and she fed it and called it George. Impy freak tech, it gave me the heebie jeebies, just sitting there in its tub, staring at me.

"Gets better," she said. "It was a DNA reconstruct, extremely expensive and rare, not plastic surgery, so I got a model on what he would look like." One of the other capabilities of George was the ability to bud off a three D reconstruction of what the person looked like. It was really good at Grausians, usable for humans, sucky for LaChan and Charee. "I talked to a friend over at the AI research division and they have this new resurrected Old TU tech called facial recognition."

"And?" I asked. She loved me begging.

"And get to the point," said Kira Friedman as she stepped out of the break room, wearing a hoodie and tights and covered with a light sweat from her lunchtime workout. The agent from Niu Irushlim was one of those Israelis that made you understand why no one ever messed with them. Smart, beautiful and deadly. I was glad to have her on my team.

"Point is, he's here in this building," said Carla, smiling like a kid that had come home with straight A's. I sometimes wondered how much that lack of oxygen had impaired her social skills. Or had she always been like that?

"Jesus Christ!" said the third man on our takedown team, Colin MacTavish. He took his feet off the desk and put down the cheap tablet. Probably reading more made up shit about the merc units, heroes of the holo. Yeah, we were an interworld team and our fourth guy, or girl, actually, Farest An- Rhanu, an honest to god Grausian born here on Alpha Prime, was out grabbing a pizza.

"What? He's working as a janitor on the second floor. Hey, everyone has to eat, even war criminals. Wait, where is everyone going?" spluttered Carla, but we were already out the door.

Chapter Two

I read through his dossier while we kitted up. Aged thirty seven, commanded an "irregular partisan unit" on a primarily human world in the DMZ during the last five years of the war. Like a lot of on the ground war leaders, he was young but charismatic. After ridding the single continent of Grausians, which I could sort of put down to war, he and his "Euroarmy" had gone on a campaign of genocide against the minority Vietnamese population. Some hundred thousand men, women and children crowded into a city and hit with illegal Imperial bio- weapons. I had seen the pictures, the slime left after the genetic weapons had broken down cell walls. It was a painful way to die. Still, only a hundred thousand. There had been over a million in Bai Laitain, including my entire family while I was in service. Mother, Father, aunts, uncles, cousins … my wife and son. I shook my head. If I couldn't get my hands on the Charee, then this guy would serve a slight dish of revenge for the innocent.

First things first, I had Kira and Colin seal each end of the second floor hallway that housed the offices of the cleaning staff. It was lunch time and Hurtenger apparently worked from three to eleven, cleaning, but we took no chances. I commed Farest and told her to watch the grounds outside, not going tactical. Then I politely knocked on the door that said "MAINTENANCE" in Common and Imperial. I guess the war hadn't gotten there yet, even a decade later.

"Yesss, what do you want?" came a hissing voice. Jeremiah was LaChan, another refugee from the war. Aliens often took human names, trying to fit into our society, but it didn't really work. Still, Jerry was a good guy who lost half his face fighting for us. No complaint.

"Hey Jerry, it's Captain Singh. Got a minute?" I called through the door.

"Yesss, hang onnnnn," and after longer than a minute the door opened. I pushed past him, gun out and scanned the small office, then the storage room in back. "Clear!" I said into the radio, "bring it in."

"OK," said Jerry, who had just stood frozen still like only a reptile based race can do, "What the hell issss this all about?"

I held up my com unit and flashed a picture of Hurtenger. "Where is this guy?"

"Ahh, I don't know. No ssssshow today. Been here for a week, decent worker. What'sssss he done to get Division Six on his asssssssss?" That hiss was annoying, but hey, he couldn't help it and it got worse when he was stressed.

"Can't tell you. Got records on him?" He did and handed them over, a thin file with application, references. "Did you check this guys' bona fides? He has to get a security clearance to work in this building."

"Sssssssssssshit Captain Ssssingh, you know how hard it issss to get anyone to do this job. I put him through but it's gonna take two monthsssss to get clearance. And I'm short handed," He was flushing different colors, another LaChan response to stress. "Am I in trouble?"

I didn't bother to answer, we both knew he was. "Let me see his locker," I said flatly. Jerry led me in his four legged walk into the back storage room and pointed to one of five. The lock was a simple combo one that I burned off with a pocket plasma cutter in less than a second. Yeah, it might be trapped, but probably not. I had checked all around for wires and the professionals know that resetting a booby trap every time you open and close a locker was a pain in the ass and deadly the one time you forget. Not radio controlled either, or else you risked a stray transmission arming it or shutting it off when you didn't want to. Nope, the trap would be when we tried to move this thing out ourselves. Not my job but I still needed to look.

I broke out in a cold sweat when I saw what was inside. Imperial antimatter demolitions munition. I knew it, had seen them in the war. Rated with a variable yield of up to ten kilotons, I'm pretty sure that it would take out the entire building as well as a good chunk of downtown Columbia. After carefully examining the control cover, I gently lifted the lid a few millimeters to see the numbers on the timer, if any. Nothing, it was a flat screen display and I wasn't going to keep lifting it. Half a microgram of hell contained in a magnetic bottle that could go off at any time. I switched over to the general TUBI net and put in a transfer call to the duty officer, Major Dillon. He got back to me right away on a secure freq.

"What's up, Singh?" he asked in his blunt way.

"I'm at maintenance on the second floor, looking at an Imperial K-36 demolition charge. Probably wired, but I don't think it's armed. I don't see any triggering devices and if I remember correctly the arming unit was separate to avoid accidental detonation." I had looked, the port for the small device was empty.

"Got it," he said matter of factly. "Can you secure the area until EOD arrives?"

"No can do, sir," I answered, "got a bad guy to catch."

"Understood. Is Jerry involved?" he asked.

"No Sir, I don't think so. He's in the outer office, Kira is chatting with him. I can tell him to lock up and go to lunch. Weapon is in a locker, I'll leave it open."

"Roger, stand fast, EOD there in two minutes. Plain clothes," and he hung up on me.

Well, orders were orders, so we sent Jerry packing and waited for the Explosive Ordnance Disposal Team to show up. When they did it was in the form of one Mantis with a duffle bag, Special Agent Wan!rst. He nodded hello, unlocked the office door, went in and closed it. Then he stuck his head out again and said, "Good hunting, hive brothers."

"OK, let's roll," I said. "Farest, take the bruiser and meet us around the back of the building." That was our unofficial aircar, a beat to crap Mistudahi that we used for undercover work. If we went screaming in there officially the target would rabbit in an instant. Likewise, bringing in a TAC team for backup would be a damn good way to spook our target.

"What's the address?" Kira asked. It was probably a fake but we had to start somewhere.

I rattled off a flop house in the crashdown district. "You've only been here three months, Kira. Colin and I could tell you some stories."

"This is where the Impy ship hit, right?" she asked as she drove. Columbia was mostly a pedestrian city, with commuter rails and slide walks throughout, but air traffic started to pick up as we headed to the outer rim. Twenty three million people, Humans, Grausians, Charee, LaChan and all the other castoff species of the Empire crammed into the narrow valley made for some interesting maneuvers.

"Yeah," answered Colin. I was too busy trying to dig my fingers into the dash. "That was back in, what was it, Captain?"

"487!" I grunted. I'm not sure you were supposed to be able to pull more than two gravities in an air car, but the bruiser apparently was capable of much more.

"Yeah, right when the Impy Third Fleet made a big push against us. So the battle was way out system, but one of their captains, dunno if it was on purpose or because the ship was so knackered, she sends the thing on a collision course with Columbia."

"Where were you when that happened?" asked Kira, nonchalantly swinging around a sewage truck.

"Me, lass? I was alongside her, pouring cannon fire from my Banshee while my backseater looked for an override of our own antimatter containment system to blow the bloody thing up. Almost followed her all the way down."

"Well?" she asked. I squeezed my eyes shut.

"Well what?" answered Colin. He was actually laughing at me.

Kira cut the speed down as the nav system told us we were getting close. "Well, did you stop the ship?"

Colin laughed and said, "I'm still here, aren't I? And there she is."

And there she was. *INS Vatuher*, one of the biggest fleet carriers ever built by the Impies, or what was left of her. The hull was over three kilometers long and she had gone in at an angle. Maybe her CO had come to her senses at the last minute, because from what I had read of reports, all the engines had been firing on reverse thrust and someone tripped the antimatter scram just before they entered atmosphere. If they hadn't, well, that demo device in our building would have looked like a spitball versus an artillery round and the Terran Union capital would be a smoking crater big enough to have ruined the planet. Might even have changed the course of the war.

The wreck itself had plowed into some very expensive suburbs, destroying many of the houses of the political elite, for which I wasn't sorry. Over the last sixteen years, despite the environmental hazards of all the crap that was onboard a modern starship, like nukes, hydraulics, coolant, whatever, squatters had moved into the area. It was now a slum for the poor, the old estates and large houses divided into tumbledown apartments. Prime recruiting ground for the Terran Marines but the Navy stayed far away. Easy to learn how to use an '89, but a lot harder to fix a stardrive. It was also a place where a lot of the aliens native to Alpha Prime had fled to when the Empire fell.

"Wasn't this your old stomping grounds, Farest, with the Columbia PD?" Kira asked. Her frustration with going slowly showed in her face. It was hard to be the new guy on the team.

From the back, a muscular double jointed arm extended and rotated to show a long scar along the forearm, patterned with surgical marks. "I received this one taking down an alien trafficking prostitution ring there."

"What did the other guy look like?" I asked. Grausains were half again as strong as humans and averaged a foot taller.

"I broke his neck like a twig," she answered, with her characteristic dry laughter. "It was glorious." There was a reason the Imperials had ruled an empire spanning a thousand parsecs for centuries, they could be a bunch of cruel bitches and in the end, they were aliens. We got along well but sometimes I just didn't understand them.

"OK, well, try to catch him, not kill him," I said. "Here we go!"

There was a reason we used the Bruiser. Colin had installed military grade fans and I had welded some ceramisteel over the doors and engine compartment. It wasn't every day that we caught a war criminal here on Alpha Prime, but sometimes we ran down leads that shot back. The bruiser would also pass on dozens of worlds as a local transport and we had plenty of budget for transshipment.

"Put it on the roof?" asked Kira.

"Let Colin jump out over the back and then we go in through the front. Remember, we want to catch him, not kill him." I emphasized the last part for the Irishman. He was a cop but also a combat veteran and sometimes we had to keep our instincts in check.

"Got it, stand by for some heavy maneuvering," she said.

"Ready up?" I asked my team.

Colin, "Aye."

Farest. "Dra."

Kira. "Check."

"Punch it."

Our bad guys run, always, because they know what awaits them is a squad of Marines with SBR-89's and a blindfold. That's why we went in slow with the other traffic and then blew our way in. Colin jumped out the side door and rappelled thirty feet down, headfirst, into the back yard, landed and unsnapped. Then we rolled over the roof and slammed down on the front "lawn".

Problem is that these places are usually packed full of people and when you go busting down the door it's chaos. Sometimes politeness works and it couldn't hurt, so I knocked loudly. Nothing. I nodded to Farest and she boomed in an amplified voice. "OPEN UP OR YOU'LL ANSWER TO SASHA ZIVCOVIC!" These people could care less about the TUBI or any other law enforcement agency but throwing around the name of the local mafioso made them shit themselves. Besides, Grausians often provided muscle for the bad guys and none of us were wearing uniforms. Our body armor with POLICE across the back meant nothing.

A timid face appeared at the door, an old woman. "Yes?" she asked in a heavily accented voice, then started speaking rapid fire in Spanish. Kira stepped forward and answered her in Common, holding up her com deck to show Santo's picture.

"Si!" the woman said and then started to open the door. I stepped forward and Kira swept my legs out from under me, drew and shot in the same motion, one round from her FM-X that made a neat little hole in the old lady's forehead. The depleted uranium sabot slug from the stubby shotgun that had started to rise from behind the door buried itself in the side of the bruiser. Simultaneously there was an explosion from the back of the house and Colin's voice broke over the coms in an agonized yell. I cursed myself for not calling backup, slapped my com and yelled, "OFFICER DOWN, DIVISION SIX, THIS POSITION!" and then I followed Farest and Kira through the doorway as their weapons barked. There were two gunmen on the floor of the hallway, one still breathing. I shot him in the head and followed the team out through the back, casing each doorway with my pistol but moving fast.

Out back was a scene of controlled chaos. Colin lay on the ground, clutching his stomach, groaning quietly. Kira was working on him with a medkit and Farest was pulling security. In the distance the plasma drive of a one man suborbital was arching out over the city. Our defenses were designed to hit things coming down, not going up and it dwindled then faded.

When I looked down, Colin's head was in Kira's lap and I could see it was no good. He had been hit with a penetrator round from a 12 gauge auto shotgun, the titanium tip punching through his armor and then a small charge blowing away his abdomen. One thing that hadn't kept pace with technology was the human body. It was still the same one that had been stopping sword blades and arrowheads five thousand years ago. His eyes were open and blood poured out onto the ground, making the skin deathly pale in Kira's headlamp. She gently reached over and closed them. Good, let his final sight be a beautiful woman.

Chapter Three

"Listen, I will tell you a mystery!
We will not all die, but we will all be changed,
in a moment, in the twinkling of an eye, at the last trumpet.
For the trumpet will sound,
and the dead will be raised imperishable and we will be
changed.
For this perishable body must put on imperishability,
and this mortal body must put on immortality.
When this perishable body puts on imperishability,
and this mortal body puts on immortality,
then the saying that is written will be fulfilled:
"Death has been swallowed up in victory."
"Where, O death, is your victory? Where, O death, is your
sting?"
The sting of death is sin and the power of sin is the law.
But thanks be to God,
who gives us the victory through our Lord Jesus Christ."

We all responded with a perfunctory "Amen!" and then
the gunshots. Three SBR-89's cracked, three times, then the
lone piper on the hill. Six burly men of Clan MacTavish
stood to the sides of the coffin, lifted the ropes and lowered
Colin's body into the grave.

"We'll get him," I said to the man who stood next to me.
He was missing an arm and an eye, lost somewhere in the
depths of space on a world not Eire. "It may take a while, but
we will."

He nodded, not looking from his son's grave. "I believe
you, but the DMZ is a large area, with a lot of planets to hide
on."

Kira spoke from behind us, her voice quiet. "He's on Holcomb IV. It's a shitty little independent, about a hundred light years outside TU territory."

Duncan MacTavish turned to look at the Israeli, searching her face. "How do you know this, girl?" he asked.

She smiled, incongruous in the somber surroundings but beautiful all the same. "I … called in some favors. Favors from back home."

I knew exactly what she had done the moment she said it and wondered what she would have to give in return. The planet of Niu Irushlim was a part of the Terran Union, but more independent than most. Their intelligence service, Mevi Haor, was good, very good and had contacts everywhere. It was Hebrew for 'Light Bringers' but I'm pretty sure the light they brought to their enemies was a burst of plasma.

"Well then, I expect justice. In the old way." He said it flatly, the tradition keeping the grief and emotion out of his voice.

Her smile disappeared and she said just as coldly, "No one needs to tell a Jew about vengeance, Mister MacTavish. Colin was my friend."

'Aye, he spoke well of you in his last letter home. If you can't get to him, I have other sons who will take up the task." He said it with a bit of pride in his voice and I knew he meant it. Although the DMZ was pretty much a free for all, I didn't want civilians to rush into a sovereign planet and get thermaled for murder.

"We'll get him, Duncan. You have my word," I said and left it at that. Sure, we would try to bring him in. Give him a chance to surrender, even. That would probably be about the length of time it took my finger to squeeze the trigger, but it was still a chance. I am a lawman, after all.

We met Farest at the car and slowly made our way back to Collins Spaceport. I again apologized to the Grausian for making her wait in the car, but she said she paid it no mind. "People have long memories, especially out in the provinces. It would do me no good to explain that I am from Alpha Prime, in fact might be worse, given the Celt's history," she said.

"What do you mean?" I had no idea what she was talking about; this was the first time in my life I had been on Eire.

It was Kira who answered as she drove. "You don't know about the Great Rebellion? Seems like there was a spot of trouble between the Old TU and this planet about a month before the Imps came and smashed everything. The Fleet got caught with its britches down, totally out of position to defend Earth and Alpha because they were on their way here to put an end to it."

Farest smirked and said, "It wouldn't have made a difference, my ancestors were unstoppable, praise to the Empress!" She was just trying to get a reaction out of Kira, who failed to rise to the bait.

"Better you stay in the car anyway," I said, "there are a shitload of veterans here. They'll tolerate you at the port, but not at a social gathering."

"Understood, Captain."

We boarded the shuttle for the short burn up to the DIV 6 courier boat, Kira piloting it like it was some kind of trans atmospheric fighter jet, then got settled down for the long haul out system. The jump point for Eire's primary was about a day's travel at high G away from our position and I pretty much slept all the way pinned to my seat. Then the distortion of the Jump. boring time in transit and we were dumping speed far out from Holcomb IV. It was a beautiful planet, brown and gray with very little blue. I punched it up on the database and sat down to read as we passed by a ringed giant.

Holcomb IV, settled 107 PC. Traditional Fiefdom of the Selene Family, a minor branch of Grausian Nobility. Currently ruled by Thal Lisha An- Selene. See events of 501 PC< reference Hibernia Arms. Net exporter of rare earth minerals. Population approximately 100k, balanced between most major races. Primary population center the City of Holcomb.

Well, shit, that would have been good to know before we left Eire. Hibernia Arms was headquartered there and I vaguely remembered a scandal a few years ago about their merc company using chemical weapons. Would have been good to get an intel dump from our field office on Eire.

"Kira," I said to our pilot, "what do you know about Holcomb?"

She thought for a moment. Everything action she took was a constant compromise between getting the mission done and determining if it might have consequences to her own agency. Eventually she opened up her palm and looked at the file. "There was a coup attempt there two years ago, some kind of Grausian royalty power play backed up by the Charee. The TU lost a stealth recon ship and the Charee a company of infantry and a transport. Almost started the war back up."

"I never heard of that," said Farest, who generally kept up on what was going on in the old Imperial planets.

Hell, I hadn't either. What happened in the DMZ usually stayed in the DMZ, but a shootout between Treaty Nation warships should have been all over the news. I smelled the

Terran Union Intelligence Agency Special Operations section all over it. "So what's the current situation on the ground?" I asked Kira.

"Well … my, um, other bosses, have people there who might be able to provide intel on the target." She was hesitant to reveal Mevi Haor operational secrets, but Colin has been her friend. "We've been watching the situation there because Niu Irushlim is deficient in rare earth minerals, even though we're a heavy tech planet. We do a LOT of trade through the Illyrian mission there, but the events that year prompted insertion of a *Shaul* team to keep an eye on things. There's also a company from The Irish Brigade under contract to train Holcomb's military and Dynatec Unlimited is building a training simulator facility for armored forces out in the desert. The NIDF are scheduled to rotate a brigade through there early next year, with a company of the Forgotten Legion hired to play OPFOR."

I thought about that as we cleared customs at the Holcomb spaceport. Two years ago you could have lifted on and off without anyone noticing, but apparently whatever scion of the Selene family was in charge had really put her boot down. Now there were uniformed officials, Grausian, Human and LaChan, running the place and a mixed race local security force in field brown and gray. Definitely professional, my mind noted. They even cleared the Bruiser to come out of the hold after a courtesy inspection after seeing my TU Bureau of Investigation credentials, though I hadn't said anything about our mission.

"Of coursesss," said the LaChan senior official, looking at my ID, "Rast An-Yet will want to seeeee you to coordinate whatever you are doing. Which is none of my businesses."

He handed me back my ID and dipped his long neck, the traditional LaChan sign of respect.

I wished we could have come in undercover, but sure as shit these provincial DMZ planets took their independence pretty damn seriously. Instead I asked to see the head of security at the port and I was ushered into a rear office and left to wait for a few minutes. When the door opened to admit a trim, older human in the security forces uniform wearing the rank of colonel I almost jumped out of my seat. "Holy shit, Johann Strauss! What the hell are you doing here?"

The crusty old Terran Army NCO smiled, curves of his handlebar mustache lifting. "Private Singh, looks like you've moved up in the world!" he answered, pumping my hand enthusiastically. "I haven't seen you since, well, since I got medevac'd from Barwhon! And a captain now for the Tubbies! You've done well for yourself!"

"Ah yes, that shithole," I remembered, "and don't call us Tubbies!" He had been a platoon sergeant when a young, naive draftee named Carl Singh had arrived in the 2nd Mechanized Division. The Marines got the glory and the Army got the shit, securing planets after the ground assault. That meant endless patrols trying to placate a population that more often than not was hostile. I remember the column of smoke rising from the field half a kilometer away as the platoon HQ element tripped a mine. I had heard through the grapevine that Sergeant First Class Strauss had lost both legs, though I couldn't tell from the way he moved now.

"I think we're both doing alright for ourselves," I said, pointing to the light colonel's silver leaves on his beret. "Head of port security. Not bad! But to business, I have a favor to ask." I filled him in on our quarry, giving DNA codes and holos of Hurtenger.

"I need your people to keep him from getting off planet," when he was up to speed. "He might have a single lifter, probably disguised as a cargo container here in the city and if pressed hard he'll use it."

Strauss grinned and said, "Let him try. We have a railgun ADA unit from the Blacksnakes in the heights above the city. I'm sure those boys would love to take a crack at a fast mover. It's been six months since the last smuggler got smoked."

I raised an eyebrow at that. Keeping a merc unit on station for months got *very* expensive. "Yeah, about that. I heard that the Irish have a unit here training the Holcomb Defense Forces. Is this place all mercs?"

"Ah, well, yes and no," he shrugged. "I've got the spaceport security running well and the Holcomb City PD has started to get a handle on things, but they need more training and equipment. They keep order among the miners and in the bars, that's about it. The HDF doesn't really exist yet, the first battalion should be standing up this week, actually. If you need any backup, it's going to have to be the Irish who help you."

Huh? The quizzical expression on my face must have been obvious, so I just came out and said it. "Wouldn't the planetary government have an issue with TUBI agents using their paid-for merc unit to cause shit in their city? I mean, contracts and all that."

He laughed at that and said, "You mean Thal An -Selene? But don't you see, lad, the Thal is also the Irish Brigade Company CO and mission commander!"

Chapter Four

The Grausian that sat across the desk from me wore body armor over mottled desert camo. Around his neck he had a cravat of the same color as his troops' beret, a dark emerald green. Of course an Impy could never fit a beret over his crest. Subdued black captains' bars were velcroed to his chest plate and a well worn SBR-89 was leaning, magazine loaded, up against the wall behind his desk. The creature was young, I figured no more than twenty two Terran Standard years, but he had a jagged scar on his forearm and a hard look in his eye. There was nothing in the office to suggest someone who was worth billions of credits.

Behind him, sort of off to either side, stood two Grausians in full battle rattle, one of them the biggest damn Impy I had ever seen. They were similar in color and feature, perhaps clanmates or even brothers. Unusual to see males acting as bodyguards, but the galaxy was a different place now. The smaller ones' eyes darted around the room, assessing threats, but the big one watched Selene. If his boss started to move, he would also. That was two loyal to the death armsmen.

"So let me get this straight," I said. "You're a junior officer in a mercenary company and also the ruler of this world? Leading a training mission on your own planet? And, don't take this the wrong way, you're a male ruler in a matriarchal society? Isn't that ... unusual?"

Next to me Farest interjected, "Unusual, but not unheard of, Captain. It seems Thal An-Selene has been adapting well to the new reality." She had a smile on her face and her crest was flushed brighter red than usual, standing straight up. Uh oh, I knew what that meant.

Selene looked at her for a moment, then said in Imperial, "Officer Farest, can we keep this professional, please?" The use of a human title was very pointed and her crest literally fell. Yes the world had changed indeed. A Grausian female who was interested in mating usually meant that the male had little choice in the matter.

He turned to me and said, "It's a long story, but suffice to say that Colonel Meagher has a strange sense of humor. This is my first assignment as a company commander and he perhaps thought it was amusing to place me in charge. It's a ... delicate situation and he insisted I needed 'vacation'."

"Well it actually makes it simpler for us. If we have a problem, can we turn to the Brigade troops for backup? This guy is a dangerous hombre," and I told him about the demolition nuke at TUBI headquarters as well as my murdered officer.

"I'd love to help you but you have to understand. We live on the precarious edge of two warring powers, or three if you count the New Empire. I have a duty to my people and besides, I would have to run this through my council and through Colonel Meagher. What I *will* tell you is that the Holcomb PD won't look too closely at your activities. Or those of anyone who might be helping you." He looked pointedly at Kira, who had said nothing so far. "I'd be very careful, I've heard that there are wolves about."

If I didn't know her well after working together for three months I would have missed the flinch. This young Grausian was on the bounce and apparently didn't miss a thing on his home world. I could see why his commander had put him here for this mission. "Well, Junior Captain Selene, thank you for the heads up. The TUBI appreciates it." I deliberately used his military rank as opposed to his nobility honorific.

Let him be reminded of the eight hundred pound gorilla that the Terran Union was in the DMZ and that his merc charter could be at risk.

"I understand, Officer Singh. Let's hope there isn't any violence that you can't handle. While on planet, you're subject to Holcomb law and I have no extradition treaty with the TU." Zing, right back at me. The eight hundred pound gorilla really doesn't matter when he's hundreds of light years away and he just pointedly reminded me that he was, after all, the owner of this world. Selene continued, "I would also be highly upset if any citizens of Holcomb were badly injured or property damaged during an arrest, Captain Singh."

"We understand each other," I said and he nodded, then dismissed us. Arrogant, like all Impies, but decent enough. We stepped outside and got into the Bruiser, grateful for the air conditioning as the guards waved us past the encampment gate. I noted that even on the way out the Irish mercs still tracked us with a heavy machine gun. These boys didn't screw around.

Kira's contact met us in a bar outside the miner's district, a new place that catered to tourists. Hard to believe there was such a thing, but apparently the ruling council on Holcomb was trying to diversify. Mines eventually play out and will always be targets for criminals, pirates and other military forces. Smart move on their part and the closer it tied them into what remained of the galactic economy the better.

As we waited for the meeting, Farest sat talking to some other Grausians, far enough away that the average person wouldn't associate her with us. She blended in well with the local population and she had disappeared into the city as soon as we left Selene's office, entering the bar a few minutes after us. I knew Kira had good intel, but sometimes working with the local xenos helped, too. We would take every advantage we could get. I sat across from Kira, making small talk, acting as if we were on a date. Eventually her eyes shifted focus past my shoulder and she reached up to activate the comset hidden behind her ear. I also turned mine on, only to hear a conversation in what I assumed was Hebrew. Ignoring it I glanced around to see who the player might be and zeroed in on a miner type sucking down a beer who kept glancing our way. Then I noticed that he was hammering the beer pretty hard and my danger sense calmed a bit. No operative would be drinking that much; his attention was probably due to Kira and I turned away. Then again, she was obviously with me. I glanced back and saw that the miner wasn't actually looking at us, his attention was slightly to the right, just past Kira. In the booth adjoining ours were a group of off duty Irish soldiers who were well into their cups, singing some song about a lass they had left back home on Eire. OK, this was none of our business, but … physics, not intent, rules high speed bullets and shrapnel.

"Go," I said and Kira immediately understood. She slid out from the booth and I was right behind her. Farest moved as we did, heading for the back of the bar. We passed the miner on our way out but he only had eyes for the soldiers. Kira glanced at me and I shook my head. stepping out into the bright sunlight. I tensed up and as we waited Farest I was sure there was going to be an explosion. That guy was a suicide bomber or I was getting old; I had seen it in the Army in the occupation of Barwhon. What happened instead was that the miner came flying out through the front window with a crash of glass and a cheer from several green uniformed Irish mercs. Kira actually smiled as we walked away.

"You've gotta lighten up, boss. This is a rough world on the edge of civilization, not back in Columbia."

The four mercs staggered out of the bar, one lighting up a smoke and the others jeering at the miner. "No hard feeling, but that's what you get when you mess with a soldier!" said one, offering his hand to the man on the ground. He ignored them and ran off in a sprint, a look of determination on his face. I grabbed Kira around the waist and threw us both to the ground, dragging at my pistol. Meaningless, because it was over before I could find a target. The heavy flechette gun had caught the mercenaries from the side, shredding them into bloody red dolls and splattering their flesh up against the wall. The ground car sped off down an alley before I could get a shot off.

Chapter Five

I'll give them credit, they locked the center of the city down tighter than a gnat's ass. Heavy Irish infantry, half a dozen armored vehicles, sniffers, the whole shooting match. Holcomb PD were taking witness statements and running forensics. One the mercs was still alive when the meat wagon carted him off but the others were dead right there. Desert dust had already begun to drift over the pools of blood.

"I don't understand why they do what they do,' said Kira as we watched from across the square. Behind us the Bruiser rumbled, Farest sitting at the wheel. "Those guys died for nothing. A paycheck."

Thal An - Selene stood, rifle over his shoulder, barking orders to multiple people at once. Then he turned to a short, tough looking bastard who led a squad of Irish troopers in full kit. Instead of orders he merely motioned and started off in that full speed loping run of a Grausian. They ran after him on the double despite the heat and the gear. Someone was in for a world of hurt.

"You were never a soldier, Kira," I said to her, thinking of other times. She was too young to have been in the war; Niu Irushlim had been very cautious about contributing troops after the debacle of Ophiuchi in 494. "They do it for something more. For their friends, for the adventure, the excitement. Especially for their friends though. Training, too. Don't forget that most of them are also Reservists in the Eire Army. The Terran Union isn't always so … Union." She had no answer to that, being well aware of TU politics. We got back in the Bruiser and rolled back to our hotel.

When we had settled in Kira brought us up to speed with what her contacts had told her. "So basically we just walked into an incipient rebellion. The miners aren't happy with Thal Selene and the Council's efforts to diversify the economy. Their union is pretty strong and there's foreign influencers meddling. Not the Charee, but probably New Empire."

"I wouldn't want to be in Selene's position. That kid is lucky to be on planet with this happening," said Farest. "Let's hope he deals with it in the old way."

"I don't think it's luck. The Irish Brigade commander, Colonel Meagher, is as smart as they come," continued Kira. "The mercs are going to need a welcoming world and a good training ground, plus someplace to move money and other commodities that isn't under the TU thumb." Whatever Kira lacked in full spectrum combat experience, she more than made up for with a stunning breadth of access to intelligence and had a brain to use it.

Just then there was a distant explosion that rattled the windows and I caught the glimpse of an errant tracer round rocketing up into the sky. A gunship made a low pass and opened up with a chain gun, waling it down a street. Farest barked a laugh and exclaimed, "So it is the old way after all! I would surely like to bed that one!" She gave a round of applause to the unseen Lord of Holcomb IV.

"Business before pleasure," I told her. "We have a bad guy to catch and if he's smart, he's nowhere near those miner idiots." I stood and paced, thinking while Kira and Farest ordered some dinner. The sunset was glorious, despite the column of smoke that lifted up from the civilian quarter. I did see a jump jet hovering overhead, silhouetted by the setting sun and my mind drifted back to the wars. It always did.

"I think the obvious question is, why here?" asked Farest. It was more a statement than a question, something to chew on. "I mean there are dozens of other planets to flee to in the DMZ if you want to get a hideout."

"He's here for a job, obviously," said Kira. She waved a hand at the view out the window. "Farest, how do you think the females who run the New Empire feel about a male Grausian inheriting one of the richest estates in Old Empire territory?"

"I see your point," I said. "It's a hit."

"Of course it's a hit," confirmed Kira. "Question is, do we let Selene know, or use him for bait?"

I pondered that for a moment, but the answer was pretty obvious. "Bait, of course. Security is already tighter than a fly's ass around him, not sure what informing him would do to help and it might hurt. And don't forget, we're law enforcement. We want to catch this guy if we can, not just get him knocked off." I said, putting aside thoughts of revenge for Mac aside.

******

We spent the rest of that evening wargaming out scenarios. Kira was in favor of just letting him do the job and catch him on the way out with his guard down. After all, what did the TU give a shit about a small planet in the DMZ, and the more turmoil the better. I saw her point, but Farest would have none of it.

"And I'm not thinking with my dick," she said, "as you humans say. First off, I don't have one and second, IF Selene gets taken out, there will be enough resultant confusion that Hurtenger can easily slip away. By the Empress, he managed to get away from Alpha Prime." Her crest turned green, she was thinking hard. "I think we need more information first."

"I see your point and this could put Selene in the TUBI's debt," I said. They agreed just as there was a knock on the door. I nodded and Kira slipped off to one side, pistol drawn. I moved to open the door and Farest was right behind me. I yanked the door open and she reached past to grab a startled Charee, yanking him in and slamming the door shut.

The four armed alien almost went cross eyed looking at the pistol pressed against his forehead. "I … I bring dinner?" he chirped. Taking his ID I glanced at it then called down to the front desk to confirm who he was.

"He's good, though for all I know there's a tac team sitting at the front desk with a gun on the manager." It was possible, though not probable. "Sometimes a waiter is just a waiter and I think that we're OK. Put the sniffer on the food and let's dig in." It was some kind of local spicy dish and smelled damn good. The nod I gave to Farest belied what I had said, this guy was sure as shit an informer, if not an operator.

Nervously setting the dishes on the small table, the waiter then bowed with a flourish of all four arms and hightailed it out of there. Just after he did and before the door closed, Farest muttered into her hand and let loose the small cloud of bugs that formed the collective consciousness of a Jutys. They weren't really bugs, per say, but close enough that they creeped me out. Trained Jutys were rare enough nowadays but they had been a favorite of the Kempo, the Imperial Secret Police, and Section Six guarded ours closer than any other secret tech. Smarter than a dog and great for tracking, they darted out through the doorway as it closed with a snick.

They would follow the Charee to whatever meeting was set up and report back through a neurolink.

Meanwhile we would try to get some rest. I took first watch, putting on a helmet that protected against flash bangs and connected to the local internet. I was surprised that they had one here at the hotel, even more so that I could get a connection. Then again Selene was trying to turn the planet into a tourism economy and appealing to visitors from the Union was a good way to do it. I maxed the gain on the sound and read up on Holcomb while I listened for anyone messing with the door.

The Jutys came back an hour later and settled on my hand, leaving little tingling sensations as tiny tendrils wove their way into my skin. I shut the news down and watched a ghostly image form in the air in front of me. It looked like whatever the viewer wanted it to look like and I tried hard to keep it neutral, an image of one of my old mentors when I first joined the TUBI. Long mustache, eyes that hinted at an Asian ancestry, Special Agent Corel had helped me adjust from the military to civilian law enforcement. Now his face channeled words to me, a neutral tone. "The target," he said, or more like the Jutys transmitted, "left this place and went three hundred paces northeast to another place. He entered and met with a female human. As ordered I/we followed the chain of contact to the target through five people, three humans, another Charee, an Illyrian and the target. He is located at this building." The picture changed from Corel's face to a fuzzy outline of a small concrete structure standing by itself in a desert setting.

"Can you lead us back there?" I asked, knowing the answer. The image was derezzing even as I watched; the Jutys was getting tired and losing the strength for the neural link. I reached over, opened its traveling container and the motes flowed into it. Well, some info was better than none.

When Kira awoke exactly on time for her watch I handed her the helmet and she checked her pistol. While she did I filled her in on what the Jutys had told me. "Plenty of cutouts, Illyrians are being used as paymasters and I still want to know what his target is," she said.

"The Thal?" I answered, half question and half statement.

"Too easy and he's off planet most of the time with the Irish Brigade, the Council is the real power here when he's gone. Look," she said, bringing up a file on her pad, "how does this guy work? We have records of him doing, what, five assassinations that we know about and six we suspect? All five confirmed were bombings, as well as four out of the other six. I think the other two were either not him or field expedient. Plus the TUBI HQ. It allows him to get away clean, put distance between him and the target."

"So you think the Council? When do they next meet?" I was running options through my head.

She checked a public news server and said, "Tomorrow, noon. The kid will be there too."

"Well that settles that. We're going to have to go to the Holcomb authorities and nail this guy before he can act." I looked at her and her face was guarded. "What?" I asked.

Kira Friedman was an agent on loan from another intelligence agency, not a cop. She had a different way of looking at things, a more direct way. "I think in the best interests of all parties involved if we were to just take him out."

I looked over at Farest but she said nothing, just continued to eat. She worked for me, but I knew she had the typical Grausian, hell even Human, feelings about honor and revenge for MacTavish. She would go with whatever I decided, though, she was an officer of the law. "Define parties. We have the Rule of Law in the Union, Kira."

"I'm going to ignore what you promised Mac's clan and remind you that, sure, we can haul him in, maybe. Once he gets back in the Union, though, whomever hired him to do this hit is just going to either neutralize him or spring him. Out here in the DMZ, clean, quick, no problem." She said it flatly and the lack of emotion on her beautiful face scared me.

"First off, there never is any clean or quick. We had him cold in Columbia and Mac paid the price for my assumption." She was a good field agent, but no, she didn't understand war and as an intelligence agent, she didn't really understand the Law either. To her it was a thing to be used, not followed, but I tried to explain anyway. "We know where he is, so we go see the Thal and keep him informed. Conspiracy to commit mass murder carries the death penalty on Holcomb, Kira, but our charges take priority. He won't get away and we'll handle it. We have a death penalty too in the Union. We'll catch him and extradite him, or even just dump him in the bruiser and jump out."

She didn't look happy, but in the end, I was the unit commander. She would do what I asked. As for the Thal, well a favor owed was a favor owed and he would know it.

Chapter Six

They came for us just before dawn. Two men that I suspected were local miners doing a favor for our target, pushing a cart down the hall and stopping just short of the doorway. One bent down and lifted the cover of the cart, hitting some kind of switch and hauling ass back to the elevator.

We watched from a button camera mounted high up on the end of the corridor and I thought for a moment about going after them, then decided not to, waiting for the explosion. If they thought we were dead, so be it.

The detonation wasn't so bad, they were miners and knew a hell of a lot about directed explosives. There was a sharp CRACK and the cart blew backwards. The door shattered into a thousand pieces, probably a type of claymore spewing pellets through what was supposed to be our room. For all the good it would do; we were already outside.

"Punch it, the target house," I said flatly. "Capture, not kill."

Kira glanced at me as the fans spun up and the Bruiser, an accusation and doubt. She wanted this guy dead because in the intelligence world, someone tried to kill you, well you pay them back. It kept things civilized and from getting out of hand. I ignored her look; The Law was the Law. She lifted the Bruiser up on fans only as I tapped a message on the screen. We were three minutes away, the city dead quiet around us in the hour before dawn. As we headed towards the target building Farest placed a call to the Thal's security. There was a rapid exchange in Imperial that I could barely follow; apparently Farest was pretending that she was wounded and Kira and I were dead. Emergency sirens sounded over the whine of the Bruiser's fans and strobe lights started flashing behind us.

Kira lifted and went to flight mode, spinning us up and over a low rise building, our target house flashing in the heads up. We had to hit it fast before he moved and there were easier ways than busting down the door. "Smoke 'em," I ordered and Farest tossed four canisters of vomiting agent at each corner of the building then jumped for the roof. Kira took the Bruiser in a tight spiraling turn, using the fans to blow the gas in through the windows. Holcomb was a hot planet so most of the upper floors were open to the breeze and the gas quickly wafted its way into the building.

We hit hard, slipped our helmets on, checked filters and exited the aircar. "We take him alive!" I told Kira but she ignored me. I did see that she pulled a tangler instead of something more lethal, though that was in one hand and her Imperial Vibroblade in the other. It hummed with that teeth gritting ultrasonic hum, usually just past the edge of perception, but it was badly out of tune and grated like a buzzsaw. I wasn't worried about the blade; she was an expert with it and it could breach a door as easily as cut off a head.

The doorway that the Jutys had followed the waiter into was closed, a heavy wooden construct with probably a steel core. I motioned to Kira and she slipped around to one side, looking for a window to gain entrance. Even though it was still dark the heat was tough to bear through my helmet, sweat rolling down my neck. I wanted to lift it off and get some fresh air but if I did, I'd be on the ground puking my guts out. I also wasn't a nineteen year old grunt anymore and my breathing was heavier than it should have been.

Farest's voice came through my headset. *"I'm in, chief, I have incapacitated three individuals on the second floor. All three seem to be miners."*

I hoped like hell that incapacitated didn't mean killed; she was as casual about killing as any Legionnaire I had known. Still, she was a cop. "Roger watch the internal stairs. Kira and I are trying to find a way -" and at that moment the front door burst open. I was ten feet away and off to one side, covering it with my own tangler. "CONTACT!" I yelled over the net and fired my first round. A tangler is kinda nasty, it puts out a web of gene modified spider silk that delivers a powerful soporific wherever it touches bare skin. The woman who came out was already choking on the incapacitating gas and she went down like someone hit her with a hammer. I went to rack the next round and there was a nerve cracking explosion in front of me.

Our helmets are designed to protect us from stun and flash / bang grenades and I was wearing body armor, but what went off in front of me was a Terran Marine issue room clearing grenade. Those suckers were designed to kill everything inside of a room with a combination of overpressure, sensory overload and fragmentation. If you didn't catch a piece of shrapnel you were so fucked up that the next thing you did get was a round to the head. Fortunately for me and not for the woman in front of me who the grenade had been strapped to, her body absorbed a lot of the effect and most of the shrapnel. I felt a piece of steel rip through my forearm, a blazing hot zip of pain that made me drop the shotgun as my entire nervous system was shaken.

Falling to my knees, vision swimming, I stared dumbly at my arm as blood started to flow. Then something hit me in the head and I fell to the ground, bones like jelly. A pair of feet clad in combat boots went past me, the person escaping taking a second to give me the finger and fire a shot into my chest. All the air whoofed out of me as I felt a sledgehammer blow on my stomach. Then there was one more input, that shrieking out of tune vibroblade in Kira's hand. What followed was like watching something on the surface from under ten feet of water.

A trained knife fighter or swordsman is almost like a ballet dancer and the shorter the blade, the faster and shorter the dance. Kira's wasn't a full Imperial Spatha, more like a short Gladius or long poniard. About forty-five centimeters of shimmering, glinting almost-there titanium alloy that was made even harder to see with my stunned senses. She seemed like some kind of Valkyrie, a pirouette of death, slipping aside as the target's machine pistol barked. First a kick to the head, knocking the mask aside, then vicious cut and then the barrel of the gun was flying through the air. A second swing took off Hurtegen's leg at the knee.

"STOP!" I managed, somewhat louder than a wheeze. Kira didn't hear me or ignored me, her blood was up and she started a broad sweep that would take off a head.

What did stop her was the rock-hard grip of Farest clamping down on her arm. Reacting as if she had been attacked, Kira twisted and thrust the blade forward, going for a stabbing blow, and the Grausian just tossed her. I mean, shit, I knew that the Impies were strong, but … The Mossad agent landed on her back and used the momentum to roll over and come back up, knife out. Then she realized who had grappled her and she instantly relaxed, shutting off the blade.

Struggling to my feet I stumbled over to the screaming man and vomiting man, who I noticed now was also missing a hand. I flipped my cuffs out, snapped them around the remaining wrist and ankle as Farest applied tourniquets and said, "Johannes Hurtenger, you are bound by law. You are under arrest by me, Captain Carlos Singh, Agent in Charge of Division Six, Terran Union Bureau of Investigation and you will be tried for various war crimes. You will be afforded all rights and privileges of a citizen of the Union in incarceration and on trial." There, it was official. Kira looked at me with a mixture of disgust and dismay, shaking her head.

From the ground Hurtenger started laughing and coughing. He was tough, I'll admit that. Farest had stuck him with some pain killers and he was fully conscious. "You should have let your dog kill me, captain. She understands. I'll be out of jail and off Alpha Prime before your termination papers hit your desk. Who do you think I work for?"

"I'm guessing some politicians who would want to cover up some of the shady shit they did in the war. You're better off in our custody, because they'll make you disappear." He was right though. We would turn him over to the courts and it was 50/50 if he ever saw a trial. Still, the Law is everything or we're nothing.

"I've got way too much insurance. You should just let me go now; I can regrow this in a month. I'll leave you all alone if you do and if you don't, once I'm out you'll never know what hit you." His face was a bloody sneer, but I got his point.

"The Law is the Law," I stated simply.

Chapter Seven

The APC ground to a halt in front of me as I drank a ton of water. The irritant had dispersed and my mask was off, hanging from my belt, with my badge around my neck. Thal An-Selene stepped out along with his two bodyguards in full battle rattle. Interestingly there were none of the Irish Brigade soldiers with him, just his personal house guard.

"Captain," he said, giving me the traditional left arm down Imperial salute.

"Thal," I answered, returning it with my own Terran Army edge of palm to my eyebrow. "As pers Section 3.7, Chapter 6, paragraph G of Holcomb Estate Law, all non-Holcomb citizens are under dominion of the Lord of the Manor while in system and are subject to the laws and customs thereof. That includes myself, my officers and my prisoner. What is your will?"

Selene looked at me, his slitted cats' eyes unreadable. Finally he said, "Thank you for studying our laws, Captain Singh. I had the finest barristers in the Union draft them. I'm in a difficult position, as you know."

"Yes. You have to appear independent of the Union and some TUBI agents just ran roughshod all over your city. May I make a suggestion?" I was ignoring Kira and Farest, even Hurtenger.

"By all means," said the Imperial. He stood calmly in front of me, double jointed arms crossed over his body armor, knees flexed in that weird alien way.

"Take the prisoner and allow us to return to Alpha Prime. Then we can negotiate an extradition treaty. It would help to normalize relations with the Union," I told him.

He seemed to think for a moment, then nodded. Two of his bodyguards stepped forward and picked up Hurtenger, who started laughing. "I've got plenty of friends here, too, Singh. Be seeing you soon enough," and he spit on me, a mixture of saliva and blood.

I put my hand out to stop Kira from hitting him and, ignoring the liquid dripping down my body armor, I stated formally, "Colonel Johannes Hurtenger, you are temporarily remanded to custody of the authorities of Holcomb Estate until such time as an extradition treaty can be negotiated." My bodycam was recording the whole thing, if it was working. "Thal An -Selene, do you accept custody?"

"I do," he said, then faced Hurtenger. "You have been charged with conspiracy to commit violence against the Head of State and other Representatives of the Holcomb Government, as well as several counts of murder of my citizens. I find you guilty," he stated. He nodded to the big bodyguard, the one named Huor. The other one, Hurin, stepped away and before the war criminal could react, a pair of immense hands grasped his head and twisted, breaking his neck with a sharp cracking sound. The body fell to the ground as he let go, that boneless thud that said a soul had gone far away, never to return. This one probably to Hell, if there were a just God.

******

"You knew that was going to happen," said Kira in an accusatory tone as she headed the Bruiser towards the spaceport.

"I did," I answered, using wipes to try and get some of the blood, spit and vomit off me. Damn my stomach hurt.

She was silent for a moment, then said, "But the Law is the Law, Captain."

"He was properly tried and executed under Holcomb Law, Agent Friedman. Do you have a problem with that?" I asked.

She smiled and said, "No Sir. I think Mac would have appreciated that. He was a law enforcement officer, as are you. I mean that as a compliment, Sir. Justice was done."

Yes, I thought, he would have. And the compliment meant a lot. The Law was The Law, but there were as many forms of Justice.

Thunder Run

J.F. Holmes

For David Drake

Chapter One

"So this here baby puts out enough power to the gun to punch a hole right through an Imperial battle cruiser!" The young tank crewman slapped the side of the engine compartment of his ride for emphasis. "And let me tell you, it's a goddamned rush to fire it!" On the angular slab sides of the tank a dancing holograph of a dragon breathed flames and the word '*SMAUG*' was stenciled on the gun tube, with more than a dozen kill rings in front of that.

"Johanson, you haven't fired at anything outside a training range and you're our mechtech, not a gunner." The gravelly voice came from up above the back deck of the M-38 Marauder, the speaker hidden behind a black visor as he used a computer to boresight the main gun. "Besides, missy," Staff Sergeant Davis continued, addressing the female Irish Brigade private who had been listening to his junior crewmember, "it won't make his dick any bigger."

The girl blushed; Eire was a fairly conservative world, very Catholic and though she was a soldier the directness wasn't really something she was used to yet. She fled with a little wave of her hand at Johanson and a bark of laughter from the tank commander. "Now get back to work, scrub!"

"Damn, Chief, why you gotta do me like that?" The mechtech had a petulant look on his face, especially with the laughter that echoed around the ship's bay. The twelve tanks of the Drakes were chained down in the hold of the *RA Itranu,* a Charee heavy haul freighter and four armed furred crewmen hustled around them. Each crew was breaking the tracks open after storage in low pressure atmo and running maintenance checks. Drop was in forty eight hours after three weeks of transit and there was a purposeful sense of energy and anticipation, relieved by the soldiers' rough joking.

"Because we got work to do, scrub. You need to be doing a systems power check on the fire control, not trying to dip your gun barrel. Like as not that girl is going to be dead by next week and I'd rather not be." He paused and said something down into the turret to Sergeant Wattabim, the gunner, then continued, "and besides, feelings get in the way of fighting."

"And fucking!" interjected the driver from the other side of the tank.

From ten feet away a high pitched voice called over, "And what would you know about fucking, Corporal Farez?" It was followed by a burst of feminine laughter and cat calls.

"And stay away from the girls on *Melusine.* You do NOT hit on the women in this unit, got it?" Staff Sergeant Davis shook his head as his mechtech gave him a pained look, turning his attention back to the gun. "Get back to work, scrub!" He had to keep his crew focused, even though they were ahead of schedule on the activation sequence.

The Marauder was almost a twenty year old design, one of the first homemade armored vehicles to hit the production lines in the Terran Union after the Massacre and the start of the Succession Wars. Old plans from before the Conquest were dusted off and integrated with Grausian tech, marrying civilian fusion reactors to a tracked chassis and a heavy duty rail gun. The original guns themselves had come from seized light suborbital patrol craft and the ballistics were a bit tricky, though the coil accelerated round could pretty much punch through anything. Surplus stuff that was proven and worked, though out of date. The tank worked if they had the power to run it and that was the mechtech's job. If Johanson kept screwing around, he was going to put his boot up his ass. At least the rail gun was gone, replaced by a 130mm smoothbore cartridge firing cannon. Damn thing worked even with the power out.

Grumbling under his breath, Private Johanson climbed up on the back deck and opened the hatch on the side of the engine compartment. His position on the M-38 was a cramped couch outside the turret ring that allowed him direct access to a bank of sensors monitoring the fusion bottle. He was a small guy, under 175 cm; bigger bodies tended to not gravitate to tanks and he was comfortable in his confines. That fact that he was within touching distance of a plasma field hotter than the surface of a star didn't bother him; if it ever got loose he'd never have time to notice. Plugging in his headset he called, "SYSTEMS TEST WARNING, STANDBY ALL SYSTEMS!"

"Acknowledged, all systems on standby," came Sergeant Wattabim's voice, followed by the Chief and then after a moment the driver.

Johanson started flipping switches and then opened up a pocket on his coveralls, pulling out a hibernation container the size of a flat loaf of bread. "Wake up, Wilma, time to rise and shine!" he called and cracked the seal. What sleepily crawled out resembled nothing more than a cross between an iguana and a crow, covered in black feathers with true hands, claws on its feet and a tail for balance. "I need you to standby in case something pops." The trillium chirped and Johanson nodded. "You know how the wires get in the cold. Let's get the bottle going first, give the dragon some juice. Batteries are getting about dry." His assistant nodded and hopped across his shoulders, standing by the main breakers. She would engage them at Johanson' call and throw them at the instant one of the sensors showed a problem.

"OK, starting the main reactor sequence in three," he said, running down a checklist. "And coming online, OK, magnets good and ignition. You think maybe some frigging day we can get an antimatter engine in here."

Several chirps in a trilling language from Wilma. "Yeah, I know," he answered, flipping another switch. "Too damn expensive and big kaboom if the containment system goes. Maybe if I get in with the Marines ..."

His thoughts were cut short by the appearance of a Charee face inches above his, screaming at him through the hatch with a bunch of what he knew were expletives. The spacer crewman wore Bosuns' rank and he had a mean attitude, reaching down and trying to hit the main containment unit shutdown. The alien switched over to broken Common and started screaming, "YOU NO START ABOARD SHIP YOU STUPID HUMAN PIECE OF SHIT!"

The private was startled and his first reaction was to shrink back into his couch. The spacer reached in with his powerful arms and one handed the tanker up and out of the hatch, throwing him bodily on the deck, screeching at him.

Staff Sergeant Davis descended on the ship's crewman like a thunderbolt from atop the turret, knocking the smaller Charee down and trying to grab him. The two melted into an indistinguishable mass of hairy arms and thrown punches as other soldiers from the tank unit and the ship's crew ran towards them.

*****

"Well, this is a fine start," grumbled the Irish expeditionary commander, who had overall responsibility for the mercenary force. The burn scars on her face were pale under the red anger that flushed her skin. Ships' captain or no, Major Iona Keely took an ass chewing like that from very few people, especially a Charee, but she admitted that the freighter captain had a big responsibility.

The Drake's company commander laughed. "If it's the worst thing we face in the next few days, I can deal with it. Besides, how the hell was that kid supposed to know about the ship aux power systems if none of the monkeys told him about it?"

"Good point. Just …" and she sighed. "Mother Mary watch over me and my temper. I almost punched him, Andre."

Captain Deveraux put a hand on her shoulder and squeezed, a friendly gesture, nothing more. "Let me get you a cup of that swill they call coffee and we can talk about how to keep everyone from killing each other over the next two days."

"If I must," she smiled back at him. "At least at the assembly area on Holcomb they had decent brew, if you can deal with some dust."

Chapter Two

At first the cold nothing of space, or the edge of it. About 27 millibars of pressure, little more than three percent of the sea level atmosphere. No sound, of course, at first. Just the curved rim of Maritaneus spreading out below. Their objective was obvious, a series of circular landing pads to one side of the triangle of landing strips. More specifically the Air Defense battery controllers that sat in the middle of the triangle. With them in operation neither the landing craft of the Irish Brigade or the cargo box that contained the Drakes could land.

Now the wind started, at first a thin whistling that quickly grew to a roar. Forty thousand feet and the buffeting started, the heat building up. Their suits were shedding material, the porous hardened radar scattering foam slowly coming loose until the ten human men and women (no xenos, of course, it was after all 2 Para) could hit the spray cans on their shoulders that melted the last away. Then drag ribbons to slow their descent, streamers that eventually broke off. Then the wing suits. In the Legions they had used inertial dampeners and anti-grav, but here a power cell would earn a quick burst from a particle beam.

One failed to deploy her wings, falling gracefully in a spin. Later it was determined, after the body had been recovered, that the Master Sergeant had been dead long before she hit the ground. A tear in her foam shielding had cooked a hole through her guts somewhere around sixty thousand and it was straight in from there. That was their first casualty and the second came when someone finally glanced up and saw the silent shapes descending against the semi-twilight of early morning on Maritaneus. The Grausian patrol leader had been taking a piss and she whipped up her rifle, took aim and fired without pulling up her pants. The round punched a hole through the corporal carrying twenty kilos of plastic explosive and he dissolved into a pink mist. Before she could get off another shot the figures swooped over a hill away from her and disappeared. She cursed as a directed EMP burst fried her radio, the sparks snapping at her face, and the sergeant ordered her people to move out in the direction of the attackers. She had no idea that they gracefully turned and headed away, ninety degrees off their assumed course.

The 2 Para officer cursed to himself as the wind whistled in his ears. The casualties had been expected and planned for, though not welcome. The patrol that had fired on them had been more than five hundred meters away and heading back towards the far end of the spacefield, pure bad luck in the darkness. It compromised their timeline though, again, planned for but not welcome. He also whispered a curse at the treaty Navy ships who sat far above and prevented an orbital bombardment, letting the inhabitants of this world sort things out in the Empire's fall. Then again, he mused, it gave his unit a contract. He deployed his chute a hundred meters up and flared to a landing, quickly stripping it away and unstrapping his gear. Then he set off on a dead run, detailing one fire team to cover the direction of the Grausian squad.

A hundred meters out and his sniper flopped down, adjusted her scope and fired. There was a soft PHUT and the Grausian kneeling outside the fire control building, peering into the darkness, dropped like a rock, the sniper round exiting out of the back of her crest in a spray of hot blood on the thermals. The team raced forward and spilled through the doorway, only the scuff of boots and the soft POP POP POP of suppressed carbines. The anti-ship missile and plasma beam operators weren't front line troops, a mix of older male and female Grausians, and none even got to move.

The Paras were in and the handler sergeant slipped a pack off her back, removing the gelatinous creature from its container. The construct slid into the fire control system, extending pseudopods like tendrils to mate with the bio-nerve control. The handler nodded after twenty seconds, seeing the animal flush red, knowing that nerve impulses were running wild throughout the plasma cannons and missile launchers of the battery. She felt a little sorrow as the hacker slowly turned black, dying as it completed its mission of disabling the systems, but that was life.

"KING," was the only word the team leader had spoken so far into his radio, giving the code word for success. That cleared the way for the shuttles to drop, bringing the Irish Brigades' Second Battalion and the rest of Task Force Dragon to the surface.

"Right, lads," he told his people. "Time to do some mischief." They melted back out into the twilight, leaving behind explosives set to detonate when anyone else entered the building. Probably that squad who had taken a shot at them, which would be good payback. Now it was off to secure the LZ for the first shuttle.

Chapter Three

"Don't feel bad for us, kid, at least we've got inertial dampeners and antigrav to keep the buffeting down. Feel bad for the poor 2 Para guys who had to drop from sub-orbit in wing suits onto an active combat zone." The words of comfort didn't help the mechtech. Johanson had never even been to space before he signed on with the Drakes, reporting to basic training at Quatra on his home world of Alpha Prime and then one lift to Holcomb for assembly. The drop there had been via a shuttle that transitioned slowly from orbit to winged flight and then landed on a runway. Right now they were strapped into their tanks, chained to the deck of a bulk hauler that used a combination of technologies to get them to the ground, more or less in one piece, but it made for a lot of low and heavy G bounces.

"So explain to me why tracks are better fans, scrub," growled Staff Sergeant Davis. He was tapping out a letter to his daughter on his comset, or pretending to. Truth was he hated reentry as much as the next man and his daughter hadn't answered anything from him in more than ten years.

Johanson knew his chief was trying to distract him and he was grateful. "Well, fans are more expensive to maintain and you try and fight in a city, you blow up some concrete dust, sensors are blind, plus it clogs the shit out of the filters. Throw a track and your crew can re-lay one, throw a fan you need a wrecker to lift it. Get a hole punched in your plenum chamber by a penetrator round and you lose air pressure plus your fan. Lose a road wheel and the crew can replace it."

"Good, scrub," said Davis. "And why a chemical gun instead of a rail gun like the Terran Marines or Impy plasma guns?"

Johanson sighed. His interest was in high tech, especially adapting Grausian systems, not old school crap. "We run a 130mm kinetic energy weapons system for several reasons. Reliability, simplicity of operation, ease of maintenance and cost of manufacture. Now if we were a Terran Marine Expeditionary unit, I'd have tri-barrel plasma cannon or a coil gun for the ammo capacity. But we'd need a complete direct support maintenance unit and we're just a merc company."

"Damn, scrub, you sound like a textbook!" interjected Sergeant Wattabim. There was laughter over the intercom system and Private Karl Johanson from Friesland was glad they weren't on the platoon push, or worse, the company net. The nickname of 'scrub' was generic for a new guy, but sure as shit he hoped that he would get something better than that when he did get a nickname.

"Nah, sarge," he replied to the gunner, "I just want to know how to do my job when the shit hits the fan." He flicked off the IC and reached over to scratch Wilma between the ears. "Das ist good, ja?" The trillium nodded; she understood the thoughts behind the vocalization and didn't need to know the language. He flipped it back on again, to get caught flipping off coms was a cardinal sin.

"- keep the heat on, scrub," he caught the track commander saying. "Maritaneus is a cold world and I hate freezing my ass off. Best thing about being in tanks is the excess heat."

It was banter to cover up the nervousness that all of them were feeling, even Staff Sergeant Davis. In less than three hours they might all be dead, punched through by a war surplus Grausian plasma blower or a red paste from some buried shaped charge. Corporal Farez, Sergeant Wattabim and Sergeant Davis had all seen the combat, either in the War or as a merc, so their fears were memories and ghosts that sat on their shoulders. For Johanson, they were imagined but just as real, tinged with a fear of letting down the crew or worse, being a coward. Looking like a fool in front of that girl from the Irish Brigade. He didn't know that at that very moment she was feeling the same doubts as she crouched down behind a wall, crying her eyes out. Her squad leader stared at her with one dead eye, the other a gory mess. At her feet was a puddle of vomit and a Lance Corporal was emptying a full magazine right next to her ear.

"Drakes," came Captain Deveraux's voice over the company push, overriding their own internal coms, *"looks like the Irish are having a hard time at the LZ. Be prepared for offensive actions rolling hot from the deck. Priority targets are being loaded; support assigned Irish units."*

"You heard the man," said Staff Sergeant Davis. "We've got Bravo Company, call sign Exile."

"Is that the one commanded by that rich Impy, Sarlone or Sarlene something?" asked Farez. Behind him in the background Johanson could hear clicks and beeps as the driver applied power to the drivetrain. He kept his eyes on his own gauges as they went from red to orange to green. One fluctuated and Wilma reached over to jiggle a wire. It popped up to green.

"Thal An-Selene," said the gunner. Sergeant Wattabim was a voracious reader of tabloids and had spent her time at the Holcomb unit assembly playing fangirl over the Grausian. It was a running joke in the unit about inter-species sex but no one knew if she was embarrassed; her coal black skin gave nothing away.

"It's just kind of weird that we're going to kick some Impy ass and one of the company CO's is a Grausian," said Farez. "I mean, I know everything has changed in the last twenty years, but ..."

"I don't give a shit, as long as he fights and we get paid," said Staff Sergeant Davis and there was general agreement. It was, after all, why they were there in the first place.

"Chief, I've got a temp spike on the reactor, nothing serious, same thing from the Field Exercise." Johanson lowered the fuel input a small percentage and the temp subsided. He wasn't worried; if the coolant let go, never mind the actual reactor, they would be parboiled in an instant and not feel a thing. If the reactor ... well, best not even think about that. Of course there were safeties, but ...

"Roger. Just keep an eye on it and our six. This is urban fighting and a rocket from a second floor in the back deck is going to kill you and immobilize us, which means we're dead. Remember, you've got control of the Interceptor system AND the rear machine gun."

"No pressure on the new kid ..." he muttered and Wilma chirped.

There was a thud and a blaring claxon that came through the seals on the hatch. "*Smaug* rolling hot," called Farez and the fifty ton tank whined forward into the screams and hell of 27th century combat.

Chapter Four

Anchor was a city under siege and Task Force Dragon was there to break it. It was a human city of two hundred thousand on a world that was home to millions of Grausian, close to the heart of the Old Empire. The mercs didn't care, at least not officially, who was in the city as long as they got paid. Unofficially, well, the majority of the soldiers were humans from the Terran Union worlds and a lot of them felt a little bit more excitement about settling old scores. Especially ex legionnaires like Davis.

"Banshee, execute Bravo," called Captain Deveraux over the radio, Staff Sergeant Davis catching his voice on the Task Force freq. He had one ear tuned to the Task Force command net and the other to the Company net, switching down to platoon or tank as he needed to and issuing commands.

"Farez, find us a hull down position and then plan an assault route to that HQ. Watti, you're weapons free to engage points of resistance designated by Exile. Scrub, keep the power coming and watch our six." Davis's voice was calm and collected, not betraying the anxiety he felt. That would pass as soon as ….

WAP! And the entire track shook as a reactive armor block blew, dissipating the oblique plasma charge before it could burn through the hull. "BLOWER!" shouted the driver, "ELEVEN!" even as he jinxed the tank sideways, throwing an unprepared Johanson against his seat restraints.

"ON THE WAY!" yelled Sergeant Wattabim in the ancient gunners' cry as the cannon rocked backwards. The problem with a plasma blower is that an untrained crew would reload instead of displacing and it lit up the firing point like a roman candle. That was the attackers' problem; the tank crews' problem was that if the blower team adjusted aim and got their second round off, or worse were operating by SOP and had two teams, well, a center mass shot that hit at the right angle would go in one end of *Smaug* and out the other.

"Fight the tank, I got shit to do," said Staff Sergeant Davis, flipping over to the platoon net. He was the senior NCO in the platoon and they had no officer; personnel resources hadn't hired anyone to replace the last damn fool. He disappeared off the interior coms, barking orders at *Melusine, Pythios* and *Panlong,* the other three tanks in their section.

*****

The first reactive charge that blew wasn't what shook Johanson and made him realize that he was in combat for real. Instead it was as he scanned the rear mounted cameras around, searching for threats while keeping one eye on the engine readouts. They were set on auto, panning around to cover the 180 degrees in the back. It was redundant, pulse radar would pick up any incoming missiles, but the Terran Marines had found out the hard way that relying too much on new computer systems wasn't always a good thing. He slapped the camera stop and zoomed on three bodies scattered at the foot of a wall, wearing Irish black and gray winter camo. The pools of red blood were shockingly violent against the snow but even worse was the sight of the girl he had been talking to in the hangar bay. She sat on the ground, leaning up against the wall, rifle at her feet, hands over her ears, screaming silently. A fireteam of her comrades bounded past with a heavy machine gun, ignoring her. She was a casualty just as sure as the two lifeless bodies on the ground in front of her.

"SCRUB, IS THERE A THREAT? WHY IS THE CAMERA STOPPED?" Staff Sergeant Davis's voice boomed in his headset, shocking him back to life.

He put the camera back in motion and babbled, "No … no sarge, negative, just thought I saw something! Just some Irish, had to ID them!" he called back in a panicked voice. There was no answer except for the tank rocking from the cannon slamming again. The crew was too busy fighting the battle. Best he get his head back in the job or he'd be lying out there in the snow himself.

The tank suddenly surged forward at the same time he heard Davis call, "Farez, put us on that hill up there, overwatch on White as they push through the road. Sector left."

Johanson watched the readouts as power demand spiked and he was thrown around in his seat. Farez pretty much had two speeds; stop and go, which he supposed was a good thing. Then he felt the tank tilt upwards and level out. A quick switch to the front camera showed a wide river valley with camouflage tents showing IR signatures. To the right the four tanks of Third Platoon were deliberately moving forward with infantry following at a run down the road. He switched back to the rear camera just as Wattabim fired another round, causing the view to jump.

*****

Staff Sergeant Davis grunted in satisfaction as Wattabim slowly rotated the turret back and forth, scanning for targets.

His platoon, call sign Red, was spread out on a low hill, watching for threats while Second Platoon, call sign White, was spread out in defilade just behind the crest of a hill, watching for enemy anti tank teams or armor threat. Intel had said they were concentrated in the siege lines, ten kilometers away from this HQ site, but Davis hadn't stayed alive all through the Succession War by trusting intel.

"DRIVER REVERSE!" he screamed as movement caught the corner of his eye, overriding Wattabim's controls and slewing the turret left where *Panlong* was supposed to be watching their flank. The coil gun round spat out by the Grausian anti-tank armored vehicle struck as the tracks sprayed dirt and penetrated the side hull of *Panlong*, a sparking TING sound that echoed over the roar of battle. Davis knew better than to ask over the radio if the tank was OK; the penetrator round had entered right at the crew compartment level and the commander and gunner were probably toast after it had finished ricocheting around inside. Maybe the mechtech in back and the driver might make it, but for now they were on their own. He did wish the track commander would hurry up and die; his wet raspy breathing could be heard over a stuck open microphone on the platoon net.

"CONTACT LEFT!" he yelled again and screamed into the turret, "FROM MY POSITION, ON THE WAY!" *Smaug* jumped backwards and the tank destroyer erupted in a ball of flame. Simultaneously its second shot hit *Smaug* on the edge of the turret, throwing up sparks and leaving a gleaning scar in the armor.

"TARGET, ANTI-TANK," screamed Wattabim, catching sight of the Grausians' wingman. She fired and the round went high as the fleeing wedge of metal crashed into a stone wall. A round from *Melusine* hit the rear hatch and it stopped dead, smoke billowing out of the chassis. The crew bailed out, running in their strange double joined way until coax plasma fire cut them down. After a long minute where no other threats showed in any wavelength Davis breathed a sigh of relief.

"Black, move out after White, Red on overwatch, Look out for friendlies on the road, over!" came Drake Six on the company net. Staff Sergeant Davis relayed the order to his platoon as *Panlong* started to burn, a brilliant torch that shot out of the open commander's hatch. The gurgling rasp on the platoon net stopped abruptly as first *Melusine,* followed by *Pythios* and then *Smaug* pulled out of line. As they fell behind the crest of the hill each trained their turret in the direction of the shattered tank destroyer, watching for more threats. A squad of infantry ran past to replace them and hastily started digging their own crew served weapons in to guard their flank.

*****

The remaining three tanks of First Platoon fell in behind Second, quickly getting covered in the mud of the torn up road. It was a cold world and winter had set in but sixty tons of tank will break through a crust of ice and churn up the dirt beneath it. That and their exhaust heat was like a furnace, melting the snow. Behind them the light infantry of the Irish Brigade rode on large 6 x 6 ATV's that allowed them to keep up with the tanks, though not too close. Their job was to assault the HQ area after the tanks had softened it up. Meaning after the Drakes had charged full speed through the area, but the approach was still at a medium pace.

The road emerged from the hills about a kilometer from the enemy's lager and Staff Sergeant Davis watched through his commander's sight. The thermals against the snow made the distant camp look like an anthill that had been hit with a stick. Trucks were revving up and some of the rear area troops were actually trying to break down tents and shelters, hastily cramming them into the back of transports. "You poor bastards," he muttered, "that's what you get for sitting in the rear with the gear, trying to get the glory without the risk." Then he thought of the crew of *Panlong* and steeled himself. It was going to be slaughter, but they were only Impys.

*****

"Scrub, make sure we're ready, gonna kick it in a minute," came Davis's voice over the intercom. Before Johanson could reply the Track Commander was already issuing orders to the rest of the crew.

"Don't tell me how to do my job, you ape," muttered the mechtech, forgetting that the channel was open.

"I will use my ape hands and squeeze your head until it pops like a grape, Scrub. AFTER you do your job," said Davis.

Johanson flipped the switch to 'listen' and cursed under his breath. Wilma chirped in laughter and he made a mock swat at her. The diminutive alien mech disappeared into the back of the fusion plant. He felt Farez kick it into gear and the transmission engaged, sending the tank forward. Scanning the readouts he adjusted the fuel flow and dialing in more coolant. He loved the machinery, but it had seen some hard use since it rolled off the assembly line on Nova Laredo and his job was a lot more complicated than it should be.

Chapter Five

The four tanks of element White split, two each to the flanks to cover the attack. The other seven formed a line abreast as the road opened up onto the snow covered field. The HQ was a kilometer ahead and the tanks threw up a rooster tail as they accelerated. The key to the success of a blitzkrieg is to get inside the enemies' decision making cycle, have them react to you instead of you to them. Once you disrupt that by attack and destruction you need to keep pressing so they can't gather their resources and stop you.

Plan Bravo was a straight through attack by the tanks while the infantry laid down suppressing fire. Once they were through they would climb the next ridge and start firing at the division laying siege to the city. The besieged forces were to attack from the other side and hopefully the Grausians would break. What happened after that wasn't the mercenaries' problem, it was the politicians.

The tanks never slowed as they went through the tents and trucks, firing indiscriminately from their machine guns and saving the main gun rounds for any armor that might show up. They turned the entire camp into an inferno and shot the Grausians that broke and ran. Others fell under the treads of the tanks, coming out the other side as a flat, bloody paste mixed with the mud. Then they were through the other side, the only damage on *Smaug* a splash mark where a rocket propelled grenade had set off one of the reactive armor plates.

Johanson looked in horror at the destruction they had left in their wake. The infantry had remounted their ATV's and followed them in, shooting anyone that even hinted at resisting. He caught a glimpse of the girl from the landing bay, no longer crying, instead shooting down a tall Grausian woman wearing an officers' silver armor plate, standing with her hands up. The mechtech kept the camera scanning while his brain reset some circuit breakers.

"INCOMING INCOMING INCOMING," started wailing over the tank's speakers and Johanson felt his gut tighten. A smart artillery round could drop a forged penetrator right through their top armor and he immediately hit the switch for the millimeter radar jammer, feeling Farez start the weaving across the field. Ten seconds into the spine jolting ride he felt rather than heard a BANG and the tank slewed violently to the right then came to a jerking halt.

"Chief, we got a broken track!" Johanson called into the intercom, then flicked the switch and said it again, feeling stupid, scared and hyper.

"No shit, Scrub, get out and fix it! Wattabim, you too and watch out for toe poppers!" the NCO immediately shot back.

"On it!" he called, unjacking the headset and hitting his seat release. It slid back, putting the hatch in line with his head. He undogged it, told Wilma to watch the gauges and swung the hatch sideways. Climbing out onto the back deck he stepped out into a world of smoke and hell, closing the hatch behind him.

The track lay behind them, twisted up like a snake. They had run over a FASCAM, a mine delivered by artillery. There were half a dozen scattered around behind them but their way forward looked clear. The gunner was already out of her hatch and climbing down the side of the turret, one hand on the tank at all times so she didn't lose her balance. As soon as she was down the turret started spinning, scanning off to the left.

"Watch for anti personnel, mon!" the sergeant said as Johanson dropped off the deck.

He froze as his boot landed three inches from a baseball sized object that had four trip wires extending from it. He gingerly stepped away and looked around for more. "Uh, what do we do when we find one?" he called out.

"Mark it with a flag for EOD and done' step on it," she said, "just remember your training, Scrub."

He did, quickly grabbing the marker kit from one of the side compartments, noticing that there were heavy caliber bullet craters running down the side of the armored skirt. He broke out a flag and pushed it in the ground more than a foot from the AP mine, slowly working his way back to the broken track. He found two more mines as Sergeant Wattabim paralleled him, checking the path of the tank. They would have to slowly move it backwards onto the track after they fixed the damage.

Johanson started to feel cold as they worked, replacing shattered track pads and laying it out flat at the back of the tank. It was heavy, an alloy of aluminum and steel with synthrubber pads. The next fifteen minutes were both the fastest and slowest in his life. It was just like a training exercise except that every now and then *Smaug's* main gun belched fire, a CRACK that hammered at his lungs. As they worked a column of Irish mercs made their way through the minefield, accompanied by an EOD team deactivating the anti-personnel bomblets by freezing the triggers off with liquid nitrogen. They made a path through and then a company of the black and white camo figures hustled past at a double time. The tanker didn't even bother to look for 'his' girl, focusing on the task at hand.

They had rolled the tank back on the track and were snaking the broken ends over the drive wheels when Staff Sergeant Davis, who had been scanning the area with the turret, yelled "INCOMING" at the top of his voice and dropped down, slamming his hatch shut.

"What -" said Johanson, who was half under the lifted side skirt. He pulled his head out and saw the infantry column scatter into whatever cover they could find. Wattabim grabbed his arm and pulled him down onto the ground, snaking her way around to the front of the tank. He started to follow her and the world exploded around him.

During the First World War on Old Terra men had been driven mad by the constant shelling of artillery. Even hidden in bunkers and protected in dugouts the constant pounding had killed men's souls just as much as it had their bodies. Johanson only experienced two ragged volleys that were badly aimed by a panicked, under fire artillery battery. Most were swept from the sky by the combined fire of *Smaug*'s interceptor gatling and a lone Irish Brigade air defense laser that had set up at the edge of the destroyed HQ site. Those two volleys, though, were the most terrifying things he had ever experienced in his short life. The last 150mm round detonated fifty meters directly over the tank's position, showering it with white hot shrapnel. It washed over a circular area, catching some of the infantry who were on the edge of the impact area. The tank itself was scoured, stripping antennas off and shredding the bags of personal equipment strapped to the back deck.

Johanson lay there, completely exposed and deafened. All he could see with his face buried sideways on the ground was a jagged piece of still smoking steel, dug deep into the ground less than two inches from his face. Beyond was the silent screaming face of Sergeant Wattabim, holding onto her leg above the knee. Below it her calf muscle was nothing more than stringy meat and sharp white bone.

A pair of boots thudded into the ground in front of him and he was roughly hauled to his feet. Corporal Farez said something to him as Staff Sergeant Davis pulled Wattabim out from under the tank, but the only thing Johanson could hear was a loud ringing in his ears. He reached up and touched his ear, hand coming away with blood. Farez looked at it, then gave him a thumbs up. Then he took a marker out of his pocket and wrote on the dull brown paint of the tank, "FIX THE TRACK".

Johanson, still stunned and looking at the gunner having her leg worked on by an Irish medic, eagerly grabbed onto the task. It was something training allowed him to do by rote, without thinking. When they rammed the last pin into the track, linking the ends together, he was astonished to see that the infantry had moved on and the was gunner gone.

Ignoring the scattered equipment, he climbed back in through the hatch and slid into his seat. He put the headset on and turned the volume all the way up, barely hearing Staff Sergeant Davis. "Say again, Chief, my ears are fucked up."

"I said to get the goddamned fusion bottle popping and give me max power. We've got a war to fight, Lucky!"

"On it, Chief," and he was. Strapped into the warm and secure cocoon of his engine compartment, sheltered from the hell outside. Wilma came over and started wiping the blood off his head with a rag but he ignored her as he made sure all the readouts were in the green. He keyed the unit to green and the tracks spun as *Smaug* raced to catch up with the battle.

Chapter Six

One of the greatest dangers to an armored vehicle is to silhouette itself on a ridgeline or above an enemy. On the other hand, it's impossible to bring your weapons system into play without a direct line of sight, so Davis played a tricky game of edging along the backside until he came to an oblique angle, shielded by the burning corpse of one of Black platoon's tanks. He didn't know and didn't care right now which of his friends were dead in there, bodies roasted to a cinder. He was angry that his gunner was wounded and glad that the mechtech wasn't. He could fight the tank without a gunner but an engine problem would leave them dead in the water.

"DRIVER STOP!" he ordered and raised the commander's seat, sticking his head out of the hatch and getting some eyes on, scanning the plain His radio suddenly crackled, the Irish breaking in on the company net.

"Stand by for targeting info," came the voice of the Irish Brigade intel officer. Davis dropped back down into the turret as a screen flashed into life, slaving itself to his gunsight. It flickered and the tank commander slapped the side of the screen, bringing it back to focus, an overhead shot of the enemy siege lines from genemoded hawk or eagle. It shifted and the view changed to orderly rows of dozens of armored vehicles.

"Yeah, that's it, you genie freak." He knew that the view was being provided by some kind of flying creature that was linked to an intel soldier. In turn the soldier was plugged into a bio computer interface. Whatever, he would take what he could get as long as he didn't have to stick his fingers into some kind of animal's spinal cord.

"Sequential fire, from right to left, sweep and zone. Pick your targets, Dragon Six out." That was fine by Davis and he directed his element to do the same in the left third of the armor vehicles. He tapped a vehicle on the screen and the gun swiveled, elevated and fired. He tapped another target before the round even hit, laughing and cursing at the same time.

*****

"Well this is boring as shit, Wilma," said Johanson. He had come down off the high of the hair's breadth escape from death and was feeling exhausted. Every few seconds the tank rocked backwards with the roaring THUD of the gun but his hearing was slowly returning. He watched dispassionately on the screen as the Irish dug in on the ridge in front of them on the military crest, slowly searching for the pretty girl. He finally found her, struggling up the hill with belts of ammunition draped over her shoulders, looking miserable and cold.

For a moment a wild fantasy came to him of cracking the hatch and inviting her into share the warmth and who knew what that would lead to. He was brought back to reality by Wilma chirping in his ear, bringing attention to a readout. He almost hit his head in shock; the plasma containment field was fluctuating wildly all over the place and power output was dropping. It was a continuous drive transmission and they either had power to the turret and electric drive wheels or they didn't, and that moment was approaching.

"Chief, we gotta pull back! I've got a problem with the containment field, might be a crack in the mag bottle!" He ignored the answer, slapping switches and yelling at the computer. The Terran Union worlds had many restrictions placed on technology by the Empire and the first run programming after the Massacre had been rudimentary at best; it showed now. There was little he could do outside the standard controls to deal with an emergency.

"SHUTTING DOWN!" he yelled into the intercom. It wouldn't be anything like an antimatter explosion if the containment let go, but the venting of plasma through a shattered containment core would fry everything in the engine compartment at least. 'At least' included him and Wilma, at a minimum. He tripped the main breaker just as the container went critical and the plasma vented out of the back of the tank in a white hot jet of flame. Then he started the lengthy reset procedure, frantically typing in commands to work around a faulty magnet that might have been more of a code problem than an actual system failure. It was a design fault that there weren't any batteries to power the tracks until they restarted, but … Wilma started slapping at the start switch for the emergency generator trying to at least get them *something.*

"GODDAMMIT JOHANSON I NEED POWE-" he heard Davis yell over the intercom, a yell cut short by a blood curdling scream. There was a tremendous simultaneous CRACK that was louder than his damaged ears could handle and the mechtech felt the entire fifty ton tank lurch sideways. Every electrical component shorted out in a shower of sparks and he was plunged into darkness. The battery powered red emergency lights flickered on and then started to shine. At the far end of the cramped compartment a matching glow

started and he realized that the paint on the wall was blistering. The glow came from the metal behind it.

With a panicked curse he grabbed at the latches for his hatch. They grated and he tried to push it aside but it moved less than a foot. "JESUS FUCKING CHRIST!" he yelled as the compartment started to heat up. He started banging on it and screaming then stopped as Wilma chittered in his ear.

"YES! GET HELP!" he screamed and she flew out of the small opening. Johanson grabbed at the supplemental oxygen mask and pulled the fire suppression manual override handle. Foam flooded into the compartment, coating him, but the heat continued to grow. He pulled himself up as close to the hatch as he could, stuck his hand out and pulled desperately at the edge.

"HANG ON BROTHER, GONNA GET YOU OUT! MOVE YOUR HAND!" The voice was female but hoarse from yelling. "GONNA CUT THE HATCH!"

Johanson pulled his hand back in, hyperventilating inside the mask as his boots began to smoke and his vision started to go black. There was a bright jet of flame over his head and then the hatch fell away, rough hands grabbing him by the deadman's strap on his coveralls and yanking him bodily out of the compartment. The woman and another soldier dumped him over the back deck to land on the ground with a bone cracking thud, pain shooting up his left arm. He cried out as they grabbed him by the shoulders and half carried, half ran him onto the back of the flatbed ATV that already contained two other wounded.

As the Medevac vehicle skittered away across the snow and down the mountain and Wilma chittered on his shoulder, the mechtech looked back at *Smaug*. Flame was shooting out of the top of the turret and his own hatch. There was no sign of Staff Sergeant Davis or Corporal Farez. Then the ammunition cooked off and the turret leapt high in the air, flipping over and cartwheeling through the sky.

"Damn, you're one lucky son of a bitch!" said the woman. "Lucky ... Johanson," she scribbled on a notepad and then shot him with some painkiller. "That's a hell of a nickname to have ..." and the world faded out.

Epilogue

"Lucky, huh?" said the Irish girl.

Johanson gave her another kiss. "Ja, Lucky."

"Better than Crybaby, I guess, but … I mean, I got my shit together, but just seeing Sergeant Calhoun dead like that…" and she started to shake with the memory.

The tanker wrapped his arm around her shoulders, took his hand and wiped away a tear from her freckled face. "Hey, it's OK, I heard you did good afterward. Fought like a demon, they said!"

"I did OK, I guess. I … I killed an Impy. One at least and I'm still alive, but, I'm going to resign my enlistment. I can't do this anymore." She seemed defeated, but then she leaned in to give him a kiss herself.

"Well, we've got time before the shuttles lift. Let's use it wisely, shall we?" he asked. She smiled at that and started kissing his neck.

Well, Lucky is better than Scrub, any day of the week, thought the veteran. He tried to enjoy the moment, but the faces of *Smaug's* crew kept staring back at him.

Milk Run

Casey Moores

"Fixer life sure beats the War, don't it?" Victor
Cernyshevsky asked. "Fixer" was their unit slang for the
FXRS, the Field Extraction and Recovery Services.

"Hells yeah, though I wish we had something to shoot at
every now and then," Jim Cho answered. "Hey, straight to
the Emerald when we get back, right Vic?"

"Sorry, pal, those days are gone, but I'm sure you'll do
just fine without me."

Cho shot a glance over his shoulder, past the litters with
injured patients attended by a trio of pararescuemen, to look
at the gunner on the opposite side. Vic didn't glance back at
him. Instead, the other gunner remained focused on the
landscape below. Cho returned his attention to his sector,
right and aft of the H2-LX Accipiter Salvator VTOL, known
in the FXRS as a 'Jolly'.

He scanned the open plains below more with curiosity
than actual concern. After so many passes across the
landscape he entertained himself by trying to find something
new. Groves of the dark blue-green trees were few and far
between. River washes of varying depths curved their way
across the terrain in multi-pronged patterns. Once in a rare
while he saw a small settlement. Earlier, he'd focused on and
memorized those areas. At this stage, they'd become
uninteresting.

"What do you mean, you're passing on the Emerald?" Cho
asked. "Weren't you hooking up with Bijou, the uber-
hottie?"

"Yes. Yes, I was."

Cho didn't look back again, but he could sense Vic smiling and blushing.

"All right, so?"

"So… she doesn't work there anymore."

"One, how the hell do you know that?" Cho asked. "And two, why the hell not?"

"Hey, Jim, we really should switch back to the main intercom."

"Vic, we ain't seen shit in what, twelve passes over the exact same spots?" Cho answered. "And I got my finger right there to switch over. If I see something I can click over faster than I can talk. Besides, I gotta get an answer to this here mystery of yours. Answer my questions, then I'll shut up and switch to main, okay?"

Vic sighed audibly over the private back-ender frequency.

"Fine. Seems some asshole stuck a baby up in Quinn. That's her real name, by the way. Quinn."

"Wait, you're saying that you were banging Bijou—"

"Quinn."

"Quinn, fine. You were banging Quinn, knocked her up and she stopped dancing at the Emerald?"

"Yeah. Seems that, being a higher class establishment, they're opposed to pregnant women getting up on stage."

"So, what, did she move over to the Frog or something?"

Motion caught Cho's eyes. He whipped his head to focus on it. A herd of the kangaroo-like reptiles, he couldn't remember the name from the briefings, bounded across the plains toward a wash. Being the first exciting thing to see in hours, he found himself mesmerized by them.

"No, she stopped dancing altogether. We had a talk and I can support her while she raises our kid. In fact, I wasn't gonna say anything until we landed because I didn't want to jinx it, but we're getting married as soon as we get back."

"You gotta be shittin' me," Cho said, dropping his voice several octaves for emphasis. "Dude, that's incredible. Horribly cliché, marrying a stripper baby mama…"

"Exotic dancer and that life's behind her. She's actually gonna go back to school if we can swing it, when the little one's older. Then I'll have my own sugar momma and someday I can get out of this business."

"And the cliché continues. You've rescued the damsel from a life of having drunk assholes drool at the sight of her, so she can be barefoot and pregnant in a tr—"

"Watch it, Cho."

"All right, all right. Congratulations. Is that better?"

"I'll take it and thank you."

Cho reached down to one of the zippered pockets on the outside of his webbed survival vest, unzipped it and retrieved his palm slate. Turning back around, he held it up, precariously balanced on one hand and aimed the screen at the other gunner.

"Hey, Vic, pan left a little."

"What? Why?"

"'Cause I'm gonna get a hero pic for this lady of yours. You can thank me later. She and your baby are gonna want pictures of their big hero man in battle."

"Eyes outside, Romeo."

Romeo was the Jolly aircrew term for the right gunner, as opposed to Lima on the left and his partner was reminding him to stick to business.

"Real quick, then I'll put it away and switch freqs and that'll be that."

"Fine. Real quick."

Vic swung slightly to his right, which gave a good profile of the gunner and the 12.7mm liquid nitrogen cooled eight-barreled Gatling gun. The left gunner shifted, narrowed his eyes and flexed.

"Ooh, dirt sexy," Cho said. "Make love to the camera. Damn, man these pics are gonna make that preggo stripper soak—"

The Jolly bucked hard to its right, throwing Cho backward and near horizontal. The palm slate tumbled out of his grip, bounced against his shoulder and fell out. It should have been tied off to his vest with a lanyard. Rookie mistake. He twisted to try and catch it, but it was too late. He heard the low, dull staccato of countermeasures dumping out.

Stacked up on litters against the walls, the patients jerked against their restraints, but stayed put. Two of the PJ's caught hold of hand grips, but the other lost his balance and flew against the right side of the fuselage.

"Romeo!" the pilot said on the main intercom. *"Did you see it? We just got a missile indication and auto dispensed. Aft right, what you got?"*

Cho had been searching to find his falling slate, but he looked back up to scan for threats and spotted a tiny village they'd passed over before. A truck had appeared in a small, horseshoe-shaped mud wall. An anti-aircraft artillery laser cannon sat on the truck bed, pointed at them. It unleashed a stream of flashes as he spoke up.

"Break left!" he shouted. He realized, with a sick feeling, that he hadn't switched back to the main intercom. As he fumbled to find the switch, Vic repeated the call for him. The tapping sound against the fuselage told him the delay had a cost.

The Jolly reversed its maneuver and kicked hard to its left. Cho grabbed a handhold to catch himself, but still strained against his harness as he, once again, fell backward and horizontal. Finally, he found his comm switch.

"Lima, was that you? What are you seeing?" the pilot asked.

"Triple-A laser, four o'clock!"

"Romeo, dammit, who's talking? Is it tracking?"

Cho could no longer see the laser fire, but an answer came in the form of orange flickers thrown up through the dust, pouring across his field of view. The sounds of scratches reverberated through the floor below him, meaning the piece had reacquired its target.

"It's tracking!" Cho shouted.

The Jolly bucked up, rolled some more, reversed its roll to level out and bunted downward. As the ship leveled, Cho searched for signs of the laser cannon but it had stopped firing. They'd gotten out of its range, notoriously short. An important factor was the insanely low altitude, just a few feet off the ground.

"Missile incoming, nine o—" The pilot never finished the call.

Everything went bright. He was thrown so hard against his gun that some ribs felt like they cracked. Before he could grab on he rolled to the side of the craft. His harness caught him but his legs went out and his butt slammed onto the floor. Cho hung for a moment at the end of the opening, dangling like a rag doll. Burning needles erupted all over his back and he got a brief falling sensation. Then everything went black.

*****

Captain Hampton, the Intelligence, Surveillance and Reconnaissance Chief, jumped from his chair and pointed to the feed that tracked the inbound Jolly VTOL formation. Both Jolly's had just made several abrupt turns before a missile exploded inside the Dash Two, the second in the formation. He watched the live feed from Dash Three as the other ship crashed into a field. The lead Jolly continued to maneuver away from the threat area.

"Sir, there's a Jolly down," Hampton said. "It's Jolly 32." As he'd been trained, he turned back to look at Colonel Knight to verify he'd been heard. In this case, there was no chance the commander had missed the message. He was looking at the same feeds and had seen the explosion amidst the formation. Every other head in the FXRS Operations Center (FOC) snapped up to look at the feed.

"Lead's reporting small arms and PSAM's," Rolle, the communications chief, reported. Portable Surface to Air Missiles were one of the most dangerous ground threats as they could show up anywhere, even worse than a truck mounted AA laser. "They're planning to teardrop back around to check out their Dash Two."

"Negative, tell them to egress the area and bring those patients back!" Knight ordered. He waited a moment to ensure Rolle passed the order. Lieutenant Colonel "Spuds" Tattimac, his operations officer, started to speak and Knight put a hand up to silence him. He watched the surviving Jolly continue out of the enemy's engagement range. When he was confident the lead Jolly was clear, he continued.

"What's the nearest Sandy formation?"

"Sandy 30 flight, sir," Hampton said. "Flight of two. Papa's lead, Powder's on the wing."

"Weapon status?"

"Full up, sir. Sandy's haven't had anything to shoot at since the big push this morning. But they're about to bingo out on fuel and return to base."

"Sir," Tattimac said, "that Jolly is gone. It's a write off, sir. Should we be risking more assets confirming it's destroyed?"

Though Tattimac acted as if the question had been meant for Knight, his operations officer glanced at the observer from the Board of Directors. For the life of him, Knight could not remember the suit's name. Tattimac seemed overly concerned with the pencil-necked, moron bureaucrat whose only job was clearly to nitpick every decision Knight made. Knight resolved to ignore the bastard and remain focused on leading the way he had since the wars.

"What about the crew, Spuds?"

"Sir... the crew is gone." Tattimac said it in a flat, matter of fact tone. It was not the hollow, sorrowful tone a normal human being would use when discussing a dead aircrew. Tattimac was an excellent manager and a great planner, but his lack of empathy made him a horrible leader. Knight had spent six months grooming Tattimac for command before he'd come to the realization. He'd resolved to reassign Tattimac to a more administrative position as soon as the contract was fulfilled.

"Hampton, zoom all the way in on that feed," Knight said. As he'd guessed, they'd already set the best picture they had available. It displayed a crashed and smoking Jolly VTOL. The fuselage had buckled, but a lot of it was intact. "Pan north a touch."

As the feed moved upwards, Knight focused on a black dot. He moved closer and concentrated on it.

"That's one of the crew," he said, raising a finger and pointing at the dot.

"Even if it is, sir, there's no way—"

"Rolle, direct Sandy 30 flight to do a low pass to check for survivors. Make sure you give them the best threat picture we have."

"Colonel Knight," the observer spoke up. "I know that you're used to operating under a budget that you never really saw and are used to getting whatever resources you need, but those days are gone. That VTOL cost forty million Terran credits. With that loss, this contract is now operating on a very slim profit margin. The gunships you're risking cost sixty-three million TU credits each. Even with combat loss insurance, if you lose just one of those gunships—"

"Sandy's," Knight said. "We call them Sandy's in here and the VTOL was a Jolly."

"Colonel, you can call them whatever you like, but I'm telling you that—"

"That you presume to tell me how to do this job that I've been doing since before you were spawned from whatever nerd factory created you? Fixers, do we leave our own behind?"

"No, sir!" the entire room replied. Knight noted the only two exceptions were Tattimac and the pencil-neck. Knight tried not to dwell on the time he'd wasted trying to develop his operations officer.

"The user will reimburse us thirty-five percent of combat losses per the contract. Insurance will give us another twenty-two point five. If we can rebuild whatever we recover, we'll be fine. Even if not, I can still get good deals on surplus from my supplier."

He returned his attention to Rolle. "Sergeant... you heard me. Get those Sandy's overhead."

"Yes, sir." Rolle got on the radio, directed the Sandy's to the crash site and passed the list of threats that Jolly 31 had reported.

"Copy all," Knight heard the Sandy 30 lead reply. He recognized the voice of Papa and grinned. If the enemy was still active in the area, Papa would end them.

*****

Captain Candace "Papa" Cummings listened to the radio call and watched the data feed populate in a display. Her mind fought to remember the crew roster, trying to work out who was on Jolly 32. She thought she knew the answer but didn't want to be right. A moment later, that information filled in on her display. She cursed.

"Powder, you got all that?" she asked her wingman on their private formation frequency.

"Two," he responded. It was the appropriate response to all queries from the formation lead. It could mean either affirmative, that the message was received, or both. This response meant both.

The information feed displayed the coordinates of the crash site. With a tap she highlighted them and then hit an icon that set those coordinates as the next waypoint in her flight director. The navigation cursor shifted and she banked to follow it. As they'd been on the same corridor between their airbase and the operating area that the Jolly had followed, it wasn't far.

She'd never conversed with any god before, but now she prayed it wasn't as bad as it looked. Tension built up in her shoulders. She took long, deep breaths and focused on trying to stay calm. She failed.

"Powder, break off for overwatch," she said a few minutes later as they arrived overhead. "Lead's heading down for a low pass."

"Two."

He moved aft and left out of the tight wingtip formation he'd been maintaining. She cut her thrust to idle, racked the controls to invert her FR-AX Fulminis II gunship and pulled hard to point the nose straight at the ground.

It took less than thirty seconds to drop ten thousand meters. When the ground screamed towards her, a hard jerk on the controls leveled the ship off at a hundred meters AGL— above ground level. The gunship groaned in anger at the stress on its wings. Leaving the thrust at idle, she banked sharply to the right to re-orient towards the crashed Jolly. While doing so, she descended another fifty meters and bled off airspeed. A target cursor in her HUD helped her identify the crash site. Papa set up a slight offset to get the best angle, set the gun camera to record and toggled it to pan over the area as she passed by.

The wreckage itself was clear and made her grimace. Smoke still billowed out of it and debris was scattered all around it. On the other hand, it wasn't flattened or completely blown apart. The overall structure was somewhat intact, which gave her a glimmer of hope.

"Lord, or whoever, please let me see inside that cockpit. I beg you," but the crew area remained obscured by smoke. As she was about to break off, the FOC called to ask if there was a crew member to the north of the wreckage. Papa straightened up and snapped her head in that direction to look. Her thumb toggled the camera in that direction.

Warmth flowed through her body as she identified a figure. There was no telling if they were alive or dead, but there were no signs of blood and they at least looked intact. Reason told her it was most likely one of the gunners or perhaps a PJ from the back, but hope told her there was a slim chance it could be the pilot. With another tap, the data system relayed the feed to the FOC.

A stream of bright orange flashes appeared in front of her. On instinct, the pilot yanked back, jammed the thrust to max and went vertical. The taps of ground fire rattled against the gunship's skin, but no warning alarms illuminated.

"Powder, you got 'em?" she called to her wingman.

"Two," he replied laconically.

Papa rolled the gunship back over and nosed down just in time to see her wingman pour fire, lead, laser and missiles into the source of the ground fire. Normally, he would deserve berating for wasting ordnance. In this case, she knew that, for one thing, he was low on fuel and could only make the one pass. Anything he didn't use up would remain on his wings for the trip home. For another, the fuckers deserved it. As he zoomed through the area, a missile launched from the south.

He finished his strafing and bombing run and pitched back up into the sky. Countermeasures dumped out behind him and the missile bit off on them. It exploded a short distance behind him, close enough that the fragmentation might get him.

"Powder, status."

"Minor damage, but I'll make it," he said. *"But that's it, Papa. I'm not quite Winchester, but I am Bingo. RTB'ing."*

She'd assumed as much. It was hard to dump all your weapons on one target without plain jettisoning them, but she didn't expect him to push his fuel status any further. Either way, it was better that he Return To Base so he wouldn't be around to stop her from doing something really stupid.

"Lead copies. I'll make one more pass and follow. See you back at the ranch."

Lucky for her, he knew better than to question her fuel status. Rolling about to zero in on the missile launch site, Papa fired two of her four Infernus missiles and followed them with a healthy dose of laser fire from her Executor multi-barrel laser cannon. Sporadic ground fire replied during her attack run. This time a few damage alerts populated on her display but nothing immediately serious. The area exploded in two successive fireballs from the missiles. As the smoke cleared, she lanced anything that moved.

"Sandy 31, say fuel status." The FOC was calling. A simple tap on that radio shut it off.

Flying a pass for damage reconnaissance, there was nothing but charred wreckage and blackened corpses from her attack. Rage unsatiated, Papa hoped there were more of them to kill. In a slow, wide circle, the pilot scanned for any movement, vehicles, or people. A group of some non-human species huddled together and made a mad dash out of the area. It was clear they weren't Grausian and were likely a family of indigents, so they weren't worth her attention.

"Sandy 31, you are directed to return to base immediately!" This call came on the interplane frequency, but it wasn't Powder. The FOC must've realized she'd turned their radio off and switched frequencies. A few more taps punched all of her radios off. The silence was kind of nice.

A line of dust spewed up in the distance that could only mark inbound vehicles. Staying low, she angled forty five degrees off of the line. Once well past the leading edge of the cloud, a teardrop approach lined the gunship up behind whatever was making it. As the distance closed, the picture on her gun camera showed two trucks rolling up, full of Grausian troops. Achieving target lock, two Infernus missiles leapt off the wings, one for each truck. Her Executor poured burning light through the area, joined by the beat of the two 20mm Gauss cannons on the wings. As the gunship got close, she climbed a little and pickled two of her cluster bombs onto the burning trucks and fleeing figures. Hundreds of little ball-shaped grenades saturated the area. Some would go off immediately, the rest would blast at random to make the spot a kill zone for another hour.

A warning klaxon and message announced the aircraft had reached emergency fuel. Undeterred, Papa circled the area in one last search for inbound threats. Finding none, she lined up on a low wall a few dozen meters from the Jolly crash site and dumped more Executor laser and the rest of her Gauss cannon's depleted uranium shells into it. The last cluster bombs were dumped over the missile site, just in case. By design, her aircraft was Winchester—out of ammunition. It was safest to land that way.

With the last of her fuel, she returned to the crash site. A nice, flat and open piece of ground seemed the best place to touch down without blasting rocks into the aircraft and the potential survivor. Slowing to a near hover, Papa eased the aircraft down. As the gunship settled the engines whined and cut out from fuel starvation.

Papa realized her actions would end her career with the Fixers, but she couldn't really care. At the very least, the Fixers didn't administer lashes or execute their members the way the Terran Marines did, even if the TUMC Search and Rescue had always been kinder and friendlier than the Line

Regiments, or at least they'd always said so in the recruitment vids. Regardless of the potential punishment, her actions would have been the same. Job, lashes, execution be damned... she had to know if the pilot was okay. Their love had carried her through six years of bitter war and would carry her through the rest of her life, however short that may be.

*****

The Sandy remained fixed on one position in the screen surrounded by dust plumes. A scroll to the left of the aircraft showed flight instrumentation information. The airspeed flickered between zero and two knots and the height above ground level (AGL) slowly dropped to zero. The dust plumes dissipated. The operations officer stalked up to the screen and pointed at it.

"Is she landing?" Tattimac asked. "ISR, is that what I'm seeing? Did Papa just land?"

"Sir, I believe so," Hampton said. "It's obvious she went well past Bingo fuel, sir."

"Sergeant Rolle, still no answer from her?"

"No, sir." Rolle repeated the same calls to Papa over and over again, switching through the various frequencies she should have been monitoring.

Knight looked down the roster of active aircraft. Two other flights of Jollys were outbound from their pickups and a third flight was inbound to one. Two Kings were forward with the user, in the midst of loading up damaged equipment. Three flights of Sandys were covering the Jollys and the Kings. As much as he wanted to, he wouldn't pull another

Sandy flight away for this. He couldn't justify leaving those assets unprotected just to throw more into a bad situation.

"Spuds, gin me up the alert King with a PJ, Raven and Dagger team," Knight said.

"Now we're risking a dropship, too?" Tattimac replied, with a belated, "Sir?"

"You saw the feed; Papa expended every piece of ordnance she had making sure there wasn't a damn thing left alive there. Besides, there's no indication they had any high altitude air defenses."

"Noted, sir, but high altitude air defenses don't always announce themselves before they show up. The threats that took that Jolly down sure didn't. Plus… one each ground teams as well? That'll limit our ability to support the contract if anything else goes wrong."

"Contract be damned!" Knight said. "If the high and mighty Forgotten Legion had secured their lines as well as they said they had, we wouldn't be where we are."

"They've mitigated surface to air threats as stipulated, but they're not going to take responsibility for some rogue Grausian teams sneaking behind their lines. They'll expect that's exactly the sort of threat that an armed rescue company, a former TUMC SAR unit, should be able to handle. In the meantime, if they make a call and we don't support, even though we've got the resources, they'll hold us in breach of contract."

"They breached it themselves when they failed to uphold their end. The contract stipulates we have a right to protect our own assets."

"Colonel," the bureaucrat said, "one man and a junked VTOL does not constitute our own assets. That gunship might, but your pilot clearly disobeyed orders and is risking that gunship— "

"It's called a goddamn Sandy!"

"—outside of your control, which is an internal issue. The Forgotten Legion does not stand for support units failing to back them up, especially considering their history."

"Is there a point in all this, or do you just like hearing yourself talk?" Knight asked.

"Well, Colonel," the bureaucrat continued, "if money is withheld pending a legal battle, which the user has demonstrated on more than one occasion they are willing to do, that will mean—"

Knight snapped his fingers and pointed at Sergeant Vasquez, his security chief.

"Get him out of here, Vasquez."

"Yes, sir," Vasquez responded. The tall, muscular man moved towards the bureaucrat without drawing any weapons.

"Tossing me out won't make any of this any less true," the bureaucrat continued. He raised his hands in innocence but maintained his conceited expression even as he followed Vasquez' guidance towards the exit. "You should have followed my advice, Colonel."

The last word was spat out, dripping with condescension. The man stepped through the door, followed closely by his escort. Knight let himself relax as he watched the man leave.

"Sir, the alert King— King 05— is starting their launch sequence."

He acknowledged and said, "And make sure the alert Sandy's are up to date on everything going on."

"Richard…" Tattimac said in a pleading tone. Among closely ranked officers, the use of a first name was the standard way to get another officer's attention before making what leadership courses called an assertive statement.

"Et tu, Spuds?" Knight sneered.

"Sir, I know you hate the Board as a general rule, but it might be wise to consider his point."

"Continue to generate that King and somebody tell me how soon we can have more Sandy's on station," Knight said. Then, he dropped his chin and rubbed his eyes. "Spuds, I respect you. So, I'll let you tell me what you think."

Tattimac glanced around the FOC at the others, who all pretended to ignore the conversation. The operations officer walked close so that he could speak in a low voice. Knight clenched a fist, but kept it hidden at his side.

"Sir, we're not Marine Air Wing SAR anymore. We're a mercenary company—"

"I know that very well, Spuds. If you'll remember, I'm the one who formed this company and I'll be damned if some little pissant is going to come here and tell me how to run things."

"Understood, sir. But the Board owns the company, not you and we have a contract to fulfill. I know it's important to make sure we take care of our own, but we have to manage the assets to make sure we don't short the user."

As if summoned by Tattimac's words, Centurion Vasilis, the Forgotten Legion's liaison officer, spoke.

"Colonel Knight." Knight was surprised that he'd stayed out of the previous discussions but was glad the man hadn't given the bureaucrat any ammunition. "The Legion is transmitting a new pickup request. They say we'll have several ten lines shortly, one for personnel and a few for equipment."

Tattimac remained stone-faced, but Knight sensed him repressing a smirk.

"Sir," Tattimac said, "the King you just alerted is loading up with our last standby PJ team. You've got to make a call, sir."

Knight locked eyes with Tattimac and fought to restrain all expression of emotion.

"Who's the pilot?" Knight asked.

"Major Routt, sir."

"Once you pass him the latest threat picture, tell Jim to head to the crash site and drop the PJ's and Ravens as close as they can get. As usual, the Daggers have authority on their placement."

Tattimac sighed and slumped his shoulders in defeat.

"War's over, Richard," Tattimac said. "There are no more generals to give you a medal, promotion, or a pat on the back for making the tough calls. The only thing we answer to now is the user and the Board and I'm pretty sure you're going to piss them both off."

"And I'll take responsibility for doing so, as a leader should."

It was something Knight didn't think Tattimac had ever learned.

*****

Papa, in a rush to exit, almost pulled the canopy jettison handle. She stopped herself after remembering the system was designed to release a canopy in flight, where it would be blown backward and away by the airflow. On the ground, it could detach the canopy in an emergency, but it would sit there until lifted away by the pilot or a recovery crew. She flipped the switch to raise the canopy in the normal way.

While waiting for it to open, she plucked the PW-93C carbine needler from its sleeve along the right wall of her cockpit. After verifying it was activated and armed, it was slung over her shoulder. Papa twisted to reach the buckles to her go-bag. If anyone was alive, the medkit would be crucial. After unhooking the carabiners, it took a little work to shimmy the bag out from under her seat. When the canopy locked open a single switch killed the power to the aircraft and the lights and displays went dark. Everything became quiet. Papa took one more deep breath and tried to clear her head.

Before getting out, experience told her to scan outside for threats. Finding none, the pilot climbed out of the cockpit and down the side. On the ground, she unslung the carbine and squeezed into the shoulder straps of the go bag. Her head remained on a swivel on the trek towards the crashed Jolly.

It was a mess. Any hope of survivors onboard disappeared when it became clear the entire inside was charred. Her approach slowed on the discovery of burnt, shredded corpses in the two pilot seats. She stared at the body of Captain Drescher, the right seat pilot and commander of the crew. There was no reason to get closer and check for signs of life. He was dead, flames still licking up from burning plastics.

Strength left her. Papa fell to her knees. Her breath became rapid and shallow and she cupped her face in her hands. Recent, vivid memories piled into her mind. Memories of pressing up against him, skin against skin, with nothing but sheets covering them. Eyes closed, Papa prayed to nothing in particular that it was some kind of misunderstanding, or a bad dream, or anything other than what it was.

With one last deep breath, she tensed up all of her muscles, opened her eyes and stood. Nothing had changed. A combination of anger and apathy pushed the flood of memories away. Several blinks and rolls of the eyes worked the tears out. Weak and light-headed, she staggered towards the wreckage where the left gunner's blackened body was slumped over his gun. How some joke they'd prefer to go. The gunner ethos revolved around their weapons and sex. Their arguments usually revolved around which they preferred more. If there was such a thing as an afterlife, she wondered if the gunner's spirit still felt that way.

Further back, in the small cargo compartment, two columns of three litters stacked up on each wall. The twelve Forgotten Legion patients and the three pararescuemen had fared no better, a jumble of corpses that had been scattered and burned all over the compartment and she saw the effect of the missile that had impacted and detonated inside. There wasn't a whole body in there.

A mere five feet from the wreckage, her legs stopped working. She didn't collapse again, but some unseen force kept her from getting closer. It occurred to her that she should go inside and verify everyone was deceased, but it just wasn't going to happen. Had it been any other crew, she could have. But not this one.

The body tossed out to the north returned to her mind. The only unaccounted for crewmember was the right gunner. It took a lot of focus not to fall over while backing away far enough to circumnavigate the Jolly. Going around the aft end helped avoid the temptation of looking at the pilot again.

The Jolly had dug a short, wide channel in the ground. Putting the pieces together, she decided it had flown close to the ground, as expected if it were getting shot at. When the missile had gone off inside of it, it must have killed the engines. If it had landed in a slight pitch up attitude, it would have crashed at a low enough velocity to make that impression in the ground. Even so, it was surprising the Jolly hadn't rolled or flipped on impact. If the crew hadn't been killed by the blast, they probably would have survived. It was excellent piloting, but it hadn't saved anyone.

On the other side, the gravelly terrain trended upward. The loose gravel and sand were interspersed with clumps of yellow grass and spiky bushes. A hundred meters away, backtracked from the Jolly's final route of flight, the right gunner lay face down and motionless. Per the data burst, it was either Cho or Chern-something-ski. Outside of hearing their pilot talk about them, she hadn't really known either well enough to recognize them— especially face down.

On her way to him, Papa took stock of his situation. His upper back was slightly singed, but not charred like all the others. His harness looked intact, but the strap which had connected him to the Jolly wrapped around him and trailed a few feet to his side. The end of it was jagged and blackened.

The harness strap must've been cut by the explosion and the gunner tossed out. It was miraculous that he hadn't been burnt any worse from the explosion inside the Jolly, but she'd seen stranger things in her time.

What was still unknown was how he'd landed. Even with the helmet, if he'd landed on his head, his neck would be broken. Regardless, there was a strong chance of spinal injury. As such, moving him was a bad idea even if he was alive. She crouched next to him and lifted his right arm to check for a pulse. He had one.

To see if he was breathing, she shuffled around to his head. His mouth hung open and his head rested on its right side, supported by the helmet. Unzipping and reaching into her left breast pocket, Papa retrieved an old but trusty signaling device— a mirror. When held up to his mouth, it fogged up. He was breathing.

Having confirmed he was alive, it was time to do what she had been avoiding-- to fire up her radio and contact the FOC. She could only hope that the old man would be more focused on coordinating their pickup than on berating her for disobeying the order to RTB.

After collapsing, legs crossed, next to the gunner, her thoughts wandered off. Her hand fumbled into one of her vests pockets for the comm brick but had trouble finding the strength to grab it. She wrapped her arms around herself and broke down. Visions of her best moments with Drescher flooded into her mind while tears flooded down her face.

After a few minutes, which felt like hours, she pulled out her brick and passed the ten line information.

#

"Ten line information coming in now, sir," Rolle reported.

"It's about damn time," Knight said.

"It looks like she's just sitting there?" Tattimac said.

"Put the ten line up so we can all see it," Knight ordered.

"Yes, sir."

One of the screens switched to an information feed.

The FXRS "ten-line" was modeled after the nine-line that Terran military forces had used throughout the war and much further back through history. In the transition to becoming a mercenary unit, a line had been added at the top for the client to define the priority of the request.

Lines 1, 2 and 3 denoted the priority, the location and the comm frequencies— information they already had.

"Line 4..." This was the line on which everyone focused. "1AH, 18XH."

The despondency in the FOC was palpable. Some gasped and others slumped into their chairs in defeat. Out of the nineteen humans who'd been aboard the Jolly, just one had survived. Papa had listed that one as urgent, meaning they needed medical care as soon as possible.

"What's the ETA on King 05?" Knight asked. He glanced at the screen that tracked its progress. It didn't look too far out.

"Twelve minutes, sir," Hampton said.

"Line 5— S." The patient required a Scoop litter, meaning Papa suspected a spinal injury. The ISR reinforced that it meant the patient was the one who'd been tossed clear.

Line 6 was redundant in this case— that there was one patient who couldn't walk.

"Line 7— U." The enemy situation was unknown or unobserved. This was actually encouraging, since it implied she thought she'd killed all the observed enemy forces. The ISR feeds had implied as much as well, but the reassurance was nice. There were a lot of feeds to watch and a limited number of people to watch them.

Line 8 outlined standard signaling equipment. Line 9, meant to allow users to identify the allegiance of the personnel, reiterated that the patient was a member of FXRS. Line 10 denoted there were no nuclear, biological, chemical, or other technological threats.

All of that information could've been passed over voice communication and sometimes it was. However, the data burst was proven to be the most efficient way to pass the information, especially since FXRS survival bricks pre-populated a lot of the data and only required a few lines to be updated and verified.

Three of the intel feeds, including the one watching the downed Jolly, glitched out at once and turned to static. "Just lost feeds four, five and seven, sir!" Hampton said. "Switching channels."

The room hushed again as Hampton tapped away on several different slates. "It's no good, sir. Comm relays from those assets are being jammed."

"Are we still in contact with the King? Or any other nearby King?"

"Yes, sir," Hampton said.

Sergeant Rolle, anticipating the next request, said, "Sir, I'm requesting all airborne King's initiate alternate laser comm relays."

"Good job, Rolle."

It would take crucial minutes before those relays came online. Even then, the connections would be intermittent, as long-range laser comms always were in an atmosphere. However, what bothered him more than that was the fact that communications jamming never happened in a vacuum— it was a prelude to enemy action.

"Launch the alert Sandy's," Knight said. "King 05 is still what, eleven minutes out?"

Mental math told him the Sandy's would take five minutes to launch and another ten to arrive on station. That meant the King would be alone for about four minutes. They had a decent defensive systems array, but little offensive capability.

Even at high altitude, whatever else the Grausians had out there might have something that could reach out and touch the King. He didn't need the bureaucrat to tell him it was a seventy million credit asset.

"Ten minutes, forty seconds, sir."

"Will Powder be recycled in time to make it a three ship?" Knight looked at

"No, sir. He took a bit more damage than he reported. It'll take hours to green up his Sandy."

Knight avoided looking at Tattimac and presumed the operations officer disapproved.

"Colonel Knight," Tattimac said in a soft tone, "until the Sandy's are overhead or we know if anything's inbound, I say we hold the King off. If they had one team buried behind the Forgotten Legion's lines, we know they could easily have more. Especially since the jamming would serve to prove as much."

Knight glanced at Tattimac, thought for a second and nodded.

"Good input, Spuds. Rolle, tell Routt to hold well clear until the Sandy's arrive."

*****

Movement on the horizon snapped Papa out of her agonizing reminiscence. A scan of the horizon revealed a series of tiny dust plumes. Flipping up her rangefinder binoculars, she counted five skimmers heading towards her from a little over two klicks away. The sky fan tail and shiny metal gave them away as Grausian. With grim disgust, she realized her comm brick had lost all signals. There was no way to send a distress message.

Until that moment, she'd taken it for granted her people would show before another group of Grausians would. That belief was incorrect. Papa cursed and looked at the unconscious gunner with irritation. A dried ravine stretched a hundred meters further up to her northeast but going there had seemed a horrible idea. Moving him could hurt or kill him.

For several seconds, she scanned the sky for any sign of FXRS or Forgotten Legion aircraft. There were none. In bitter resignation, she stuffed the comm brick back into its pocket, tossed her go bag back onto her shoulders and slung her rifle.

"Well, I hope your neck and back are fine," she said to the gunner. With a grunt, she rolled him over. Squatting low, Papa grabbed the handles on the back of the gunner's harness and heaved him backward with every ounce of strength her legs could muster. The pair rumbled about twenty centimeters through the sand and gravel. As fast as possible, she reset herself and repeated the maneuver and again and again.

Her rifle slid off her shoulder several times along the way. Eventually, she gave up and laid it out on the gunner's chest. There was probably a better way that some grunt would have known, but that grunt could suck it.

With resignation, Papa accepted there was no time to erase the obvious trail they were leaving. It just meant they'd have to keep moving once they got into the ravine. Being tracked was not an if, it was a when. All she could do was try to buy time for her people to show up.

The whine of the skimmer's engines was audible by the time they were within a meter of the ravine. She took a second to survey the drop off. A steep two meter downslope led to the bottom. The approaching skimmers became visible with her Mark One eyeballs.

After a moment of thought, she grabbed his feet and dragged until he was perpendicular to the edge. After re-slinging the rifle a sharp kick rolled him until he tumbled over the side. Happily, it had been a sandy slope and not a rocky one, so the gunner didn't smash his face on the way down. Papa scooted to the edge and slid down after him. Halfway down, one of her feet caught and she flew forward, slamming hard onto the ground next to the gunner. Her nose bumped against the dirt with a crunch and her vision exploded with stars.

The stars didn't last but the pain in her nose did. Her hands went to her face and felt for blood. Whatever the Grausians had with them would certainly be able to smell blood. One hand pinched the broken nose together while the other fumbled to dig out some gauze. Ripping small strips out of the gauze was frustrating and time consuming, but better than leaving a long red trail to follow. After spending a lot more time than she would've preferred, two massive clumps of gauze hung out of her nose.

"I gueth I detherved that after what I jutht did to you," she said.

Papa stuffed the supplies away and returned to dragging the gunner. The smoother, sandier dry river bottom made it easier to drag, but they only made it another dozen yards before the whine of the skimmers ceased. Papa stopped, held her breath and listened as best as she could. There were no yips, pants, or growls, which would've meant Grausian hunterbeasts. The silence didn't rule out a lot of other kinds of genetic monstrosity. The dragging resumed with even greater haste as there might be little to no warning if such things caught up with her.

A welcome, familiar roar sounded overhead. A flight of Sandy's. Streams of emerald laser fire crisscrossed into the air from south of her position. Multiple screams of varying pitches denoted a missile battle between the ground and the air.

Over the top of the ridge, a Sandy shot into view and rocketed off to the east. The noise of the ground air battle continued. The glorious, beautiful Sandy banked around to make another run. A second Sandy streaked by, trailing smoke.

As the first gunship lined up to make another run, rocks tumbled down the ravine. A light brown, dog-sized spider-like creature skittered over the side and slid down the gravel towards her. A decicrus, one of the nastier Grausian creations. Two long pincer arms reached out to her in anticipation and four fang-like mandibles around its mouth clacked and salivated.

Without thinking, Papa flipped the rifle up and jerked the trigger. One millimeter needles zipped out and tore into legs and abdomen. Ichor oozed out from the punctures and several legs snapped. It staggered as a more controlled burst tore into its mouth. The creature collapsed and tumbled onto its back, its legs curling inward.

She'd received the intel briefing on them countless times, but this was the first time she'd seen one in real life. The Old Empire Grausians used them for area denial and to clear populated areas. If a swarm of them swept through a city, they wouldn't even leave bones behind. The most relevant information was that decicri were always unleashed en masse. If there was one, there were dozens.

As expected, several more of the creatures emerged around the edges of the sunken riverbed and tumbled over the sides. In desperation, Papa cradled her rifle into her right arm in order to shoot while continuing to drag the gunner.

For the most part, she failed at both. The rifle bucked all over the place. Her shots were wild and few hit the growing collection of decicri. Her left hand burned as she gripped tighter and tighter to pull the gunner. For all that effort, she didn't move much.

A great boom echoed through the air. She looked up to where she thought the Grausians were and saw nothing. Off to the left, smoke billowed up in a column. One of the Sandy's had gone down.

There wasn't time to think about it as the horde of decicri encroached well inside her comfort zone. She released the gunner and grabbed the carbine in both hands. With a good kneeling stance and the rifle well braced, Papa focused a solid burst into each one, one at a time. Some paused to eat the dead ones, but plenty more climbed over and drove towards her. She couldn't kill them fast enough and they were approaching at a run.

The rifle clicked empty. She deftly dumped the magazine with one hand while ripping the next out of a Velcro pocket with the other. By the time she slapped the new magazine in, the decicri were closing in.

Papa cursed herself for not checking the gunner's pockets for grenades. Most gunners kept some secured inside zippered pockets. With her teeth clenched, she considered how useful they would be at that moment.

It occurred to her that the sounds of the air ground battle had ceased. If one Sandy had been shot down, the other would have been ordered away. Colonel Knight never allowed the Sandy's or the Jolly's to operate independently.

Papa was alone. The decicri would sweep over her within the next minute and rend her away to nothing. She could only hope for a quick death— perhaps they would crack open her headfirst, so she wouldn't be alive while they devoured the rest of her.

The whole thing had been idiotic on her part. She'd envisioned landing, finding Davis alive and saving him the way they did in those stupid drama shows. Instead, she was there, in a ditch, dragging some gunner whose name she wasn't sure of and who might've been killed just from being dragged. Either way, they would both be dead soon.

An explosion detonated in the dead center of the mass of decicri. The concussion sent tremors through her body and left her ears ringing. Decicri piled through the remains of their fellow, biting and clawing. Her finger clenched tight to the trigger.

As the ringing in her ears died off, the telltale staccato of a SAW90 opened up from somewhere behind her. The charge of the decicri stalled out as their legs shattered and their bulbous heads and abdomens were riddled with holes. The rounds tore through their chitin and light gray fluid splattered everywhere. It didn't get them all, so it seemed prudent to keep shooting.

"Sup, ma'am, you order some cavalry?" crackled over the radio.

Papa shuddered. Of all the assholes who she didn't want to show up and save her, Sergeant John Asmar ranked at the top. She ceased firing in the slim hope that a decicrus might make it through and kill her. That way, she wouldn't have to thank him.

Two more explosions amongst the mass of decicri sealed the deal. With a sigh, she turned her head and watched a team of six Ravens, Sergeant Asmar in the lead, as they rumbled down the other side of the ravine and stomped towards her. Three PJ's and three Riggers followed close behind them.

Riggers were used to help rig, repair, or set up equipment for extraction. She presumed that once things were quiet, they'd get to work securing the remains of the ships. The thought led her to wonder whether her ship was still intact or if it had been destroyed by the Grausians.

She recognized one PJ as Senior Sergeant Rob Disney, one of the most experienced and respected among the Fixers. He moved straight to the gunner and checked for a pulse. After the briefest moment, Disney used a knife to tear the cloth off the gunner's arm, retrieved a needle from his kit and slid it into a vein. Another PJ knelt on the other side of him and they spoke to each other in low voices. Disney made eye contact with the PJ who was helping Papa and he nodded his head.

"You did a good job, ma'am," her PJ said. "There's no way he woulda made it if you hadn't done what you did and you sure were tearing up those decicri when we found you. You've sure earned the nickname Psycho Bitch, haven't you?"

Sure I did and as a result, I'll be out of a job soon, she thought. Out of fear that she'd kick their ass, no one called her by the callsign she'd been given on her induction into the SAR. Everyone called her by the more socially acceptable Papa Bravo, which had been reduced over time to simply Papa. Right at that moment she was too zoned out to care that he'd called her by her real moniker.

Her mind wandered back to Davis. Everything around her took on a surreal quality, as if she wasn't really there.

"You alright, ma'am?" the third PJ said. He didn't look at all familiar, but he had the same clean shaven, eager young boy look that most PJ's had. He knelt next to her and his mouth was moving, but she didn't really process any of the words. The PJ grabbed her rifle and helped her to her feet.

Disney and the other PJ snapped together a makeshift litter for the gunner and eased him onto it. Two of the Riggers picked him up. The Ravens formed a perimeter facing the Grausians and the whole group moved in the opposite direction.

Papa remained in a daze as they moved back. At some point, more Sandy's were flying overhead. The PJ had ushered her into a Jolly that she hadn't even noticed. She craned her head up and saw the Jolly's wingman flying a dog bone pattern overhead to cover them. As they lifted off, she saw blackened, smoking areas where the Grausian skimmers had been. A King dropship roared in on its four massive thrusters and settled into a field near the downed Jolly. Her Sandy had been blown apart by the Grausians. Further to the south lay the smoking wreckage of the Sandy that had gotten shot down.

She gave half a thought to who it might have been, but found she lacked the brainpower to give it any real consideration. The sound of the Jolly's twin fans and the reverberation through the aircraft's structure lulled her to sleep.

*****

Rolle stood up with a grin from ear to ear.

"Sir, Captain Scanzanillo reports his Daggers have suppressed all the air defenses and disabled the Grausian skimmers. They're not going anywhere and they're sitting ducks for any Sandy's we send at them. He reports his team will keep sniping at anything that moves and says he'll gladly go in and finish them all off if you want."

The FOC erupted in cheers and clapping. Even Tattimac seemed content with the outcome, though he could only muster himself to give a slight nod while maintaining his grim expression. The Forgotten Legions liaison smiled and Knight hoped there was a chance to smooth that relationship over as well.

Though the intel feeds hadn't come back up yet, Sergeant Asmar had reported that Papa and Cho, the only survivor from Jolly 32, had been secured and were both in stable medical conditions.

"Excellent news, sergeant," Knight replied. Even in the war, the Dagger teams had always proven to be a magical solution to any given problem. Assuming you could infil them in one piece, the rest was just a matter of time. "But tell them they've done their part. They can sit tight and wait for our next flight of Sandy's to show up."

Centurion Vasilis stood up and made a gesture meant to get Knight's attention.

"Go ahead, Centurion," Knight said.

"Colonel, the Primus is on the horn." The Centurion jabbed a thumb toward Knight's private office. "Should I direct it to your quarters, sir?"

The expression on his face told Knight the answer should be yes. Knight nodded. Then, he snapped his fingers and pointed at Tattimac.

"Spuds, it's all yours."

Tattimac nodded in reply.

Knight entered his meager office and closed the door. Using his slate, he connected his earpiece to the Forgotten Legion line. Taking a long, deep breath he dropped into his chair and activated the connection.

"Colonel Knight."

"Richard, this is Daren." said the commander of the Forgotten Legion. *"I'm guessing you know why you're getting this call?"*

"Of course I do. I presume your people are squawking about our failure to support."

"That's right. Now, you've done a good job for us up until now and I understand you encountered some Grausian teams who hid out behind our lines."

"Yes, that's exactly what happened. In case your liaison hasn't passed you a full picture, I lost one of my Jolly's, two of my Sandy's—"

"I hear one of those losses, and the events following, was self-induced?"

Knight clenched a hand into a fist and closed his eyes. "Well, one of my people broke SOP's and took it on herself to land and check for survivors."

"Sounds brave and stupid. I'd give her lashes and a promotion if she were one of mine. But that's beside the point. I have my men on the front out here fighting a much larger battle than what you have going on. All they know is that Forgotten Legion troopers are dying in the field because your VTOL's and dropships are focused on recovering your own."

Knight, still alone in the room and only on audio, pounded his fist onto his desk. "What would you have me do? They wouldn't be doing that if your troops hadn't left a mess of

Grausians back here behind what you considered secured territory!"

"*Wait just a goddamn minute, Colonel,*" shot back the former Legionnaire. "*Your Fixers are advertised as capable of defending themselves. I remember how the SAR used to run during the Civil War and it was always a blessing to have them assigned to us. Much better than those unarmed Medicus Airlift that got doled out to most legions and like I said, you were doing a damn fine job here until that shit went down. Now, as I was trying to say, I can understand that you had to do what you had to do and take care of your own. I would've done the same if I were you and I can't fault you for that. On the other hand, this isn't the war. I have a contract that delineates how much support I'm supposed to receive. As you said, you lost twelve of my troops... troops who were alive when they left the battlefield in your care. I have ten lines that have gone unanswered for longer than stipulated and for all that, I'll have to apply the penalties for the contract. I understand your position, I really do. But just like you have to cover your own, I have to cover mine.*"

A chill flowed through Knight's body. The profit margins were already gone. The loss of a Jolly and two Sandy's had already dropped them into the red and additional penalties would only make it worse.

One man. I could've left it at the loss of a single Jolly, but I pulled in all those resources for one man who could just as well have been dead. During the war, no one would've questioned a single damn thing I did. Hell, this was an average day back then.

"*War's over,*" Daren continued, "*and we've got troops who have to get paid. If you're not holding up your end, you get less payment. That's just how it is now, Colonel.*"

"Understood, Primus. The contract is the contract. Is that all?"

"Can I count on you to resume your support of my Legion?"

"You can."

"Then yes. That's all, Colonel. I'm glad to hear you recovered your man. I hope it was worth it. Out."

Knight disconnected and rubbed his temples until there was a knock on his door.

"Yes?"

The door swung open and Tattimac stepped through, his face as pale as a ghost.

"Spuds, I left you in charge. You shouldn't need my approval for—"

The words caught in his throat as he noticed Sergeant Vasquez and a security team standing behind him.

"Sir, I'm here to relieve you."

"What?"

Tattimac straightened and licked his lips. He looked terrified by what he was saying. "Sir, the Board representative sent a coded transmission directly to me. The Board has unanimously decided to remove you. You are no longer in command of the FXRS."

The Empress's Price

Armondo Borboa

"The Massacre", as the treacherous destruction of the non-Grausian legions is popularly called on human worlds, has been portrayed in endless fictional media. Plays, books, vids, holos, recruiting posters, Terran Union military propaganda. None, however, have provided a true firsthand account of the events as viewed by the Terran Fleet command staff at the moment. Few survived the initial attack and even fewer the next fifteen years of war, but through careful research and reconstruction of surviving records, I hope to provide a somewhat accurate account.

Many thanks to the estate of Lieutenant General Suki Nakamura, TUFSC, for providing access to her personal unpublished notes on the Massacre. Also, for the personal interview with Colonel (R) Thomas Meagher, TUMC, Marine Security Platoon Leader on the *USS Caledonia* at the Massacre.

~ *Cause and Effect, A History of the Succession Wars*
by Dr. Armondo Borboa
Professor of History, University of Cartagena, Nova Hispania
Major (R), Terran Union Fleet Strike Command (Spaceborne)

CHAPTER 1

"Four times within a few years I held the rank of Primus Pilus. Four and thirty times I was rewarded for bravery by my commanders. I have received six civic crowns. I have served out twenty-two years in the army and am more than fifty years old."

— Service record of Roman Centurion Spurius Ligustinus, as recorded by Livy

Date: 484 PC (Post Conquest)
2626 AD (Human calendar)
Re: Six years before the Fall of the Grausian Empire
Glarius System, Glarius VI
Capital world of the Old Grausian Empire

"You have got to be kidding me, Max."

The other man in the room shifted stubbornly in his chair but otherwise said nothing.

"You're the hero of the hour." Vice-Admiral Robert Franks leaned back in his chair and propped his boots up on the desk before continuing, "Hell, you're officially a 'Hero of the Imperium' now, with capital letters and everything! The galaxy is your oyster and you're up here pouting?"

Despite the accusatory question left hanging in the air, the two off-duty men were both content to sit in otherwise companionable silence. Their collars were laid open and the bottle of golden-amber Scotch Whisky resting on the work desk between them had been half-emptied since they first sat down.

Much like their forbearers had done since time immemorial, the pair were dealing with the lingering mental trauma of recent combat action in the traditional method of human soldiers everywhere, with smoldering cigars and full glasses in either hand. They were busy drinking their troubles away while gray-blue smoke formed a distinct cloud layer a few inches over their heads. The only outside sounds that penetrated the Vice-Admiral's private office were the battleship's conventional space engines thrumming gently in the distance, while routine ship's messages sounded over the intercom.

Not hearing any denials from his friend, the human Navy officer tried a different tack. "Look, Max. Just let me spell it out for you the way the Terran Union and the Joint Chiefs see it. You are the one who stepped up and took charge of the ground force, practically single-handedly saving the invasion from total disaster when senior leadership got toasted in orbit. You improvised and executed a worldwide, multi-pronged Operations Order, all while dodging fire and on the run. On top of that, you're the one who kicked in the palace doors on 'Callan the Usurper' while she was in the middle of broadcasting a rant so clichéd, it was essentially an evil villain monologue.

Pausing for dramatic effect, the Vice-Admiral put both hands on the desk, leaned in and said with solemn intensity, "Oh and let's not forget that last little thing you did, the part where you fought a royal Grausian in single combat to the death and saved an entire planet of twelve billion innocent sentients from her doomsday weapon. I'm telling you; I don't know if that makes you a genuine military genius or comic book superhero."

Still getting no response from his friend, he finally deadpanned, "It made for great watching, by the way. Best viewer ratings of the whole evening, I spilled my popcorn and everything," which finally generated a chuckle from the other man. "You've got to give me something here, buddy."

After a few more moments of silence passed, the Terran Ground Forces Brigadier General slumping in his chair finally took a couple of deep puffs on his cigar and tossed back his glass before angrily spitting out. "That's just public relations spin for the masses and you know it, Robert. What I really did was to pull a third-tier contingency plan directly out of my butt, so that at least we would go down swinging. This after the Terran Fleet," he pointed an accusatory finger at the other man's Navy uniform for emphasis, "left us twisting in the wind.

Taking in a quick, sobbing breath that caught in his throat, Max almost tearfully choked out between gritted teeth, "Yeah, it worked, ok? My Hail Mary battle plan worked. I took charge, won the battle and ended the war... and it "only" cost me three-fifths of the force to make it happen. May God forgive me, seven hundred thousand of our people dead. We didn't even find most of the bodies, Robert! The majority of my men are now either buried in unmarked graves or simply floating around as radioactive dust, drifting on the winds of that stinking mud pit of a world."

Max's growl of rage and pain had risen as he spoke until his voice was practically reverberating off the metal bulkheads of the office. "As to the rest of it, the last thing I want right now is to receive the formal thanks of the Empress for executing her daughter like... like... I don't know, like some kind of Imperial gladiator fighting a Bio-Savant in the Grand arena, all in the name of saving her precious Grausian Empire!"

Giving his friend a moment to regain his composure, Franks temporized, "OK, I'll grant that you've got a legit point there about meeting the Empress. Might be a bit awkward, in a social sense," while refilling his friend's glass.

"I get where you're coming from here. I really do," Franks said with compassion before his voice became firm again. "However, your tender, butt-hurt feelings aside, what else you got for me, champ?" When Max finally looked him in the eye, Franks continued. "I mean, I can't just go to the Fleet Admiral and tell him, 'Hey Sir. The legendary James Maximilian Viktorovich, Max to his friends, Victor to his peers... soulless, murdering bastard to his foes... the single biggest swinging Richard we have in the allied Terran Union and Charee fleet, suddenly doesn't wanna go down to the surface for some glad-handing because he feels bad about how hard he put down the rebellion!' Not gonna happen, pal. I like my job way too much to do that, even for you."

"OK, you want a legit excuse? How does this sound?" Taking a sip of his refreshed glass while organizing his thoughts, Max eventually began to sketch out an idea. "The instructions we received say all able-bodied senior leadership is 'Ordered and invited to attend the festivities' which means every Field Grade Officer and above will be on the surface, getting drunk and swapping the same old lies as always. It also means that you're going to have nothing but Lieutenants, Ensigns and mid-level NCOs up here running the fleet."

When Franks shrugged in acknowledgment, Max added. "Technically, I'm still in medical recovery from catching more than six inches worth of vibrosteel in my guts. Glad you enjoyed the show, by the way. That said, you're going to need at least some minimal adult supervision in place to make sure the reprovisioning operation doesn't turn into an orbital traffic jam. Or even worse, a fifty ship pile up directly over the Imperial capital that would justify every nasty thing the senior races say about us. Might as well be me, right?"

Taking a deep puff on his own cigar, Franks again leaned back in his chair to look up at the bulkhead ceiling while he considered the other man's words. "OK, that's at least something I can work with. I'm paraphrasing here, but Joint Forces Regulation FS-1060, Article 3, Section Six, Paragraph 7-2, says that '...when different services are deployed together... absent contrary orders... the highest-ranking combat Officer present will take command... regardless of branch...' so-forth and so-on. So, if the rest of us are down on the planet having a good time, there's really no reason we can't leave a stick in the mud like you in charge up here."

"As a matter of fact, now that I think about it, you really do need some Flag-level Command time added to your sheet." Franks continued. "You might be the newest 'Hero of the Imperium' but that doesn't mean you get to keep that shiny new star on your uniform without eventually checking off a few boxes on your Fitness report."

"Let's see here..." Dropping his feet from the top of the desk and leaning forward, Franks punched up his friend's Officer Personnel File on his desk comp. "According to this, you need at least two more major operations under your belt this rating period to justify making your brevet rank permanent. As the senior surviving officer of the Pegasus invasion, your command of the ground force covers one major ops requirement." Peering over the top of his comp, Franks said with a grin, "Lucky thing you survived, right?"

Not getting the hoped-for rise, Franks continued. "Shepherding an entire fleet reprovisioning as the top dog would count towards the second one. At that point, your brevet rank becomes permanent and you can basically start writing your own ticket."

"Thanks, Bob. I knew you'd eventually see it my way," Max said in a tone of visible relief, quickly setting down his glass before his trembling hand spilled anything. "Besides, I've had enough handshakes and backslapping just from the folks here in the fleet since we got off that damn planet to almost throw my shoulder out. The last thing I need is more of the same down on the capital world from a bunch of Legion douchebags."

"Speaking of Legion douchebags, let's switch topics just a bit here, Max," his friend began in the most reasonable tone he could manage. "You really need to listen to me this time. We both know the military is just 'politics by other means' to the Grausians and if there's ever going to be a hope of earning full autonomy for the Terran Union, we need to get more of us into the hierarchy of the Empire. That's where we can finally make a difference for humanity."

"I don't know what you're talking about," said Max, although he fully knew what was coming.

"You're my G3 - Operations Officer, but let's be honest," Franks replied. "With your combat track record, I should be the one working for you. If you'd just be willing to play the political game a bit more often, we wouldn't be talking about how to keep your one star. You'd probably have two or three of these bad boys already, like yours truly," he said, rubbing his fingers across the two stars adorning his own uniform.

At the other man's eye roll, Franks pressed on. "Look, we've been best friends our whole lives and we both swore we would someday move the needle for humanity. We volunteered for induction at the same time, went through Boot Camp together, got selected for Officer Candidate School in the same cycle... let's see, what else?"

Putting down his glass and ticking off on his fingers, Franks continued, "Officer Basic Course, Maneuver School, War College, Staff course, Battalion command, Fourth Legion Assistant Commander, all that good stuff. Logically, we should be at the same rank. But instead of requesting additional Legion assignments after your mandatory tour, or at the very least jumping over to the Terran Fleet like I did and running a squadron of your own, you decided it would be more fun to stay with the human ground troops and drag your knuckles in the dirt for as long as possible. And now, your career progression is suffering for it."

Waiting for the other man's muted concession, Franks added, "More importantly, we're both on the wrong side of forty. At our age, you shouldn't still be making combat drops or wondering when the next flathead with a popgun is going to shoot some more bits off you. Even with Grausian healing techniques on tap, one of these days you're gonna break something that simply can't be fixed, regrown or replaced. Let's face it, you're getting old, buddy. Nothing and nobody lasts forever, not even a piece of crap Spaceborne Paratrooper like yourself."

"True, everything you said, including the getting bits shot off me," Max finally, grudgingly, admitted. Taking another deep puff on his cigar and blowing the smoke directly at his friend across the desk, he continued with a smile. "On the other hand, like you yourself just pointed out a minute ago, all the senior leadership floating safely in orbit got toasted at Pegasus. At least on the ground, I can see who's shooting at me."

At his friend's grimace, Max decided to twist the knife in just a bit more. "But what the hell. The longer I can keep from becoming just another fat, knob-polishing and button-pushing admin puke like the guy I'm looking at right now, it's all good."

"Hey, screw you. I'm not fat, that's just bureaucratic insulation," Franks said in a semi-hurt tone, playfully underscoring his words by slapping at his small but growing belly for emphasis. "OK, hero, tell ya what I'm going to do for you. I'll go talk to the Fleet Admiral about your request to take charge of the reprovisioning operation... as soon as I can manage to sober up, and we'll see how it goes from there. In the meantime, proceed under the expectation that you'll be in charge as Acting Joint Forces Commander and the primary Beachmaster for the resupply mission once we make orbit."

Consulting his desk comp again, Franks said, "You're currently berthed on the *Macedonia*, right? That actually works for our intent. She's a Heavy Missile Cruiser, which means she's big enough to be equipped with a Leonidas-class Battlespace Operations and Tracking System in her CIC, as well as the integrated, 360° big board display screens."

At his friend's blank look, Franks explained, "What it means is even a broke-down, borscht-eating, Russian Cossack landlubber like yourself can play traffic cop for the combined fleet. If we moved you here to the flagship, you'd be running operations on our one and only Theaterwide - Comprehensive Command and Control' system the Grausians magnanimously allow Fleet Strike to borrow so we can push individual ships around in combat. It's a complex system and takes a hell of a lot of experience just to make sense out of the display, much less use it."

Neither man commented on their disgust with the T-C3 system, a genetically engineered and purpose grown intelligent creature hardwired for life into a ship's sensors.

"Since the Grausians keep all of the best stuff for themselves, the rest of the fleet is stuck using five-hundred-year-old tech developed way back when we were still independent. Fortunately, that works out, since you'll only have to worry about keeping track of twelve squadron commanders instead of four hundred odd individual ships. *Macedonia's* BOTS is sufficient for you to see the big picture, hammer out a loading plan, tell the acting commanders who has priority, de-conflict any problems that come up, stuff like that. Don't worry, those kids will know what they're doing. On the other hand, you've only got a few days from the Gate until we arrive in orbit for you and your people to familiarize yourselves with the system. So, go grab your command crew and make it happen, hero."

Throwing back the rest of the whiskey in his glass, Max took one last puff of his cigar and carefully snuffed out the end to smoke later in private. He then proceeded to stagger to his feet and snap to formal attention, giving the best salute he could manage in his inebriated state. Formally, he recited, "Vice-Admiral, orders received and understood, sir."

When his friend returned his salute, Max grinned and added, "By the way, I'm keeping this," as he grabbed the bottle and promptly headed out.

"You owe me a big one, jackass, and don't slam my door!"

CHAPTER 2

Date: 484 PC (Post Conquest)
2626 AD (Human calendar)
Re: Final approach to the Gamara Fleet Armory
Glarius System, Glarius VI
Capital world of the Old Grausian Empire

"OK, folks. This is it," Max said to the group of Officers and NCOs gathering in an anteroom just outside the *Macedonia*'s command section. He ostensibly wanted to give them a quick pep-talk before taking their stations, but he was really just talking as much to pump himself up as anybody else. "Everybody ready to go forth and do great things for Empress and Empire?"

As the Terran Union's designated Joint Forces Special Operations (JFSO) Commander, he had a nominal staff of three dozen individuals that were all likewise qualified Tier-1 Special Forces operators from across the spectrum of human military services. This number included a number of hard-charging aliens 'loaned' to him on a permanent basis. However, due to the horrific combat losses the allied ground forces had suffered at Pegasus, his remaining staff of only twenty were forced to wear multiple hats just to keep the machine from breaking down.

In addition to their normal roles as his JFSO command staff, a few had been tasked to also function as the combined fleet's temporary Ground Force HQ command staff, while others had been loaned out as the Admiralty's J-3 'GO' staff, i.e., the Joint (Multi-Service) Planning, Maneuver & Fire Support - Ground Operations staff. Now, with his tasking as the acting CO for the fleet reprovisioning, he was again asking his people to step up and accomplish a task that wasn't in their job description. In this case, they would function as his liaisons to the various Squadron Commanders and department heads of the fleet, translating his Army-speak into the appropriate Naval terms and orders.

However, like all such groups, years spent in the fires of constant warfare had forged them into more of a family than a group of subordinates and co-workers. That gave them a familiarity with each other that military protocol normally wouldn't allow members of such disparate rank.

"Wait a second, 'Empress and Empire' my ass, Sir. I'm pretty sure we're only doing this because you didn't want to attend the big shindig down on the planet," laughed Major Suki Nakamura.

"How the hell does she read me so well?" Max wondered once again in amazement. "Ok, granted I didn't want to go down to the surface. On the other hand, maybe I just really wanted to keep you from fending off marriage proposals with those fancy Vibro-knives of yours again. Which we all know is exactly what would happen if I let you off the chain and you got a few drinks in you."

"Hey. It was just the one time," protested Suki innocently, while dramatically tucking a nonexistent stray hair back into her elaborately braided coiffure. "Besides, I thought we all agreed to never talk about that again?"

"Sorry Ma'am, but the general called it," snickered Command Sergeant Major Thomas (Tommy) Stevenson, the group's senior NCO and primary Operations Sergeant. "Those Charee noblemen bidding to add you to their harems like you were on the concubine auction block or something was downright hilarious. This after they'd already seen you carve up some smartass Grausian Legionnaire like a roasted turkey. And there you were, drunk as a skunk, waving your knives around and challenging each of them to honor duels to and I quote, *'prove themselves worthy of a human female.'* That story is never gonna get old." Behind him, his perpetual sidekick and the group's primary heavy weapons expert, Sergeant First Class Ajay Michaels, a towering giant of a man almost as large as a Grat, was holding his belly and giggling like a little girl at the shared memory.

Pulling one of the knives in question out of a ceremonial sheath on her right hip, Suki balanced the scalpel-like blade upright on a finger before rapidly spinning it in a complex pattern, causing the rest of the group to unconsciously take a step back. A family heirloom, the Ka-Bar style, synthetic obsidian vibro-knife (and its twin on her left hip) had an edge only three nanometers thick, making it five hundred times sharper than the finest steel blade, even without the ultrasonic generator turned on.

"Don't get me wrong, fellas. I was completely flattered by the generous bride price they were willing to pay you guys for my hand. Would have made all of you cackling hyenas insanely rich, I'm sure," she said in a sweet tone, belied by the nasty look she gave each human male present while continuing to flip the deadly knife around like a carnival juggler.

In addition to her primary duty position as the Special Operations command group's Communications Officer, Suki was an expert in all things sharp and stabby. Notorious for her mercurial and whimsical personality, she served double duty as the fleet's senior hand-weapons instructor and had personally trained each member of the team in close-quarters knife & stick work, dishing out beatings and laughs in equal measure. As good as he was in a fight, Max had no illusions whatsoever on what the outcome would be if Suki ever got pissed off at him.

One thing Suki did not find funny, however, was a growing fashion trend within some circles of Grausian societies' more established races. The Empire's structure as a Matrilineal Stratocracy, combined with humans' natural talent for war, had resulted in Terrans becoming a dominant percentage of the Empire's total armed forces over the centuries since they'd been forcibly integrated. This in turn led to human military women being seen as desirable trophy objects by some members of the upper class and nobility.

Although 'exotic' harems, (i.e., multi-species) tended to be acquired more for the status they conferred rather than for any realistic attempt at cross-species procreation, the especially class-conscious Charee had begun to use increasingly coercive methods in the last century to acquire their human concubines. Fortunately, despite their status as a second-class species, nothing in Grausian law said human women had to go willingly or without bloodshed involved. Although not a xenophobe by nature, Max knew Suki had long ago made it her personal mission in life to prove what a bad idea it was for other species to covet human women. "A girl simply has got to have her standards. And four-foot-tall monkeys just don't do it for me, no matter how many arms they have or planets they might own."

"Ok, Suki. I'm sure your, uhh… point... is taken by everybody," interjected Max while unobtrusively keeping a sensible distance between himself and his pet sociopath. "Now, put that pig-sticker away and let's get this party started. Everybody, fall in. Sergeant Major, they're all yours."

Quickly forming up in a well-rehearsed drill, Stevenson marched the group in an orderly procession into the command deck before dismissing them to the individual workstations most closely aligned to their individual military specialties: Operations, Intelligence, Security, Tactical, Communications, Engineering, etc.

The process of Naval duty watch handoffs, even the number of hours per watch, tends to vary from ship to ship depending on any number of factors; the size of the crew, mission requirements and the commander's particular leadership style being just a few. But one aspect all handoffs have in common is the incoming brief, where the person about to be relieved gives their replacement a detailed rundown on their station's current status, ongoing tasks and anything else of note. Briefings can take anywhere from a few minutes to a full hour, depending on how much data a particular station might deal with. However, the most important consideration of all is that at no time should a warship ever be deprived of any critical function or capability because of an empty seat somewhere.

Although he would be in overall command of the fleet, there could only be one master of a ship at a time and it was inappropriate for Max to be on the deck while the captain's duties and command keys were handed over. Keeping one eye on the ships' chronograph, Max impatiently cooled his heels outside the blast door entrance while his people assumed their duties. For this operation, the ship's acting commander would be his staff's Executive Officer, Lieutenant Colonel Jennifer (Jen) Marie, while he focused his attention on the fleet.

Waiting for her in the command chair at the top of the central dais was Commander John Reilly Pasco Jr., the current captain of *Macedonia* and a descendent of a long line of Navy men. Having worked for Admiral John Pasco (Senior) a decade or so back, Max remembered being told their family could trace its lineage all the way back to the Signals Officer aboard Lord Admiral Nelson's flagship at the battle of Trafalgar. Named after his famous ancestor, CDR Pasco was being groomed for great things in the Terran Navy. At the same time, his prestige was built entirely on his own merits, having earned a solid reputation as a hard-working sailor that always brought out the very best in both his ship and crew.

Thanks to the (by intent) excellent acoustics in the CIC, Max was able to hear every word that passed between the two officers. Stepping up to the bottom step of the dais, Jen saluted and recited the script she memorized the night prior, an ancient litany that was old before the earliest chemical rockets had lifted the first warships from the Earth's gravity well. "I am ready to relieve you, sir."

She in turn was answered by Pasco with the traditional reply, "I am ready to be relieved." More so than any other human military service, the Navy was committed to its customs and traditions, including the exact wording for a command handoff while underway.

The use of the term "sir" and who renders a salute first when transferring command occurs without regard to the relative ranks or normal duty positions held by the officers involved, in this case an Army Lieutenant Colonel saluting a Naval Commander of equal rank.

Unlike the Old Earth navies, and perhaps to their detriment, the Imperial system required that flag officers had to spend time commanding units of different services. It wasn't odd to find someone who had commanded a ground battalion to be immediately placed in command of a navy warship. It was as much to prevent cults of personality in commanders that might threaten the regime as it was to encourage cross service knowledge.

That said, Max favored a lot less formal protocol when running an operation, but he and his team were functioning in a Navy environment now so it was up to them to do things the 'Navy Way' Max thought wryly to himself. *'When in Rome, I guess.'*

Standing up from his chair, Pasco took a lanyard from around his neck and said, "I relinquish the master weapons key," before handing it over. He repeated the procedure with the launch codes and jump key, as well as verifying that Jen's biometrics were logged and activated for the ship's executive computer control systems. Jen echoed every step of the checklist procedure, as both a confirmation as well as an acknowledgment.

With all the accouterments of command in hand, Jen began the last portion of the verbal dance with, "I relieve you, sir."

Pasco replied with, "I stand relieved" before announcing to the room, "Attention in the CIC, Lieutenant Colonel Marie has the deck."

After another exchange of salutes and a handshake, Jen finished out the exercise with her own announcement, "This is Lieutenant Colonel Marie, I have the deck," before taking her place on the command chair and nodding to Tommy. He in turn nodded to Max, letting him know the room was ready for him to assume his own duties. *"Senior Officer on the deck,"* boomed out Tommy, now the acting Chief of the Boat (COB) as Max stepped through the hatch.

"As you were," replied Max to the room before beginning his walkthrough.

Taking a cursory look around as he briefly inspected each station, Max compared the reality of what he was seeing to what he had researched in his refresher prep for this assignment. Back in the time of wet navies, surface warships would have a Combat Information Center (CIC) situated deep in the armored guts of the vessel for protection, with an exposed navigation bridge placed up on top of the superstructure for maneuvering and observation. Since the distances involved in space combat had all but rendered the Mark One eyeball irrelevant, windows were now only used for aesthetic reasons. Thus, the functions of the CIC and navigation bridge had been combined into a single large command center onboard modern space going warships.

Additionally, military planners had determined a circular, tiered configuration, with everybody facing outwards towards their sectors of responsibility was the most efficient layout for warfighting in 3-dimensional space. There were several ergonomic reasons for this design, but mostly because it allowed the command crew to situate themselves to the ship's orientation, as well as helping them keep track of vectors relative to the ship's direction of travel.

Right in the center of it all was the captains' chair, an elevated workstation on a small, raised dais, sitting just high enough to allow the watch officer to see all the information needed to run a fighting ship by simply looking around the 360° electronic CIC Bridge. As the senior officer present, Max had every right to take the chair for himself. However, he and Jen had agreed to let her take the chair while he would stand watch at the battlespace plotting table, being that a flat electronic map was more akin to what he was accustomed to as a ground force CO. Were he on a bigger ship, there would be an entire staff suite dedicated to Fleet Operations but here they had to make due.

Inspection completed, Max called out to Suki, "*Comms*, signal to the Terran Union and Charee fleets that I have assumed command and to prepare for reprovisioning operations as previously detailed. Report when all have acknowledged."

After being relieved, Pasco had waited by the plotting table to talk to Max as a courtesy. "Glad you and your people managed to find the CIC, sir. I was worried your ground-pounders might get lost once you got past the galley. However, I hear from my staff that your team seems to know what they're doing, so at least you are off to a good start."

"Not at all, Lieutenant Commander," Max replied with a grin. "I made sure to send my Pathfinder forward an hour ago to scout the way in and lead us forward. By the way, any words of advice for my staff and myself?"

"Well, I would never presume to tell you how to run your operation, sir..." Pasco equivocated.

"Come on, spill it. If you're anything like your old man, I'm sure you have all kinds of nuggets of wisdom to match any situation imaginable."

"Well, this is more for your XO than for you, sir." Looking over his shoulder, Max summoned Jen over with a quick nod of his head. "Back when I received my first command, my dad gave me a bit of advice that his father had given to him and that I'm sure grandad got from his own dad and his father before that, etcetera," Pasco said with a slightly embarrassed grin on his face. "He told me, 'Always remember your ship isn't just your ride. She's your heart and soul. When everything eventually goes to hell, your first duty is to the ship that will take your people home. Not to me, not to your family, not to any individual crewmember, but to the ship.' We humans imbue our ships with female characteristics for a reason, Sir. Treat your ship like a lady and she will take care of you.' And make no mistake, the *Macedonia* is a lady. Remember that and you'll do OK."

Taking the other man's words to heart, Max replied, "Thank you, Commander. We will do our best to keep that in mind."

Right then, Suki called out, "All squadrons acknowledge orders and are standing by, General. Also, Gamara Fleet Armory sends to all ships, *'May the blessings of the Third Divine Warlord go with you'* whatever the bloody hell that means. and says we may begin reprovisioning operations at our convenience."

"So much for small talk," Max said to Pasco. "Well, you had best get your people down to the planet before they drink all the good stuff."

"Right you are, Sir." To the room, Pasco said, "Everybody that's headed down, fall in on me."

Waiting until the last crewman left the deck, Max looked over his shoulder again to ensure Jen had taken her assigned seat before turning to his own board.

"*Communications.*"

"Sir."

"Signal the fleet. Let's get this party started."

CHAPTER 3

Date: 484 PC (Post Conquest)
2626 AD (Human calendar)
Re: Mid-reprovisioning operation
Gamara Fleet Armory
Glarius System, Glarius VI

At some point after the Earth's Second World War but prior to the first primitive warships patrolling human-occupied space, some brainy German military scientist had calculated the optimal balance between the number of men involved in any particular military activity and the acceptable number of accidents and deaths caused by said activity. *'Clearly,'* a bitter Max muttered under his breath, *'that bastard must have been involved in a resupply mission.'*

Thanks to the Gamara Armory's extensive fleet of semi-sentient cargo drones, robotic warehouse docks and advanced bio-nets operating at trillions of calculations per nanosecond, the resupply operation for the more than four hundred warships of the combined Terran Union and Charee fleets was expected to take no more than approximately six hours. This was just enough time for the balance of the force to transport down to the surface, conduct a massive Pass in Review military parade for the pleasure of the Empress along the Grausian Grand Conquest Boulevard, throw back a few drinks at the Victory Palazzo and then make their way back up the gravity well to their assigned ships.

Naturally, it hadn't worked out that way.

As per their usual sense of importance, the Grausian capital ships assigned to their fleets had insisted on jumping the line and being the first serviced, disrupting the carefully orchestrated master plan and causing unanticipated delays for the rest of the force. Naturally, as soon as they were supplied with their allotment of food, fuel and munitions, the Grausians immediately boosted out of orbit and headed for the system's nadir jump point with nary a backward glance.

Despite that rough start, the operation had otherwise gotten quickly back on track… and then four hours in, the first of a series of "accidents" had started. Six of their Heavy Carriers were badly damaged when automated cargo drones loaded with munitions tried docking with fighter craft launch tubes, detonating on impact and making entire wings of Bearcat fighters and Manticore bombers unable to deploy from their flight pods. In addition to the six CV-H's, twelve other warships had suffered lesser collisions, each in a rapid succession of less than ten minutes before Max's prompt order for a safety halt had stopped all operations.

The Gamora Harbormaster immediately claimed the collisions were simple programming cascade failures caused by human negligence *"…inevitably triggered by you allowing those huge dreadnoughts to resupply out of their designated order, which put all your smaller ships that followed increasingly out of position."* Max was forced to bite back the venomous retort he wanted to spit at the Harbormaster's blatantly obvious attempt to shift the blame. Telling senior Grausians exactly where to stick it was never a healthy career option.

An hour later, fleetwide operations finally restarted, but the damaged ships were going to require months of repair time in dry dock to get them fully operational again.

Having at least a few minutes until the next disaster cropped up, Max looked up at the main overhead projector a minute ago, all the senior leadership floating safely in orbit got toasted at Pegasus. At least on the ground, I can see who's shooting at me."

At his friend's grimace, Max decided to twist the knife in just a bit more. "But what the hell. The longer I can keep from becoming just another fat, knob-polishing and button-pushing admin puke like the guy I'm looking at right now, it's all good."

"Hey, screw you. I'm not fat, that's just bureaucratic insulation," Franks said in a semi-hurt tone, playfully underscoring his words by slapping at his small but growing belly for emphasis. "OK, hero, tell ya what I'm going to do for you. I'll go talk to the Fleet Admiral about your request to take charge of the reprovisioning operation... as soon as I can manage to sober up, and we'll see how it goes from there. In the meantime, proceed under the expectation that you'll be in charge as Acting Joint Forces Commander and the primary Beachmaster for the resupply mission once we make orbit."

Consulting his desk comp again, Franks said, "You're currently berthed on the *Macedonia*, right? That actually works for our intent. She's a Heavy Missile Cruiser, which means she's big enough to be equipped with a Leonidas-class Battlespace Operations and Tracking System in her CIC, as well as the integrated, 360° big board display screens."

At his friend's blank look, Franks explained, "What it means is even a broke-down, borscht-eating, Russian Cossack landlubber like yourself can play traffic cop for the combined fleet. If we moved you here to the flagship, you'd be running operations on our one and only Theaterwide - Comprehensive Command and Control' system the Grausians magnanimously allow Fleet Strike to borrow so we can push individual ships around in combat. It's a complex system and takes a hell of a lot of experience just to make sense out of the display, much less use it."

Neither man commented on their disgust with the T-C3 system, a genetically engineered and purpose grown intelligent creature hardwired for life into a ship's sensors.

"Since the Grausians keep all of the best stuff for themselves, the rest of the fleet is stuck using five-hundred-year-old tech developed way back when we were still independent. Fortunately, that works out, since you'll only have to worry about keeping track of twelve squadron commanders instead of four hundred odd individual ships. *Macedonia's* BOTS is sufficient for you to see the big picture, hammer out a loading plan, tell the acting commanders who has priority, de-conflict any problems that come up, stuff like that. Don't worry, those kids will know what they're doing. On the other hand, you've only got a few days from the Gate until we arrive in orbit for you and your people to familiarize yourselves with the system. So, go grab your command crew and make it happen, hero."

Throwing back the rest of the whiskey in his glass, Max took one last puff of his cigar and carefully snuffed out the end to smoke later in private. He then proceeded to stagger to his feet and snap to formal attention, giving the best salute he could manage in his inebriated state. Formally, he recited, "Vice-Admiral, orders received and understood, sir."

When his friend returned his salute, Max grinned and added, "By the way, I'm keeping this," as he grabbed the bottle and promptly headed out.

"You owe me a big one, jackass, and don't slam my door!"

on the forward bulkhead. The live broadcast of the celebration parade down on the planet was showing on the main screen but his mind was replaying a scene from earlier in the day. About half an hour after they had first kicked off the Op, his team's Grausian engineer, Tala-lo Ot-Laqatta, (Laq for short) had come to him with a troubling observation.

After more than a decade of fighting various brushfire conflicts and the Civil War together, Max trusted Laq with his life. So, when the Grausian approached in the middle of the operation with his Intel Officer, Major Jim (Joe) Puller, in tow to ask for a private moment to speak about an urgent matter, Max was more than willing to make the time to listen.

"Sir, when the Gamara Fleet Armory sent us the blessings of the Third Divine Warlord, it wasn't just a polite courtesy," Laq stated, her beaklike nose quivering in agitation. "It was a reference to our religious pantheon, the Seven Divine Warlords, each of whom teaches us a different martial value. The Third Warlord's primary lesson is about fidelity to your master, even unto the maw of annihilation! The scriptures of Parra tell us how he expected his loyal warriors to hold the line against their bewitched fellows, the ones who had been possessed by the Spectral Demons' unholy bio-corruption. The loyal warriors knew they must be willing to fight to the death, in order to protect the innocent villagers sleeping peacefully down in the valley from the most savage of butchery."

Pausing a moment trying to understand, Max finally responded. "I'm sorry, Laq, but I just don't get it. What do any of your religious teachings have to do with us here and now?"

"Sir, once you strip away all the theology and mysticism," Puller explained, "the story pretty much boils down to the mountain army of the Third Warlord poisoned by some kind of chemical or biological agent. Their enemy turned the mountain army into little more than psychotic killers. The warriors still in the initial stages of infection were ordered to form up at a chokepoint down the trail and block the army from leaving the mountains at all costs. Those loyal warriors did as they were ordered, knowing even if they held the line, when the Third Warlord arrived with a fresh army from the plains, he would slaughter all of them, loyal and mindless alike, in order to prevent the infection from spreading."

"Joe, check the cultural database. See if this "blessing" has ever been given to human troops before and how it turned out. Thank you for this information." Dismissing them back to their stations, Max tried to keep the dire warning in the back of his head, but more pressing concerns kept him focused on the task at hand for the next several hours.

Now, with the fleet resupply running smoothly again, he had a chance to ponder the earlier warning. Looking over at Puller's station, he caught his Intel Officer's attention and asked an unspoken question with a simple look. With his bushy white eyebrows scrunched together in frustration and disgust, Joe responded with the barest shake of his bald head, he had been unable to find anything.

Although Laq was undeniably a Grausian, she was also an Int-em Erata, the lowest tier of their society, the alien version of an untouchable, a non-person that was seen but never acknowledged. Despite this, even the lowliest untouchable still had access to information and technology that was restricted from the lesser races. Ever pragmatic, three centuries ago the human military had created many Grausian-specific Military Occupational Specialties and career paths in the hopes of absorbing as much institutional knowledge as possible from their Grausian conscripts.

Members of the Int-em Erata were heavily recruited by offers of generous incentive pay and modern, safe housing for their families, but primarily by the type of respect they could never hope to earn from their own people. These new MOS's included positions on Research & Development groups as well as Special Operations teams, as the ability to use advanced (but restricted) technology in the Empire's constant wars of expansion was often the key to mission success. As humanity's influence in the militaristic Empire had grown, so too had a high profile career in an elite human unit become the single best way for a member of Laq's caste to raise herself (and her descendants) above the lowly station they had been born into. Having seen how grateful she was for the respect and opportunities given her, Max suspected Laq's loyalty to humanity far exceeded her loyalty to the Empire.

As such, when Laq said there was something to worry about, Max was willing to take it on faith that there was something to worry about. Combined with the unexpected crippling of 12% of their airpower, on top of orders sending their senior people and the bulk of their troops down to the planet, it was enough to send cold chills of terror down his spine.

Looking back up at the main board, Max saw the last units on parade approaching the royal entourage's stand for the Empress's review. Making a sudden decision, he turned to Suki. "Major Nakamura, bring a tablet and come here please. COB Stevenson, you too and bring Sergeant Michaels with you," he said before ascending the few steps up to the command dais next to Jen.

As soon as all the indicated personnel had joined them, he hit the privacy screen to mute their conversation from any unfriendly ears. "I don't know what's going on, but I have reason to believe we might be in trouble. Jen, without sounding a Condition One alert, I want you to get the ship ready for action. I know we're running with a skeleton crew but do your best. Ajay, get down below and start kicking over every rack with a warm body in it. Tell them it's a repelling boarders drill but issue a full combat load of live rounds. Tommy, as soon as he leaves, secure this deck and quietly pass the word to each of our people to watch their backs. Suki, contact Admiral Franks on his personal comm and pipe it up here on a secure line. Also, get on the horn with the commanders of the rest of the fleet. Encrypt it eyes-only and give them the same instructions and warnings I just gave everybody else. Any questions? No? Good. Make it happen, folks."

Dropping the privacy screen, Max watched his people casually walk away to carry out his directives, walking without undue haste to avoid arousing suspicion. Taking advantage of the momentary solitude, he looked around the CIC. Normally staffed by up to seventy-five Officers and Specialists, there were currently only about fifty or so sentients manning it on the two levels. Excluding the members of his command group and other humans, roughly half of the remaining Officers and technicians were Imperial Grausians, with the rest being a couple of non-Imperials as well as a smattering of various other alien species. If things came down to a firefight, it would get ugly in the close confines of the command deck.

The beeping of his wrist com interrupting his thoughts, he looked down to see Suki staring intently at him. Seeing she had his attention, she touched her headset and spoke in whispered tones so that even the Charee commo technician sitting next to her wouldn't overhear, "Message sent and acknowledged throughout the fleet, sir. Also, Admiral Franks is on the line."

Glancing back to the main viewer, Max saw the very last unit was done marching. Next would come the billowing of hot air from various VIP windbags to the assembled troops before the banquet celebration kicked off. "Robert, are you there? It looks like the parade just wrapped up."

"What do you mean, 'Just wrapped up'?" the tiny voice said from the command workstation's speaker. *"The parade was over an hour ago, buddy. The troops were stuffed to the gills out on the landing fields and should have already loaded the shuttles. The Officers and senior NCOs are sitting down in the banquet hall for our own feast. The Empress should be up any minute. You're missing out on a hell of a party. You should at least tune in and watch it."*

"I am tuned in. For some reason, they delayed the transmission. At any rate, a few screwy things are going on up here that just don't feel right."

"Again with your gut feelings," Frank's laugh boomed even through the micro-speaker. *"You worry too much. Look, I'm going to put you on hold, they just announced the Empress's entrance. Stand by."*

Grunting in frustration at being cut off, Max looked back up at the main viewer. Noticing he was off his call, a young human Ensign at the tactical board announced, "Sir, two minutes ago we detected a series of troop shuttle launches from the planet. It looks like they're sending our people back up the well a little bit early. They should be within our envelope in the next ten minutes."

"Wait, what?" Looking over at the plotting board, Max saw their near airspace still filled with cargo drones on their automated courses regardless of the approaching shuttles. "Damnit. *Comms*, contact those troop shuttles and wave them off. *Navigation*, stick them in a parking orbit until we can figure something out."

Taking a moment to think, Max said to the room at large, "I don't know about anybody else, but I'm getting mighty tired of the unexpected continually biting us right square on our fourth point of contact. *Tactical*, give me a full system scan, let's figure out how many birds are already in the air and how many more are coming up out the well."

The young Ensign acknowledged with an "Aye, Sir" and got his section working. Within thirty seconds, Max heard a confused, "What the hell?" float up from one of them along with a sudden flurry of activity. Silently counting out another thirty seconds to himself, he was about to demand an update from the unknown junior Officer when Jen came back up the central dais and whispered, "Ensign Jasutara," as she sat at the command station.

"Ensign Jasutara, what do you have, son? Give me something to work with here." In reply, Jasutara straightened up and used one of his pincers to point to an overhead screen, "Tossing to #3. Sir, we have about a quarter of our troop shuttles coming up the well in this first wave, but not all of them are squawking our transponder codes. About three dozen of them are reading as Grausian troops, not human or CLu'Lachan."

Max responded with, "What the hell indeed."

"There's more, Sir. Zooming out to system-wide view, viewscreen #4. Highlighted in green, you can see the Grausian capital ships that left us are heading to the system's

Nadir jump gate. Based on their present location, they must have gone to full conventional speed as soon as they were out of our near-range sensors. From their approach vector, it looks like they intend to link up with another group of Grausian vessels that are... well... Sir, by their formation and the backed-up traffic around them, it looks like they're interdicting anybody from leaving the system." By now, the Charee Ensign was clearly panting. "Also, we have an additional Grausian force interdicting the Zenith Gate, with a third force making flank speed directly towards us. Intercept is in less than forty five minutes."

The silence that descended on the command deck in the wake of the Ensign's pronouncement was deafening, while Max had an all too familiar sinking feeling in the pit of his stomach. Into this quiet, the line to Admiral Franks came alive again with the sounds of gunfire in the background. *"... can you hear me? The parade, the victory celebration, all of it, we were set up!"*

CHAPTER 4

Date: 484 PC (Post Conquest)
2626 AD (Human calendar)
Re: "The Massacre" first battle of the Succession Wars
Glarius System, Glarius VI
Capital world of the Old Grausian Empire

Waving a hand at Suki, Max ordered her to put the call on the bridge loudspeaker while rapidly switching his gaze between the three screens displaying the ongoing victory celebration and both tactical maps. "I hear you, Robert. What's going on down there?"

The sound of distant explosions could be heard going off before Franks could reply. *"When the Empress showed up, she demanded to know where you were. When the Fleet Admiral said you hadn't come down, she ordered him to join her on the stage and just executed him right there. She shot him full in the face, Max! Her Legionnaires were waiting in the wings, they began slaughtering everybody. A few of us managed to get away. We barricaded ourselves in an adjoining office, but I don't have to tell you that hand weapons aren't going to last long against heavy infantry."*

"Sir, I'm getting reports from other ships," Suki interjected from her station, "They're echoing what Admiral Franks is saying to us from their own personnel on the planet. This is legit going down."

Right then on the main viewer, the view switched from the parade fields to the scene that Franks had mentioned playing out, but not at all in the way he had described it.

Within days, a number of independent news organizations, as well as thousands of individuals with a technological aptitude, would easily determine that the Empire-wide broadcast had been manipulated to make the humans look bad.

But by then, it would be far too late.

On the screen the Empress and the Fleet Admiral walked out onto the stage together but it was the latter who pulled his sidearm and attempted to execute the Empress. She wrested the weapon away and shot him in self-defense, whereupon the humans in the audience rose up against their CLu'Lachan and Grausian compatriots, screaming in a feral rage, tearing at them with their teeth and bare hands before the signal finally cut out.

"*Communications*, Red Alert the fleet," Max immediately commanded. *Tactical*, activate the full BOTS system and engage Friend or Foe identifiers."

Separately, Jen grabbed the ship's intercom, "Sound General Quarters, General Quarters. All hands, man your battle stations. Set condition 'Zebra' throughout the ship. This is not a drill. I repeat, man your battle stations. This is not a drill."

As soon as the commands were out of their mouths the entire bridge erupted into chaos and destruction. Of the eighteen Grausians on the command deck, sixteen of them were Imperials who had been seconded to the allied forces but were still loyal to the Empress. Like Laq, they had been raised on the stories of the Seven Divine Warlords and understood the hidden cultural meaning taught by the blessings of the Third Warlord. They knew what was expected of them and were determined to fight and die as the ancient loyal warriors had once stood at the mountain pass.

Unfortunately for them, they were Imperial warriors, not Terran combat Infantry.

Human Soldiers and Marines, as well as their auxiliaries, work as a team. They train to react and execute as a single entity, achieving far more as a unified group than would ever be possible for a collection of individuals. This was the martial philosophy that made human forces dominant in battle versus the Empire's other militant races. Warriors may fight with immense passion and bravery, but ultimately, they still fight alone for personal glory.

Of the sixteen Imperials who pulled their weapons, eight focused on Max to the exclusion of all else, screaming the name of the Empress and shooting indiscriminately at the central dais. In the same situation, human Infantrymen would have instead split their fire to effectively engage multiple targets and take down as many of their foes as possible. Not that it made any difference, since Max had already chosen the better part of valor, diving headlong behind the captain's station as blaster fire and slugs tore through the space he had occupied just seconds earlier.

The massed shots all but vaporized the front of the platform, as well as the #6 viewscreen to the rear of it. Between the two exploding consoles, Max was showered with burning plastic and charred components as he tried to burrow through the deck while still fumbling for his own gun. In the initial confusion, the Imperials targeting him ended up masking each other's fire in a vain attempt for glory, with one accidentally shooting a pair of his own comrades in the back while trying to kill Max.

Four Grausians never even fired a shot, managing only to grab their firearms before the nearby humans assaulted them, with one physically thrown to her death from the higher deck by the COB.

The last four Imperials were from the Commo and Intel sections and were intercepted by Suki as they rose up from her workstation quadrant. Firing off a pair of front snap kicks to create space and stop their forward momentum, she pulled both knives and waded into the fray with a shrieking Kiai' that nearly peeled the paint off the closest bulkhead. Despite being armed with their own hand weapons, three of her foes were still completely eviscerated before their bodies even hit the deck. The last one jumped away over the workstation, only to stumble and fall dead on the other side with a thrown Vibro-knife still jutting out of the back of her throat.

Three of the Grausians shooting at the command station hit Jen when she jumped in front of the General to shield him, killing one of her murderers even as she herself died. Another gave Max flash burns from a near miss when he poked his head out to return fire. The rest died as they moved forward, caught in the crossfire between a group of Charee as well as two of their fellow Grausians, including Laq herself.

Without even missing a beat, Max quickly brought the deck back under control. "*Stations*! COB, clear out this mess. Suki, status of the fleet?"

Eyes rolling with manic delight at the mess of guts and offal piled at her feet, Suki tapped her headset to send out the query. A moment later, still grinning past the alien blood splattered on her face, she replied, "Sir, various reports of widespread fighting on a number of the larger ships with Imperial specialists on board. Fleet is standing by for orders."

Ensign Jasutara looked up from his board and spoke again. "Sir, the Grausian shuttles accelerated to attack speed when we waved them off and they made it inside our defensive umbrella while we were... ahh... distracted. They've been identified as assault-variant Imperial shuttles, some of them have already made contact and are cutting through airlocks. ETA, 30 seconds until the first ones breach."

"Ok people, clearly we've got problems," Max said to the room, stating the obvious to make sure nobody would remain frozen in shock. "Work the issue, people. I need solutions."

"*COMMUNICATIONS.*"

"Sir?"

"Call our friendly shuttles in, order them to dock with the ships under assault and have them repel boarders.

"*TACTICAL.*"

"Sir?"

"Order any remaining shuttles to lift up off the surface under emergency power. If they are squawking our ident, confirm with a visual and a challenge & password. If not, blow them out of the sky."

"*CAG.*"

"Sir?"

"Launch all ready Bearcat and Manticore wings. I don't care if you have to stick nuggets and drone pilots in the cockpits. If they can fly, stick them in a bird and get them in the air."

"*PLOTTING.*"

"Sir?"

"Get us the hell out of here. Find us a course that keeps us out of the Orbital Fort's defensive arc for as long as possible."

Turning back to the open channel, Max shunted the feedback to the command workstation's comm and called to his friend, "Robert? Robert? You still there?"

"I'm still here, but not for long. They blew through a wall and took the outer office. The few of us left pulled back to the secure conference room, but it won't hold much longer than the office did. They aren't bothering to take prisoners, pal. We're about done here."

"I've got the fleet spun up and we're moving out," Max replied. Neither man wasted time with false platitudes or hopes of a miracle. "Both jump Gates are locked up tight, we have a third force breathing down our necks and Legionnaires from the surface attempting to board. Also, we just put down an insurrection by the Imperial Grausians in the CIC. You should be up here, bro. I'm out of my element, I don't know what else to do."

"Sounds to me like you're already doing what you do always best, pal. You find a way to survive and keep on fighting, no matter how insane the odds. But maybe for the first time in your life, let me give you a bit of advice that you'll actually follow. Set your course to go past the asteroid ring and in between the two gas giants. If you're lucky, there will be an unused jump point to nowhere located in the Lagrange point between the two bodies where their gravity cancels each other out. There's no telling where you'll end up, but anywhere is better than here. Your plotter is good, let him figure it out."

Immediately, Max relayed his friend's instructions to the human navigator before asking for an updated status on the fleet. Without even being tasked, Suki had stepped up to fight the *Macedonia* while still handling fleet comms. "Sir, thirty ships report being breached, including us, fighting continues.

Friendly troops have been rerouted to assist them. Additional friendly shuttles are coming up from the surface and will attempt to meet us en route. Incoming mobile force is moving to intercept us along our course. Estimate thirty minutes until we're within their firing envelope."

"*Navigation*"

"Sir?"

"Is there any way to gain some distance on them, to give us time to look for a jump point?"

"Standby."

In the few seconds before the navigator spoke again, Max noticed the connection to the surface had been broken. Looking back at Suki he saw a rare frown crossing her face as she met his eyes, an expression that told him more than enough what had happened.

"Sir, I've got an unstable jump point in system that will be open for the next two hours, but it will scatter the fleet all to hell out-system. The real problem is that we're just too heavy and the hostiles were already at speed before we started running," the navigator finally said. "We'll be ten minutes inside their envelope before our slowest ships are running at flank speed. Even worse, they will be shooting right up our backside the entire way in. Our own drive wakes will blind us to ninety percent of their fire."

"What do you mean by 'too heavy'? I thought our ships were just as fast as theirs?"

"We are, Sir. Significantly faster, actually. The problem is that our Capital ships, the battleships, heavy carriers and large troopships take too long to get up to speed. Even our heavy cruisers like the *Macedonia* can accelerate four times as fast as a Battleship."

"Sir, message coming through from the enemy force," Suki called out. "Battle Comp has identified them as the First Grausian Fleet."

On any other day, knowing who was bearing down on them would have shocked him to his core. Today, it was just another red entry in his personal ledger. "Put it through to the main viewer."

As the image solidified on the screen, he felt his hackles rising in anger. If this was to be his day to die, there was no way he was going to do it groveling, especially not in front of THIS particular Grausian. "Good evening, Primus. Fancy meeting you here."

Primus Enha An-Sathren, Praetor of the Grausian First Fleet (the Golden), Legate of the Realm, third in line for the throne and cousin to the sitting Empress. Also, at one time a mentor and advisor to a much younger Lieutenant James Maximilian Viktorovich.

There was actual sorrow on her face as she addressed him, *"Max, you have no idea how much it hurts me to be here, to be the instrument of your destruction, my friend."*

"You think you have it tough? You should try it from where I'm standing."

"I am so sorry, Max. I did everything I could to put off this reckoning, but the Empress, she just went wild with rage upon receiving the report from Pegasus. Although you fought her war and saved her Empire, she simply could not live with the knowledge that her beloved eldest daughter was humiliated in personal combat and killed by a mere human male."

Although his poker face remained intact, Max felt a chill deep in his soul. Was he ultimately responsible for this betrayal, for all this unnecessary death and destruction?

"I know you are a proud soldier. Let us end this matter in honor, even though the reason we fight is dishonorable," Sathern reasoned. *"Halt your fleet, turn them around and face us. Fight and die in a manner that you may go before your ancestors proudly, with your wounds in the front rather than in your back."*

Max stood there for what felt like an eternity of indecision, but it was really only seconds. The calculation was simple. Even if they had been fully manned, the Grausian Golden fleet outgunned them three to one, if not more. To turn and fight would be suicide, plain and simple. Conversely, to keep running with their capital ships slowing them down was also suicide, except much like the old sniper joke, they would only die tired.

However, there existed a third option.

Recalling Pasco's last words, *"... your first duty is to the ship that will take your people home,"* Max dusted off a favorite military aphorism that had guided him his entire career, *'One problem at a time is a dilemma, two problems at a time just might be a solution in disguise.'*

"You want a fight, Primus? I'll give you a fight you'll never forget. Viktorovich out."

As soon as he was sure the connection had been broken, "Suki, give me fleetwide."

When she gave him a thumbs up, he keyed the transmitter, took a deep breath and began, "All hands, this is General Viktorovich. As I'm sure everybody is aware by now, we seem to be in a spot of trouble. But we can deal with this. We are going to survive; we are going to come back here someday and we are going to make them pay for what they did to our friends." Max glanced down at the surviving bridge crew as he spoke, to see what effect his words would have.

"The Grausians expect us to die valiantly in a doomed last stand. So instead, we're gonna piss 'em off by escaping their little mousetrap. All Capital ships and any smaller vessel that isn't under positive control, you are directed to set your ship autopilots on a collision course with the Golden fleet, all batteries to continuous sustained fire. Lock your drive engines all ahead flank, break your control keys, scramble codes and abandon ship. You have..." looking to the navigator for an update, he continued, "You have exactly eighteen minutes to make it happen and get yourselves aboard another ride home before we boost out of here at best speed. All fighters and bomber wings, your job is to provide the ramming ships air cover on the way in. Make one, I say again, MAKE ONE PASS, dump all your ordnance and get your asses back to us ASAP. I don't give a damn about your planes, ground them in frigate bays if you have to. Your birds are replaceable, you are not. Assault Carriers, redline your engines and haul ass to get clear while the missile cruisers run interference. Good luck, all. General Viktorovich, out."

Seeing morale in the room beginning to come back as people felt hope, Max focused on the main plotting screen. Already, the fleet was splitting in two over the planet below, with swarms of Bearcats and Manticore fighter wings taking shape around the larger CV's headed on an intercept course. The line of remaining vessels began to stretch out as the quicker frigates and destroyers raced ahead in a desperate search for an escape while cruisers like the *Macedonia* hung back to provide what cover they could to the Assault Carriers, their most valuable remaining assets.

Looking over at the secondary screens, Max saw the remaining friendly transponders on the surface had finally turned black. This brought back memories of the last time he had been forced to leave his dead behind on an alien planet, turning Max's cold anger into a fiery rage.

"*Gunnery*, I want kinetic strikes all along the length of the Grand Conquest Boulevard and on the Victory Palazzo. Keep firing until we pass out of range. I don't want a single human or CLu'Lachan body left intact enough for them to hang on the palace walls."

"Sir, Kinetic strikes are circumscribed by royal edict on non-hardened targets..." the Gunnery Officer began.

"Son, I don't think the Empire's rules apply to us anymore. Do you?"

Gripping the damaged and smoking console in front of him so hard his knuckles cracked, Max remained glued to the screens as tendrils of silvery lighting began reaching out to the surface of the planet. Hundreds of solid tungsten rods were launched at hypersonic speed, each impacting with the force of a small tactical nuclear package. As the first blooms of destruction arose on the planet, a significant portion of the fleeing allied fleet began to curve away into its' own arc of travel on the #3 screen.

Before Max could formulate a question to his staff, Suki called out, "Sir, the Charee are disavowing your authority over their forces across all frequencies and are signaling their continuing fidelity to the Empire."

"Confirmed," said Ensign Jasutara. "The Charee ships are refusing fleet orders and are grouping up into a separate formation but continuing their direction of travel."

"Get me the highest-ranking Charee on the horn," Max demanded.

"Sir, the Charee are refusing secure tightbeam communications," Suki informed him. "They will only respond to us on an unsecured channel." To this, Max said without preamble to the open line, "What the hell do you folks think you're doing over there?"

"General Viktorovich, this is Captain Hollmenez. I am most sorry, but we Charee cannot support your actions against the Empire, nor your personal dispute with the Empress. If you had any honor, you would immediately surrender yourself to the mercy of the realm rather than continue this madness."

"If the Empress wanted my head, all she had to do was ask for it, Captain. Can't you see this is larger than just one person? They divided our forces and deliberately weakened our fighting capabilities before this all even started. This isn't a personal grievance, this is the destruction of our ability to defend ourselves," Max reasoned without much hope. The Charee had always been an ambitious but myopic race, divided in their loyalties even to each other and focused more on individual goals rather than the long-term security of their species. It was abundantly clear they intended to abandon their human allies at the first opportunity.

"Sir, incoming fire from the First Fleet," said one of the Charee techs, "Hits on multiple ships." A human tech reported, "There goes the *Iowa,* she took out two Impy carriers. Dios Mio!" There had been two thousand sailors and Marines still fighting aboard the Terran battleship when it impacted the Golden fleet, her death was marked seconds later by a flare of brilliant light flashing on the viewscreen.

Immediately, desperately, the Charee Captain spoke again, talking as much to the listening Grausian ears as to Max *"General, I repeat. We cannot support your disloyal actions here today. Good luck to you, may whatever Gods you worship watch over you. Charee fleet, out."* At this pronouncement, the remaining Charee followed Ensign Jasutara's example by slowly raising their multiple limbs in surrender before Max snapped at them, "Get back to work, all of you. Do your jobs and we won't have any problems."

"Sir, incoming message from our lead elements," Suki announced into the sudden quiet while at the same time deliberately moving over to stand directly behind the largest group of Charee. There was a burst of radio static over the loudspeaker, then a very young, female Gaelic accented voice said, *"... is Caledonia, we found it! Sending coordinates now. We're jumping, hull integrity compromised, see you on Eire or in Hell!"* and the first of the frigates disappeared off the plotting display. Moments later, another vanished and then more in rapid succession as the fleeing ships desperately raced for their only hope of salvation.

Focusing once again on the tactical screen, Max saw the horrific number of still manned fighting ships engaged in a lopsided battle to cover their retreat, as well as the dozens of strung-out troop shuttles that hadn't been able to dock with the retreating fleet in time. Taking a precious moment for himself, Max uttered a silent vow to the soul of his dead best friend Robert, to his XO Jennifer Marie, Commander Pasco and all the rest, both the living and the dead they were leaving behind, then picked up the mic and transmitted, *'I swear, someday we will come back here to avenge you. We are going to pound the Empire back into the stone age and I'm going to personally carve humanity's name right into the Empress' black heart.'*

He hung the microphone back in its cradle and then looked around at the bridge crew, his friends. No, his family, but more importantly people who were going to be needed in the coming fight.

"Sergeant Major," he ordered, all familiarity gone, "I'm ordering you to take my staff and have them board a shuttle to the fastest frigate we have. No arguments."

"But Max-" Suki started to say, face draining of color.

"Major Nakamura, you will follow the sergeant major onto a shuttle, taking as many of the lower enlisted sailors as you can with you AFTER accounting for all staff. Then you get the fuck out of this system and back to Terra." His voice was cold steel and brooked no argument.

"Yes sir, I understand," her voice equally hard but a single tear running down her blood splattered cheek.

Far more softly, so only she could hear, he said, "if I don't make it back, tell Alicia that I'm doing my duty. She'll understand. I am NOT going on a suicide mission, but this is going to be tough."

Suki nodded, stood ramrod straight and saluted. Not the Imperial way, left arm out and down and right hand clasping left elbow, but in the old Terran way, knife edge of her right palm touching the corner of her eyebrow. He returned it and then turned his back to her, barking orders to the fleet.

When they were gone, Max was surprised to see Laq still sitting at her station. He motioned the Grausian over and when she did, he told her to sit. "Thank you, my friend," he said simply, taking her heavily muscled hands in his.

The lowborn Grausian nodded. "What the Empress did was ... dishonorable, General. Not only that, it was ... inept. You would have pulled it off better. And my family is on Alpha Prime, they will honor my name. My daughter, Farest, is attending the police academy in Columbia and perhaps she may graduate with a name of distinction, if only among your people."

"Let us hope that we are there to see her graduate." The general sat and pondered for a moment, his brain going a mile a minute.

"Max, we're away and on course to rendezvous with the destroyer Johnston," came Suki's voice on the coms. *"Hit them hard and get back to us, boss. Nakamura out."*

"Good luck and I'll see you as soon as I can," he replied, then stared at the plot. The *Macedonia* was passing through a debris field, a small moon destroyed in some long ago conflict that still followed the orbit demanded by physics and it gave him an idea.

"Laq, did you ever hear of the Tunguska Event?" asked Max. Knowing that the xeno probably hadn't, he continued, "in 1908, Old Earth calendar, a meteor detonated in the wastelands of my ancestors' country. It exploded with the force of a twelve megaton nuclear weapon. We don't have any heavy kinetic bombardment weapons, but we do have all those logistics tugs. Imagine if something similar were to happen to, say, the Imperial HQ? Several hours after this battle was over?"

The Grausian grinned, crest green with pleasure. "Not the Palace?"

"Oh no, Laq. I want the Empress to choke on this for a very long time. I fear all she has done is to awaken a sleeping giant and fill him with a terrible resolve."

Beneath their feet the deck of the *Macedonia* began to hum with power. "Indeed, general. It has been a pleasure serving with you. Perhaps one day my people and yours will fight again under the same banner." And the Grausian stood up in her curious double joined way, walked over to her station and sat down to wait.

Epilogue

University of Cartagena, Nova Hispania
512 PC

As is well known, the sacrifice of one half of the human crewed fleet by suicidally engaging the Grausians while the other ran left a core of ships with skeleton crews to build a new Terran Union Navy around. The fact that the Charee crewed ships fled and did nothing to help created a bitter hatred that led to the Union striking their home worlds first. The Charee ground forces were never a large component of their military so the Empress discounted them in her calculations. The CLu'Lachan, as the smallest political unit of the combatant nations, suffered immensely even with their warlike traditions, losing all three of their ground forces regiments while inflicting immense damage to the ambushing legions.

The next fifteen years of fighting, until the Treaty of Kepler Sigconis in 499 PC, were the most brutal and destructive the galaxy had ever seen, the first true interstellar war. Even though the convention against mass orbital bombardment was never broken, it was bent on occasion. Even so, whole planets were devastated through purely conventional means. Trillions of credits of material were destroyed and the casualties ran into the billions. Economically, the system of trade between planets ground to a halt and individual worlds that became cut off saw mass starvation. It was the greatest catastrophe for humanity and the xeno races since the Grausian conquests.

The last decade has shown a rise in nationalism and a fierce struggle among corporate entities to control the wealth of the former Grausian worlds. The treaty fleets have managed to keep major violence from spilling from system to system but small wars have continued to plague the common people.

If you enjoyed this book, please leave a review on Amazon and check out our other great Military Science Fiction!

www.cannonpublishing.us

Follow us on Facebook at
The Command Post

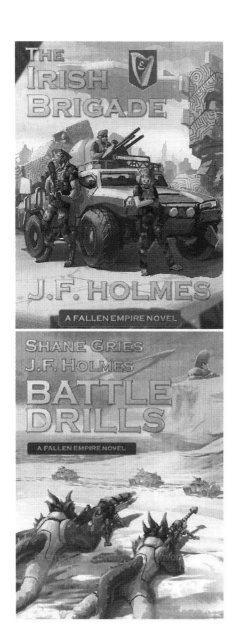

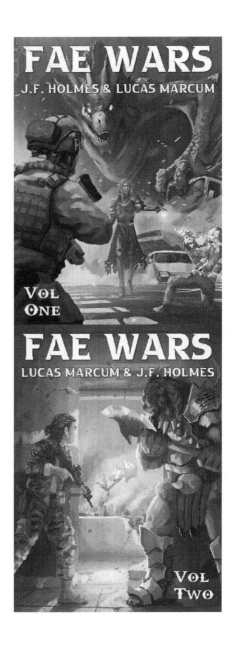

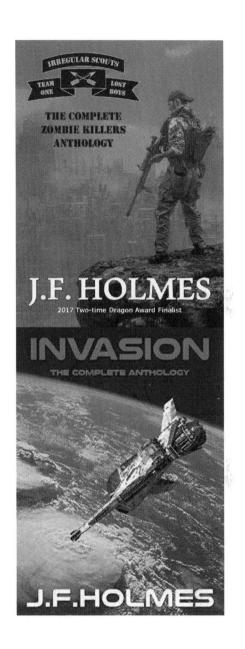

Appendix A

Timeline

Calendars—The Terran Post Conquest Calendar is used in the books. The Grausian Calendar cannot be matched (without a ton of calculating) because it's based on a 247-day year. To match our current calendar, add 2142 years.

Future History (all years are given in PC, or Post Conquest)

Yr. 1 (2143 AD)—Terran Union (consisting of eleven settled planets) conquered by the Grausian Empire in 01 Post Conquest. By 50 PC, the Terrans have become an integral part of the Empire, but there has never been a cessation of rebellious elements.

100 to 280—Grausian Empire is at the height of its expansion and power. Pax Grausia. Massive settlement of humans in imperial worlds mixing with alien races. Some planets closer to the old Terran Union are majority human. High restrictions on technology, kept at Terran 21st century level throughout the Empire. Artificial Intelligence and high level computing banned.

Between the years 300 to 400 Post Conquest, the Empire increasingly looked towards the center of the galaxy for their interests and outward fell more and more into the periphery of Imperial attention. The Terran Federation was the last actual conquest of a subject race; The Illyrian worlds, existing more than 250 LY Outward from the furthest TU world, gave tribute, but never had Grausian occupation.

As attention shifted more to the center and the Grausian population lost its vigor due to the wealth rolling into its coffers, the Legions were increasingly made up of humans and other races. The main leadership stayed Grausian, but the rank and file of the troops were increasingly Human, LaChan and Charee, among others.

300 to 400—Dynastic struggles and civil wars cripple the Empire.

412— Split of the Grausian Empire into Old and New. New capital moves toward the galactic center.

Over the next eight decades, the "provinces" became increasingly independent, though the Grausian nobility remained on their estates and continued to rule from the sector capitals. There were three actual rebellions by subject planets, but they were localized. From 454 to 467, the Terran and CLu'LaChan administrative units were actually 'ruled' by Governor Thal -Sjar, but were reabsorbed when he was assassinated in 467.

400 to 490—Collapse of Old (edgeward from the center of the galaxy) Empire due to Civil Wars.

479 to 483—Rebellion of Callan the Usurper, breakaway of the Terran Province and many other worlds who remain loyal to the Empire. Victory of the Restoration Fleet.

The fall of the Old Empire became precipitous in 479 when an Imperial Princess, third in line for the Old Empire throne, launched a rebellion directed at the overthrow of her mother. With support of agents of the New Empire and the backing of some fleet units manned by Charee, Callan waged a brutal war for four years that saw the devastation of entire planetary systems, use of orbital bombardment, biological warfare and nuclear / plasma weapons. At first the Terran Union planets attempted to remain neutral, but the increasing casualties of Terran Legionnaires who still fought in the Empress's armies and a biowarfare attack on the human system Tau Ceti (which left the two M class worlds uninhabitable and caused eleven billion casualties) made them throw in the side of Imperial forces.

With the addition of Terran ship production capabilities and an infusion of new recruits into the Legions, the rebellious worlds fell one by one, until the space & land battle of Pegasus Prime in 483 PC resulted in the defeat and execution of Callan.

484—Assassination of the Terran Fleet High Command at Restoration celebration on Glarius by the First Legion, on orders of the Grausian military high command.

In 484 PC, Empress Krarri IV invited the victorious fleets and legions to a celebration in the capital of Glarius. During the height of the festivities, the Empress' First Legion, which was still composed of all Grausians, committed a complex assassination which decapitated the leadership of both the legions and the fleet. The First Legion initially resisted, claiming such an action to be craven and dishonorable, but relented on direct orders of the Empress. At the same time, assault troops attempted to board all the Terran crewed vessels, resulting in seizure or destruction of over 2/3rds of the Terran and CLu'LaChan ships, as well as the loss of 90% of the veteran Human and LaChan troops.

What followed was the start of the Secession Wars, which had two distinct phases.

485—The Terran Union declared independence and ejected all imperial administrators on the original twelve TU worlds. Launches preemptive / retributive strike at Charree home world high command, neutralizing Charree forces and issuing neutrality ultimatum under threat of orbital bombardment.

486 to 487—Terran offensive seizes control of three imperial sector capitals. Styled as a war of liberation, many subject races rise up and act as crews on captured imperial ships and new Terran ships.

487—Imperial forces attack and occupy a LaChan world in the battle of Rigel, in an attempt to control the Rigel transit point, which linked directly back to the Imperial Capital of Glarius. The system quickly becomes a focal point of Imperial and Alliance forces and added the CLu'LaChan to the Alliance. Although the Terrans controlled the system, the transit point remained in the hands of the Imperials and the Union wanted to avoid casualties in a very mixed population. The ground offensive on Rigel III took almost a year and close to a million casualties.

488—Terran Union seizes Rigel transit point in a commando raid and launches a surprise attack through and into the Glarius system. Terran and CLu'LaChan forces defeat Imperial forces and conduct a planetary siege.

488—Siege of Glarius, capital of Old Grausian Empire, by a force of allied Terrans and CLu'LaChan. Siege is lifted by an expeditionary fleet of New Empire naval ships. Allied forces are routed but the New Empire fleet takes enough damage to make pursuit impossible and withdraws.

489—The Empire is defeated at the Battle of Grendel III with major losses for Imperial Legions.

490—Second Siege of Glarius. The New Empire is unable to send another relief fleet. Eventually, the last Empress is forced to abdicate her throne under imminent threat of capture by allied forces. In her final address, the Empress demands all loyal Grausian Imperial subjects either follow her into exile or die fighting a holding action. Most choose the former, bringing their technology, riches and mobile infrastructure to the New Empire. The Sack of Glarius is a massacre perpetrated against those Grausains too poor, or simply without the means, to evacuate. Period of chaos follows, including efforts by the New Empire to retake territory.

490—Evacuation of many Grausians to the New Empire. New Empire Fleets fight actions to prevent the Union forces from seizing any systems that contain transit points to New Empire territory.

490 to 499—Succession Wars. Three- way struggle between Terran Union, CLu'LaChans and Charee. Illyrians remain neutral. Occasional forays by New Empire forces.

491—LaChan and Terran alliances dissolve over direction of effort. The LaChan want to focus on rehabilitation of Rigel, Terrans want to expand control over as many former Imperial planets as possible.

493—Charee break their treaty with Terrans, launch multiple attacks on non-Terran Union planets. Swing CLu'LaChan over to their side with promise of aid for rebuilding.

493 to 498—Five years of warfare between Charee, Terrans and former Imperial forces. CLu'LaChan switch sides twice, depending on who they see as the possible victor.

493—Orion Nebula TU vs. CA (Fleet action / Charee victory) first action of the war after withdrawal of New Empire forces.

493—Pleiades Jump Point engagement TU vs NE (Fleet Action / TU victory), New Empire attempts to influence the war. The New Empire withdraws.

494—Terran drop onto Ophiuchi, three- month ground engagement results in Charee withdrawal.

From 493 to 495 PC, the Terrans were generally in the defensive, since they had just finished a brutal campaign against the Old Empire and the Charee had taken them by surprise. After 495 though, the balance began to switch back towards the Terrans. From 496 to 498 the Charee lost most of their original gains in systems, but many of the worlds fought over were devastated. In 498 the CLu'LaChan switched sides again to Terra, but then went neutral after the cost of the war became too great.

498—The lines stabilize with a series of hit and run engagements; both sides are exhausted. In late 498 PC, before the treaty negotiations began, the New Empire Admiral Thal Bestia launched an attack in the Gamma Draconis system, attempting to cut off several Union worlds from the majority of the Terran Union sphere. The Union Ninth Fleet responded immediately and a ferocious battle took place at the Gamma Draconis jump point. Ultimately, the Grausian fleet was defeated and Thal Bestia died in the wreckage of his flagship. The Ninth Fleet suffered grievous casualties, but managed to capture several Grausian ships, including a battleship and several cruisers.

498 to 499—Treaty negotiations on Kepler Sigconis brokered by the New Empire. All three sides agree to fall back to a set number of worlds which have a majority of their species populations:. 27 for the Terran Union, 14 for the Charee and 6 for the CLu'LaChan. All worlds outside of these territories fall into a "Demilitarized Zone". Fleet and ground actions are forbidden on these worlds, to be enforced by random patrols by each nation. Independent worlds can petition to join one of the political units, but none do.

499—Massive demobilization of the Terran Union military in expectation of a peacetime economy.

500—Treaty of Kepler Sigconis between three warring sides, brokered by the New Empire. All sides exhausted, massive demobilization of ground forces. Navies are barely functional after twenty years of war. Illyrians start building a trading empire. Dozens of buffer worlds between all star nations are left to fend for themselves while major nations consolidate and rebuild. New Empire forces withdraw a thousand light years towards the center of the galaxy, leaving Old Empire worlds to fend for themselves.

500+—Rise of the Private Military Companies.

As of 500 Post Conquest (Terran Reckoning), there' is an uneasy truce between all the races in the territory of the Old Empire. Each primary political unit is jockeying for position and influence in the DMZ. To that effect, mercenary companies are often employed as proxies to influence events, since actual national militaries will break the truce. They are sometimes hired by different factions to settle disputes in the turmoil left behind by the dissolution of the Old Empire, engage in corporate wars and recover Grausian technology.

Appendix B: The Grausians

When humanity made its first moves out into space the Grausian Empire was in its heyday and far past the technology level of the new Earth colonies. They were aware of humanity, of course, but focused more on an ongoing war of extermination, a crusade in essence, against another species that were further down the Orion Arm. So for a century they let the Terrans explore and settle new worlds. In 2097 a Grausian diplomatic ship landed on Earth and forbid crossing a certain line, claiming that they were forbidden to interfere with humanity's development.

Perhaps they actually meant it, but the history of the Grausians was one of conquest, not of peace. In 2146, after finishing up their genocidal war against the Yusan. They turned their attention to the Terran Union. The TU was caught unawares, engaged in a cold civil war between Federal and planetary authority, and the rest is, as they say, history.

The Grausians were and are a warlike species, evolved from a plains dwelling sauropod, perhaps what might have eventually happened on Earth but for the Yucatan meteor. Standing approximately seven feet tall on average, they have an odd double joint system that allows them great flexibility and strength, though the joints are delicate. Their life spans were on par with a humans until genetic engineering extended it to about fifteen decades. Their skin is leathery with a fine down of feathers. Their eyes are similar to a cat's or a lizard, with an inner membrane instead of lashes. Atop their heads is a crest of filaments similar to hair, but much more connected to their nervous system. Like a gecko, the skin on their crest can change color from green to blue to red and back to their normal skin color.

Perhaps the most important dissimilarity between humans and grausians is their distributed nervous system. There are several "nodes" which a similar, though smaller, than a human brain. This does nothing to effect their intelligence and speed of thought but does provide resilience in the face of CNS damage that would kill a human being.

Socially, at least as far back as records go, the Grausian Empire society has been matrilineal and matriarchal. This also applies to their politics. During the early years of the Empire the Legions were composed of both females and males. However, the female grausian brain, such as it is, is more in tune with political machinations, and they came to rule the Empire and provide much of the officer corps of the military. It was a very rare male by the time of the Conquest who rose about Centurion.

The Empire itself was, to a remarkable degree, similar to Earth's Roman Empire in late Antiquity, even to the point of the original configuration splitting in the face of civil pressures and weaknesses. Of course it is purely a Terran euphemism to use the words "Old" and "New" when referencing the Empire, since the Grausians themselves consider it one political unit, continuous through history. Along the same lines it is much easier to translate the Grausian words into "Primus, Centurion, Legion," etc.

The Grausians have been a huge influence on Terran culture and the other Xeno races that were under their rule, but the same is true for the Grausians themselves. What type of culture that develops, especially in the DMZ worlds left adrift outside the emergent political entities remains to be seen.

Cover Art by Logan Arts

Made in United States
Orlando, FL
09 February 2022

14629572R00157